About the

Mac Alexander was born in the valleys of South Wales.

At school he learned that, apparently, he could do better.

He's done so much better. He still lives in the South Wales valleys.

How Hard is it to Kill? is his second published novel.

www.macalexander.co.uk

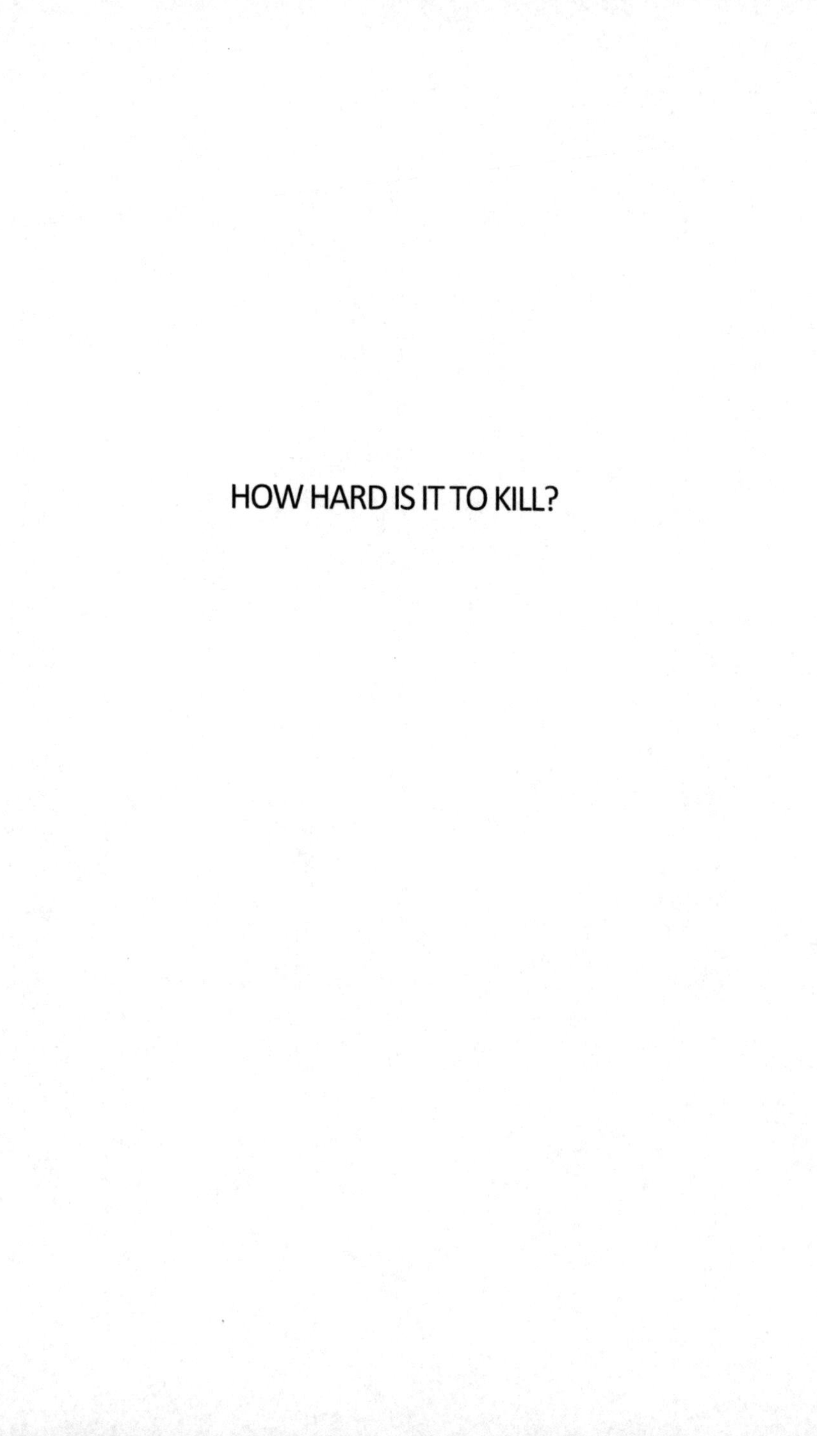

HOW HARD IS IT TO KILL?

MAC ALEXANDER

HOW HARD IS IT TO KILL?

BOOK 1 IN THE T.S.A. SERIES

Vanguard Press

VANGUARD PAPERBACK

A CIP catalogue record for this title is available from the British Library.

ISBN 978 1 80016 344 7

Vanguard Press is an imprint of
Pegasus Elliot MacKenzie Publishers Ltd.
www.pegasuspublishers.com

First Published in 2022

Vanguard Press
Sheraton House Castle Park
Cambridge England

Printed & Bound in Great Britain

Dedication

To Holly.
It was your turn.

Acknowledgements

I'd like to offer my thanks to Dai Covid, nineteen, for giving me the peace and quiet to finish this project.

I'd also like to thank my long-suffering wife, Rose (not nineteen), who's had to put up with my disappearance from normal life.

TUESDAY

In the glowing aftermath of a successful crusade, this always happened. It could have been no more than ten seconds after the bullet had perforated the man's forehead, splaying his brain-matter over a large part of an unloved, bent and buckled garage-door, that Niko became as hard as over-frozen ice cream.

"Shit!" Niko said, the word echoing around the carefully selected darkness, chosen for its complete lack of illumination. He took a few steps forward, stood astride the wide-eyed corpse, looked up to the starless, April London sky, and let out a sigh.

"Shit!" he repeated, waving his gun in the general direction of his crotch. "For the love of God why do you always do this to me?" He then placed the Glock, his weapon of choice, back in his jacket pocket, and, in an effort to ignore his discomfort, concentrated his eyes on the lifeless form below him.

The corpse stared back, a few bloody bubbles forming at its mouth, but it offered no reasonable explanation in response to Niko's question. Its explaining days, limited as they may have been, were now things of past wonderings.

Niko, in the forlorn hope his manhood had some conscience, attempted to persuade himself the man he had just dispatched had a family: a loving, beautiful wife called Isabella, he mused, who was of Argentinian descent and still carried a hint of accent with two — hell, make it three — adoring children. Two girls and a boy: Maria (ten), Sofia (eight) and Mateo (six), the latter named after the man's hero-worshipped grandfather.

It didn't work. The bulge in Niko's trousers refused to subside.

"Oh, come off it," Niko said, trying to push the protuberance down with the palm of his hand. "Have you no respect for the dead?"

The truth of the matter, as Niko and his swelling knew, was that the corpse below him had no loving family of any description, and certainly none from anywhere as exotic as Argentina. The information Niko had gleaned over the last two weeks suggested the man had never voluntarily strayed much further than the boundaries of Hackney Wick.

"Ah, what the hell," Niko said, giving up on his efforts. "I guess, Mr Phallus, you and I both know this man, whose brains I have just removed, isn't worth a spit. So, let's just get this thing done. Maybe I'll give Cherie a call when we're finished and get her to get rid of you. You'd like that, wouldn't you?"

With a huff of resignation, Niko retrieved a pair of surgical gloves from his jacket pocket, snapping them onto his hands with just a hint of drama. He kneeled at the side of the corpse and systematically began removing all personal items from the man's pockets, carefully setting them to one side. Niko glanced at the name on the man's driving licence — *Martin Bead.* Niko, as always, had gone to great lengths to ensure he was ending the life of the right person, but there was always a sense of relief when it was confirmed he'd found the correct mark.

"You know, one of these days, Martin," Niko said, "I'm sure T.S.A. will give me more to work on than just a bloody name and number."

From another of his own jacket pockets, Niko removed the burner phone he'd collected earlier in the day and pressed one button — the star button.

At the click of a connection, Niko spoke.

"This is Operative Four reporting that number…" he checked the number he'd scrawled on a scrap of paper, even though he remembered it well enough, "…two, three, four, six…" Niko paused for dramatic effect and lowered the tone of his voice "…has been duly eliminated." He slightly slurred the 'ess' in his best Sean Connery imitation.

Niko was aware there was little need for such detail. From the beginning, he'd been informed he needed to say only the victim's number, followed by one word — *done.* Brevity, he had been told, was a T.S.A. principle. No mess. No fuss. But how boring would that be?

Niko liked being Operative Four. He had always believed even numbers held the higher status over their odd colleagues. If numbers had a caste system, Niko believed odd numbers would be ranked in the same category as the *'untouchables'* in India. God also made the stars, the sun and the moon on the fourth day, and where the hell would we be without the stars, the sun and the moon? No, being Operative Four suited Niko just fine. He was sure he would never have taken on the gig if he'd been told he was going to be number three, or five. How Bond had ever coped with being 007 was beyond him. Niko would bet his bottom dollar that James hated Fleming for that particular indiscretion.

"Tell me," Niko said to whoever was on the other end of his phone, "are there three other people doing this job, or is there only me and I'm the fourth person to have taken it on? I mean, take William the Fourth, for example. Now, four Williams didn't sit on the throne at the same time, did they? He just so happened to be the fourth William to come along and get the gig. So, I have to ask myself, if I *am* the only person doing this job, like William the Fourth, what happened to the other three?"

Niko had asked questions of this nature each time he had completed a successful kill. Every time the response was the same. Silence.

"Not very talkative tonight are we, Delores?" Niko had decided some time ago that the person on the other end was a woman and had called her Delores after a social worker he'd once had dealings with. She'd never said anything of any interest, either.

"Come on, Delores," Niko continued, "this is the sixth time we've spoken, so we're way past the third date. By now we should be falling madly in love and ravishing each other with total abandon." Niko glanced down at his swelling, which was still refusing to go away. "Trust me, *I'm* ready. So, how about a simple hello? Or, 'Hi Niko, how are you tonight?' Go on, Delores, you know you want to." Niko waited but knew there would be no response. There never was.

"Ah well," Niko said to the silence. "Have it your own way, Delores. Now, let's see…" Niko picked up the dead man's belongings, one item at a time, and placed them into a plain, plastic carrier bag. His *quarry*, as Niko liked to term the people he was sent to dispatch, rarely carried much, and Martin Bead was no exception. "One driving licence," Niko advised whoever was listening. "One set of keys on an 'I heart Spurs' fob. A half-eaten packet of extra-strong mints. A cheap mobile phone. A small address book," Niko quickly ruffled the pages, "with very few entries. A well-worn, brown leather wallet containing…" Niko emptied the contents onto the ground, "…twenty-four pounds and two credit cards. And that's it."

The phone went dead.

"Pleasure talking to you as always, Delores," Niko said. "Take care."

Later, Niko would follow the drill and deliver the items, including the phone he'd used, to a run-down car-breakers in Lewisham. His instructions were always the same. Within two hours of the kill, no matter what time of day or night, he was to drive into the yard and drop the carrier bag into the boot of whatever vehicle was parked outside the main office. Under no circumstances was he to talk to anybody at the yard.

This last point had so far been mute. In Niko's five previous visits he'd not seen a soul.

Niko often wondered why T.S.A. insisted on including this element of the job. Surely it would make no difference if the items were left on the body. It wasn't as if T.S.A. didn't want the corpse to be identified. Far from it. T.S.A. evidently took some pride in making sure as much of the world knew who it was dispatching, leaving the *'why'* to media speculation and public imagination. Niko could only deduce it was part of the *sport*.

Niko popped the twenty-four pounds into his own wallet. He always kept the money. A sort of tip, he thought. The biggest haul he'd had so far was a whopping forty-seven pounds and twenty pence. On that occasion, Niko had thrown one of the pounds away. There was no way he'd ever carry an odd amount. This time, he decided he'd keep the mints, as well.

"Well, Martin," Niko said. "Twenty-four quid will go some way to one of Cherie's specialities, so thank you for this. And now I guess this is goodbye."

Niko took a T.S.A. calling card from his inside pocket and placed it between the corpse's lips. The card carried no information other than a single white circle on a black background. Niko tried to guess the man's age, but he'd noticed, over time, that all men tended to look older when they'd just had half their head removed. This one was also overweight, which always made the age calculation more difficult. He hazarded it might be anywhere between twenty-five and forty, maybe even around the same as Niko's own gathering of thirty-three.

"You should go to the gym more often, Martin," Niko suggested, patting the man's stomach. "I'm sure Isabella would love to see you in better condition."

Niko checked the watch he'd taken off Martin Bead's wrist. It looked expensive; out of place. "Oh, now don't look at me like that, Martin," he said. "I'm fully aware I didn't mention the watch, but, let's face it, you're not going to need it anymore, and what T.S.A. don't know isn't going to hurt now, is it? Anyway, *you* probably nicked it in the first place."

Niko knew that exactly ten minutes after his one-way conversation with T.S.A. ended, the police would be informed, via special code, of Martin Bead's whereabouts. Ten minutes after that, T.S.A would enlighten a member of the local press fraternity. The police were fully aware of the drill and were always quick to respond to any coded message from T.S.A. on the understanding there had been no crime in the world where it had proved beneficial for the press to get to the scene before them.

Niko could already hear sirens, but then sirens were North East London's forest birdsong, and it didn't mean they were necessarily rushing to where Martin Bead's brains had just been dismantled. Even so, it was time to go. The car-breakers was less than ten miles away, and he'd never failed to get there in time yet, but ten miles in two hours around London could still sometimes be a stretch.

Niko groaned at the slight click in his knees as he got up to leave. "Maybe I should join you at that gym, Martin," he said. "Get myself in shape."

Safely back in his car, which he'd made sure he'd parked legally a few streets away, Niko rang Cherie: this time, on his own mobile.

***

An hour after Martin Bead's meagre belongings had been deposited into the boot of a reasonably new BMW, Niko's manhood, having discharged itself with the help of Cherie's expert handiwork, had finally shrivelled back to its normal resting place.

"Thanks," Niko muttered, re-buckling his seat-belt.

"Anytime, Sweetheart," Cherie said, retrieving a tissue from her leopard-skin handbag. "I aim to alleviate frustration wherever and whenever I can. Of course, if said alleviation helps to pay my rent at the same time, then everyone's a winner. Talking of which..." Cherie held out her tissue-wiped hand.

Niko counted out the agreed fifty pounds, believing the situation to be a real bargain considering it was only costing him twenty-six pounds of his own money.

"How come you don't insist on the money before you — you know?" Niko said. "I always imagined having to pay up-front for these types of services. Not after the actual event."

Cherie smiled. "I consider myself like a high-class restaurant," she said, stuffing the money into an inner compartment of her handbag. "The Ivy, maybe. Now, you wouldn't walk into The Ivy and expect to pay for your food before you actually ate it, would you?"

"No, but there's plenty of places that work on you having to do exactly that," Niko said.

"Like where?"

"McDonalds, KFC, Burger King."

Cherie punched Niko in the shoulder. Despite being pitifully thin, her punch carried just enough weight to sting.

"You saying I'm like McDonalds or KFC?" she said, turning her head away and dramatically tossing her long, blonde hair. "I'm offended. I always thought I was more like The Ivy." Through her laughter, she pretended to cry.

Niko stroked the back of Cherie's head. He wondered if the blonde was natural. Given the amount of tugging he'd given it during the act, he knew it wasn't a wig. He liked blonde, but then he liked most colours. Maybe, next time, he'd ask her if she'd consider going red.

"Of course you are," he said. "In fact, you're way better than The Ivy. If I had the choice of eating at The Ivy or eating at Chez Cherie, I'd choose Chez Cherie anytime."

Cherie turned back to Niko. "I should think so," she said. She turned the interior mirror in her direction, fished around in her handbag, and produced a lipstick, which she started to apply. "What do you think?" she asked, puckering her lips in the mirror.

"About what?"

"The lipstick, stupid. The woman in Boots said it was new in. The *Big Bang Berry* she called it."

Niko glanced at Cherie's mouth and winced. The colour reminded him of the copious amount of garish lipstick his mother used to wear.

"It made me laugh," Cherie said, without noticing Niko's discomfort, "because I thought *Big Bang Berry* for *Big Bang Cherie*. That's funny, don't you think?"

"Yeah, hilarious."

Cherie put away the lipstick. "My, my, someone's suddenly in a grouchy mood," she said. "You're supposed to feel better after seeing me, not worse."

"I do." Niko said. "I do feel better — honest. Just ignore me."

"Right, well, it's probably time I was going." Cherie caught hold of Niko's wrist and looked at Martin

Bead's watch. She stared at Niko with a quizzical eye. "This is fancy. I've not seen this before. Where'd you get it?"

"Present. Off a friend."

"You have friends?"

"Oh, very funny." Niko shifted uncomfortably in his seat. "Listen, Cherie, all this talk of food has made me hungry, and the only thing I've got is half a packet of mints. Do you want to go for a meal or a drink or something? My shout. Don't think we'll get in The Ivy, though."

Cherie shook her head slowly. "Feeling guilty, big man?"

Not for one minute did Niko believe the use of the adjective *'big'* referred to the size of his manhood, which could, at best, be described as standard. He was, however, a good foot taller than Cherie, who, he deduced, without heels, could be no taller than five-two. Niko would describe himself as having an average frame, and, in the knowledge Cherie must have to deal with some real monsters, he wondered how she didn't snap.

"No, not guilty," Niko hesitated. "Just lonely, I guess."

Cherie smiled, ruffled Niko's shoulder-length black hair, and kissed him on the cheek, leaving a smudge of *Big Bang Berry*.

"I'm sorry, Sweetheart," she said, with what sounded to Niko like a reasonable attempt at regret. "As much as I'd love to, I make it a rule never to get too social with customers. Hell, I might make you fall in love with me, and then we'd end up getting married or some shit and boy, oh boy, am I some high-maintenance beast of a woman. Why, I'd nag you so much you'd never see another hard-on as long as you lived." Cherie gave out a solitary snort and checked herself again in the rear-view mirror. "I'll gladly take some of those mints, though. They're handy in my line of work."

"Here, take them," Niko said, handing over the packet.

Cherie put the mints in her handbag, then manoeuvred herself out of the passenger door. After finding her balance on her high-heeled boots, she blew Niko a kiss through the window.

Niko inwardly grimaced at the mention of marriage. He'd only been vaguely close to marriage once.

***

When he was nineteen, he'd landed himself a job on the production line of a meat-packaging factory and suddenly found himself the only male in a sea of women who appeared to adore his slightly dark complexion. At someone's retirement do, a new girl by the name of Tuesday — apparently, she'd been born on a Tuesday and her mother was a big fan of the actress Tuesday Weld, so what other name could she possibly have been given? — approached Niko and struck up a conversation about how she thought the world would be a better place if only people got along better. She suggested they spent the night together to test the theory. They'd dated for three months, but when Niko mentioned maybe taking the relationship to the next level — the one above getting wasted and having sex — Tuesday disappeared. In time, Niko heard she was living in Orpington, getting along better with someone called Andy, who apparently liked to be called Mandy from time to time.

Like most jilted teenagers, Niko had taken the rejection hard. Three weeks after Tuesday had disappeared, following an afternoon session in which he'd drunk enough to deaden the pain of several broken hearts, Niko woke to discover he'd joined the Navy Catering Services. During his time in the navy, Niko was subsequently forced to get along better with his lieutenant-commander, a huge hulk of a man many years his senior. The lieutenant-commander also appeared to have adored Niko's slightly dark complexion as well.

***

Niko watched Cherie disappear into the darkness. "What the fuck, Nikolaus!" he said, slapping the steering wheel with both hands, the use of his full name adding gravitas to the situation. "'*Listen, Cherie, do you want to go for a drink or something? Just lonely, I guess.*' She's a prostitute for Christ's sake! She's probably had a dozen men today with a dozen more already lined up."

***

Detective Chief Inspector Stanley Wood let out a groan as he bent under the hastily strung police tape: the type of groan, he'd discovered, that crept into the vocabulary of most men his age whenever they exerted any pressure on their joints. The call from control had disturbed a rather pleasant date-night with Michelle, his long-suffering wife. At least they had finished the pasta he'd prepared, but were only fifteen minutes into the evening's chosen film — Chariots of Fire, the latest in their list of missed classics — before the call came. He'd left the house with a promise they would watch the rest of the film as soon as possible. Unfortunately, he could not give a definitive time as to when this might be. Stanley believed Michelle had fallen asleep almost as soon as the film had started anyway, though she'd never admit it.

"Okay, DI Chandler," Stanley said to his newly promoted colleague, Verity Chandler-Adebayo, who'd arrived at the scene some ten minutes earlier, having left that night's lover, whose name she could not quite recall, somewhat perplexed and no doubt as frustrated as her. "I'm looking down at a fat man with half his head missing, and something tells me, from the look on everybody's faces, that the only thing we've found on him so far is a T.S.A. calling card. Am I right?"

"Afraid so, Boss," Verity replied, handing him a coffee in a carry-out cup. "We've got some house-to-house going, but I'm guessing this is an area which doesn't take too kindly to uniform."

Stanley glared at her.

"What?" Verity said. "What's wrong?"

"You may have been bred in a multi-million-quid spread in Pinner," Stanley said. "But that does not give you the right to Lord it over this manor and make assumptions about its people. For your information, most folk around here are about as friendly and helpful as you'll find anywhere, got it? They may like to look after their own, but then that's true of every tribal patch on Earth. You disrespect it again, and I will beat you to death with my shoe."

Verity looked around to see if anyone close by could indicate to her how serious her boss was being, but they all remained oblivious to her plight and carried on with their duties as normal.

Stanley took a sip of his coffee and nodded. "Not bad," he said. "A bit more sugar next time." He looked at his watch, a present from Michelle last Christmas, which he suspected cost more than all the Christmas presents he'd ever bought her in their twenty-five-year marriage put together. He silently vowed to buy her something extravagant this year. That's if they got that far. “Right,” he said, pointing at the watch, “by my reckoning, we’ve only got a few minutes before Mr Fuckwit shows up with this guy’s identity.”

Verity laughed nervously. She still wasn’t sure if Stanley was genuinely annoyed at her. “Mr who?” she said.

“Buck Witman,” Stanley replied. “Not his real first name — that’s Lionel — but he reckons *‘Buck’* has more journalistic seriousness.” Stanley used his fingers to speech mark the word *Buck.* He immediately hated himself for doing so. He found the habit very annoying, as did Michelle, who reminded him of her annoyance at every opportunity. “Works for The Hackney Gazette,” he continued. “And, like most journalists, he doesn’t always care about the absolute accuracy of his pieces.”

“And why are we expecting him, in particular?” Verity asked.

“Because, unlike when they contact us, T.S.A. always give whatever local hack they’re using the name of the victim. Probably a ruse to keep the press on their side. Anyway, for some unearthly reason, their chosen intrepid reporter for our patch is good old Buck Witman. You’re going to love him.”

Verity made some noise of agreement. “How many is this now?” she asked, craning her neck around the host of white-caped officers circling Martin Bead’s body like vultures feasting on a downed wildebeest.

Stanley took a sip of coffee and gently pulled at Verity's sleeve to stop her from taking any further steps closer to the body.

"Counting this one, it's six in three years on my watch," he replied. Stanley noticed a hint of pride in the statement which had come out unintentionally. After all, six unsolved murders in three years wasn't something any DCI should be proud of.

"But," he added, hoping the tone had not been spotted, "T.S.A. has been operating for ten years, that we know of. One theory runs that when they've cleared as much garbage off the streets as necessary in one area, they move on to pastures new. Another is that something *'happens'* to whoever is actually carrying out the murders." He did the thing with his fingers again around the word *happens.* This time, he actually kicked himself in the shin with his heel. "Anyway, before they got to us, the Firth Park area in Sheffield had two confirmed T.S.A. murders in two years; Spring Hill in Birmingham ten in three years before that. The first was in The Gorbels, Glasgow. At least, that's the first time the calling card was used."

"Who was he?" Verity asked.

"She," Stanley corrected. "A delightful woman by the name of Sandy Mackinley. She'd been running a house that catered for those of a particular appetite."

"Young?"

"Too young. The poor girls in question were mainly Eastern European, some African. All brought to our shores under the pretence of gold-covered streets. Anyway, Miss Mackinley had popped out to the local corner store for some provisions — or at least that's the theory because no provisions were actually found — and her route back took her through a small, unlit park, where she had half her head removed with a single gunshot at close range."

"The T.S.A. way," Verity said. She became aware Stanley was glaring at her again. "I've been doing some homework," she added. "You can find quite a lot about them on the internet."

"No, you can't!" Stanley said. "Don't ever let me catch you basing judgements on anything you read off Wackapaedophile, or whatever the hell it's called. T.S.A. has not got a website, a Twitter handle or Facebook profile. Understand? Everything written about them is as reliable as a Virgin train timetable. In the ten years we've known about them, not one single investigation has ever got close to finding out who the hell they are. Even the great British media, with their tenacity and ability to find the smallest needles in the largest haystacks, has failed to uncover their identity. They're as good at remaining unknown as The Scarlet bloody Pimpernel, and they certainly do not go plastering information about themselves for all and sundry to look at. We don't even know what T.S.A. stands for. Our friend Buck has decided *'The Silencing Association'* is as good a name as any."

Verity shuffled her feet. "Okay, understood," she said. She was starting to find Stanley's wrath a little tiresome and decided to stand her ground. "But it is T.S.A.'s method, isn't it? A single gunshot to the head at close range. Leaving nothing on the body except the calling card."

"Yes," Stanley said. "But you don't need the bloody internet for that type of information. We're stood here actually staring it in the face." He waved an arm in the general direction of Martin Bead.

"Why do you think they leave nothing on the body?" Verity asked, once again being restrained by Stanley from taking a step closer to the body. "Seems a bit futile, if you ask me."

"Lord knows," Stanley said. "The brain-boffins reckon it's a power thing. Stripping people of their individuality is apparently a dehumanising tactic which shows they don't fit into the expected norms of society, or something like that."

"Deep."

"Or maybe they just do it for fun. If we ever catch one of them, perhaps we'll ask."

"So, what happened next?" Verity said.

"After what?"

"You know, after Sandy what's-her-face."

"Why don't you look it up on whatever device you youngsters decide is in fashion these days?" Stanley took another sip of his coffee.

“Because I’d rather hear it from you,” Verity replied.

Clever, Stanley thought. He recognised the tone. The one to supposedly massage the male ego; pander to the idea of the Alpha male; diffuse potential conflict. Michelle had often used the same tactic.

Stanley finished his coffee and handed Verity his empty cup, just to remind her he was the superior officer here, no matter what gender politics was at play. “Over the next two years, The Gorbels saw another four of its finest dispatched in the same manner,” he said. “Two released paedophiles, one drug trafficker, and a local thug who had been questioned about the mugging and subsequent death of a pensioner.”

Verity raised her eyebrows and cocked her head to one side. “So, including this gentleman at our feet, that’s a kill count of twenty-three,” she said. “Well, at least that’s twenty-three less idiots for us to worry about.”

“Don’t you dare tell me T.S.A. is doing us a favour,” Stanley said through a hint of gritted teeth. “We’ll leave all that type of reasoning to the likes of Mr Fuckwit and the media-industry circus. Right now, we’ve got a murdered man on our hands, no matter what dreg of society he may be. And we have a murderer to find, no matter how righteous a deed people may think he, or she, has committed. It doesn’t matter what type of sordid, unsavoury behaviour half-a-head man here has been up to: we treat him,” Stanley waved his arm in the direction of the dead body, “with the same effort as if he was the king of England. Okay?”

Stanley knew full well this wasn’t the case, and his tirade had only been half convincing at best. But if he could get Verity to treat the case with the enthusiasm normally shown by new kids on the block, then who knew what might happen? He also felt a tinge of sympathy that her first murder case would be trying to discover who’d taken out the brains of someone who, in all likelihood, was not a valued member of the human race. It was likely that if ever T.S.A. *were* uncovered, they’d be paraded around as heroes. Especially if the likes of Buck Witman had anything to do with it.

“And for your information,” Stanley added, “it’s twenty-three fewer idiots, not less. I thought you were supposed to be clever.”

“Okay, Boss,” Verity said, the supplicatory tone still apparent. “But, for *your* information, we actually know who the Scarlet Pimpernel was. His name was Sir Percy Blakeney, a fictional character created by—”

“Don’t!” Stanley said, holding up his hand. “Don’t believe for a moment you can apply whatever expensive education you think you’ve had — which, by the way, I probably helped pay for — into anything we do here. This is the real world, not some lecture in a sodding literacy class for the fortunate.”

Stanley was keenly aware that Verity was ‘*well educated.*’ He’d read it in her profile before she’d joined his unit five days ago.

***

The only child of a mixed marriage — father a God-fearing, Nigerian, consultant oncologist; mother a good old Essex girl with her own successful online fashion business — Verity had been a straight-A student at the private girls' school she'd attended and went on to gain a place at Oxford to study classics.

For some reason, she'd decided to forego a career in academia and joined the force straight from university. Now twenty-nine years old — one of the youngest DIs in the Met's history — and, if the rumours were true, blissfully single, Verity Monique Chandler-Adebayo had worked her way quickly through the ranks. Stanley had wondered how proud her father might be. Did he think police work was God's work? It would surely be without doubt he would know nothing of her slightly tarnished reputation when it came to men.

Stanley, by contrast, had been raised by a single mother with a loose grasp of discipline and an addiction to gambling and hand-rolled cigarettes.

Much to most of his teachers' despair, Stanley had been forced to leave school at sixteen in order to earn a living; a living which his mother spent furiously, trying to regain past losses, until breast cancer finally gave her the ultimate way out when Stanley was nineteen.

Subsequently struggling through dead-end jobs, Stanley just about stayed on the right side of the law. He could see the attraction of crime, but couldn't subscribe to the idea that money and materials were somehow owed to him. Stanley believed most of the thieves he'd met weren't envious because other people were richer than them; they were envious because other people weren't as poor as them. There was a subtle difference. Stanley took the view that being rich was no crime in itself, as long as the riches had been gained legally. He'd once almost voted Liberal.

Six months after his mother died, Stanley decided it was time to find a proper career and joined the army, where he spent three years marching and being bullied for a whole host of misdemeanours — his ginger hair; the slight gap between his teeth; his middle name; his inability to take orders with enthusiasm; calling his superior officers 'pricks,' and so on.

Early in his police career, the gap in Stanley's teeth had been remedied by an argument with a car-thief, who'd decided to resist arrest by throwing a well-aimed haymaker of a right hook. His top two middle teeth were therefore now false and gratefully gapless. Over time, they'd taken on a slightly lighter hue than the rest of his ageing teeth, with the result that Stanley rarely smiled in photographs. These days, he found he rarely smiled at anything.

Eventually, the army decided they didn't really want him, and it was probably best all round if they parted company.

During a drunken night with a passing friend, Stanley was easily persuaded to try the police force, based on the information that, '*Birds go absolutely mental for it when they see the uniform, mate. Absolutely mental.*'

That information had not turned out to be strictly true, although, in the intervening thirty years, Stanley had been found desirable to the opposite sex on a number of occasions, including a few since his marriage to Michelle, but, in the main, Stanley had been forced to fight long and hard for what he'd achieved, including female attention — Michelle had turned down his first two proposals — and he hated anyone trying to pull social rank on him by dint of them simply having had a richer upbringing. Even if they were as gorgeous as this one. *'Fit'* Stanley believed was the word they used these days.

***

"Okay. Sorry, Boss," Verity said. "It won't happen again. I'll keep my intelligence strictly under my hat. Even though, actually, I don't wear a hat anymore."

"Bollocks," Stanley muttered.

"No, I mean it, I—"

"No, bollocks," Stanley pointed over Verity's shoulder.

Verity followed Stanley's arm. "Bloody hell, he looks like something straight out of the movies," she whispered.

"Yeah, Dracula," Stanley said. "Listen, whatever you do, never tell this hack anything, okay? He may look like a good fart would blow him over, but he can make life very difficult. He can be very convincing, and he'll know things about you that you don't even know yourself. He may be a shit wordsmith, but he's very good at finding out information. What he doesn't know, he'll simply make up."

Buck Witman spotted Stanley and waved a hand in the air. "Stanley Arthur Peregrine Wood, my old friend," he shouted, quickening his pace towards Stanley and Verity. Stanley was sure he could actually hear Verity smiling. "It's so good to see you again. I'm sorry I'm a bit late. Traffic was mental." He offered a handshake over the police tape. Stanley ignored the offer. "And how is the lovely Michelle? I hope she's coping with — well, you know?" Buck dropped the unshaken hand. He looked at Verity. "Oh, and this must be your new recruit."

Buck stooped slightly, clasped Verity's hand, and gently kissed the top of it. "Verity, isn't it?" he said. "I do hope that visa nonsense for your father's cousin gets sorted soon. Such a messy business. I find with these things it's always a case of who you know, and, let's face it, your father knows a lot of people."

Verity snatched her hand away and wiped it on her jacket. "How the hell did you—" She was stopped from saying any more by a nudge in the ribs from Stanley.

"Let's just cut the crap, Buck," Stanley said. "Who am I looking at?" He nodded to where the body was now being bagged.

Buck removed his trilby, revealing a hairstyle that would not have been out of place on one of the original Beatles, and looked into the hat, as if the inside somehow held the answer.

"What, no small talk at all?" Buck said, looking up from the hat and winking at Verity. "Don't you want to know about my recent operation to remove an in-growing toenail? How about my forthcoming weekend away to Tenby?" He placed the hat back on his head. "I have so very few people in my life to talk to these days."

"My heart bleeds for you," Stanley said. "But I haven't got time to socialise. Especially with the likes of you. So, I'll repeat myself, just the once, before I find some reason to lose my manners. Who am I looking at?"

Buck put his hand across his heart. "Oh, you can be so impatient, Stanley Wood," he said, winking at Verity again.

"Information. Now!" Stanley reached over the tape and grasped Buck by the arm, pulling him closer. "Or I'll arrest you for interfering with the police in the course of their duties."

"Oh, Stanley, now let's not be so nasty to one another," Buck said, slowly removing Stanley's hand. "You know I don't like people being nasty. And I really wouldn't want to find myself having to print horrible things about you. It's just not in my nature. But then I guess I do have to make a living somehow." Buck let the threat hang for a moment. "Look, why can't we just all be civil? Wouldn't the world smell sweeter if people stopped shouting at one another? How do you fancy all three of us getting together one night? Just for a nice, friendly chat. We could shoot the breeze and tell this delicious creature all the things we've been through together." He once again winked at Verity.

"Mr Witman," Verity said. Stanley recognised that tone again. "It's getting late, and I'm sure we've all been pulled away from something we'd rather have been doing. I know I certainly was. Oh, and look," Verity held her palm upwards, "it's just started to rain. So, if it's not too much trouble, could you just give us whatever information you've got about our victim and then we can all go on our merry way. Oh, and by the way, you wink at me one more time and I won't just arrest you, I'll take your eyes out with a rusty spoon."

Buck looked at Stanley and laughed. "Feisty one you've got here, Woody," he said. "I think I'm going to like her."

Buck pulled his Mackintosh around him against the steady fall of rain. The coat didn't really fit his painfully thin frame and could have easily accommodated another body, but it had become Buck's trademark piece of apparel and he was rarely seen without the cream-coloured coat. For one thing, it gave him plenty of pockets, and it was from one of these pockets that Buck now produced a small notebook. He flipped a few pages.

"Okay," he said, "seeing as you asked so nicely." He cleared his throat dramatically. "Martin Bead, forty-three-year-old, single man—"

"Thanks," Stanley interrupted. "We'll take it from here."

Buck's eyes widened. "Sorry?"

"I said, we'll take it from here."

"But don't you want to know—"

"Nope." Stanley crossed under the police tape, nudging Buck out of the way in the process, and started to walk away. "Come on, DI Chandler," he shouted over his shoulder. "We've got work to do."

"But I know everything about this man!" Buck shouted.

"So do I," Stanley shouted back as he reached the driver's door of his service vehicle.

Once in the car, Verity asked, "So who is he?"

"You'll see," Stanley replied, starting the engine. "When we get back to the station, we'll run his name."

"What if nothing comes up?"

"Oh, it will," Stanley said. "Let's just say Martin Bead is a name I recognise. Anyway, T.S.A. has never taken out anyone who isn't on some sort of register or list somewhere. At least not yet."

"Real knights in shining armour."

Stanley snapped his head “I told you to leave that bullshit to the media,” he said. “T.S.A. has no authority to murder. Especially not on my watch.”

“Sorry, Boss,” Verity said, sighing heavily. “Um, if you don’t mind me asking, what did Witman mean when he asked about your wife? He said he hoped she was coping. Coping with what?”

“Mind your own goddam business,” Stanley replied, then quickly thought he’d best offer something to avoid further discussion. “Probably meant how the hell does she cope living with me.”

After a few moments of silence, Verity started to giggle.

“What’s so sodding funny?” Stanley asked. “I don’t see anything funny.”

“Peregrine,” Verity replied. “Really? Where the hell did that come from?”

“Again, mind your own business. And if you mention it again, I’ll make sure you spend the rest of your career giving out parking tickets.”

Stanley had once asked his mother about his name to be told that Stanley and Arthur were names of maternal grandfathers, but that Peregrine had come from the midwife at his birth commenting he had shot out of his mother as fast as a peregrine falcon.

***

Stanley was right. The police central computer had plenty of information on Martin Bead.

"Wow," Verity said, looking over Stanley's shoulder at the screen. "That is one heap of bad, right there."

The final piece of information confirmed Martin Bead had been released from prison only two weeks prior to having half his head removed. He'd served half of a three-year sentence for the armed robbery of an all-night convenience store on the Mile End Road. The owner of the store had died of a heart attack two days after the robbery. Pre-trial, the prosecution had argued that having a shotgun pointed at your head, with the threat that either the store's takings or the store owner's brains would be leaving that night, was the major contributing factor to the man's death and wanted to go for a charge of manslaughter. Unfortunately, the CPS had decided it would be too difficult to prove, and the best they could go for was the actual armed robbery. Even that, they'd suggested, was pushing it, on the grounds that the gun hadn't been loaded properly and it was lucky Martin Bead could not afford a decent defence lawyer.

"I worked on that robbery," Stanley said. "Martin Bead was a right piece of work. A career criminal. Not a very good career criminal, but a career criminal all the same. Unfortunately, we ended up in court with one of the more liberally minded judges on the circuit. You know the type? Even a hardened criminal is a victim, forced into criminality by the harsh realities of modern life, etcetera, et-bloody-cetera, blah, blah, blah.

"Everybody except Judge Lenient thought we'd be getting rid of Martin Bead for a decent stretch. Eight, maybe even ten years. But no, the right honourable Ming the Merciful decided three was enough. If I'd known good old Martin had been released early, I'd have gone and said hi."

"So, what next?" Verity asked.

"We do the best we can to try and find who killed him," Stanley replied. He stood up from the screen and retrieved his jacket from the back of his chair. "Martin Bead may have been a first-class arsehole, but it doesn't mean someone can just snuff him out like a candle. First, I need some sleep. Martin Bead will be just as dead in the morning. Why don't you go home and get some rest?"

Verity gave out a solitary laugh. "Oh, trust me, if the handsome thing is still where I left him, there'll be very little rest happening."

"Too much information, DI Chandler," Stanley said. "Too much information."

***

Deep down, somewhere Niko couldn't fathom, there was a disc. He could feel it; he just couldn't see it. Was it growing? Niko couldn't tell, but he knew it was black.

How could it be any other colour? He took another swig of his lager followed by a long drag on his joint.

"I've got a disc growing in me, Mr M," he whispered. "Can you feel it?"

The cat — full name Mr Mephistopheles, a tabby stray Niko had picked up many years ago — purred gently as it lay on Niko's stomach.

"Of course you can feel it," Niko said. "You're a goddam cat. You sense things us humans only dream of feeling. Although, perhaps you're slowing down, eh? How old are you now? Fourteen? Fifteen? Sixteen?

"Now, if I had my way, there wouldn't even be a number fifteen. Horrible number." Niko took another luxurious toke. "So, answer me this, Mr M, why are the numbers eleven and twelve not oneteen and twoteen, eh?" He gave the cat a quizzical look as he blew out smoke his body couldn't take. "My thoughts exactly," he said. "Anyway, let's see, you're probably nearing a hundred years in human time. Shit, that's old. Hell, I doubt even my grandparents lived to be that old, and they were Greek! And we all know how long Greek people live. Just look at Aphrodite, for God's sake. Well, maybe not for God's sake. Maybe Zeus's sake, or Chronos perhaps. Or is it that Greek people just look old? Perhaps they have such shitty lives chasing fish around, they age before their time."

The cat stretched itself.

"You've heard of Alexander the Great, right?" Niko asked. "What am I thinking? Of course you have, all cats know their history. Hell, you might have even been one of his cats in a previous life. But did you know, despite being Greek, he was only thirty-two when he died? Of course, there would have been no fish-chasing for him. He would have had people to bring him everything he needed. So, if he wasn't chasing fish about, what did he die of, I hear you ask. Well, apparently, Mr M, he got ill after a drinking session and clocked-out a few days later. What's great about that? Even I've outlived him, and nobody calls me great."

Mr M purred gently.

"Anyway, let us give thanks to everything sacred that you are actually a cat. Because, my four-legged companion, if you were human, you'd undoubtedly be in a home for the terminally forgotten by now, being fed pulped garbage on a spoon by some drugged-up twat who liked nothing more than to stub his cigarettes out on your bare feet.

"Look, my point is, neither of us are getting any younger. Granted, we've both outdone Alexander the Great, but maybe those fine senses of yours are getting a tad dulled by age, what do you think, eh?"

Niko had a sudden realisation he may well be talking about himself. What if he went to pull the trigger one day and his eyesight let him down, or he suddenly developed a tremor in his firing hand? Missing the quarry had never been discussed — in fact, very little had ever been discussed — but he had the feeling that even if his intended target would be pleased about the fact that he, or she, was still breathing, T.S.A. certainly would not.

The cat didn't move.

"So, old and wise feline friend of mine, tell me something." Niko took another drag and pushed thoughts of failure to one side. "What the shit almighty is this disc thing? Is it my soul? Is it cancer? Is it the Devil himself residing somewhere around my pancreas?"

The cat still didn't move. It blinked slowly.

"Ah, what the hell. I can see you're not in a talkative mood tonight. Might as well have called you Delores. Anyway, I need another tinny, as the Australians say. So, come on, old-timer — shift your arthritic bones."

Niko gently pushed the cat off himself and got off the sofa. Mr Mephistopheles gave a whine of disapproval as it landed on the wooden flooring and slowly made its way over to a nearby chair. It bumped into the leg of Niko's ornate coffee table on its way to continue its musings.

Niko retrieved a can of Fosters from the American-style fridge in his designer kitchen and made his way to the large, mahogany desk in the corner of his spacious living room. "Fair play for the Australians, Mr M," Niko said. "They may struggle with social decorum, but they sure know how to make a lager." He raised the can in salute.

The desk (eight foot by four foot) sat atop a large, expensive-looking rug (ten foot by six foot). The rug had not actually been that costly; more a haggled purchase from a Lebanese on Camden Market who just so happened to sell other products he could not display, and that Niko was smoking right now. But it wasn't the cost Niko cared about: it was the dimensions.

Even by even, just like the desk itself, and who could fault the number ten in any equation? In Niko's eyes, the number ten was the God of all numbers. The Zeus of integers. The coolest number in the known universe. The number that walks into a party and steals the girlfriends of all the other numbers. Yes, he liked being Operative Four, but oh, how he would have loved to have been Operative Ten. Niko had always told himself he would retire from his current line of work once he had dispatched his tenth quarry. Yes sir, the minute that tenth arsehole hit the floor, he'd be on the phone to Delores.

'Hi Delores — Operative Four here. I'm dropping the mic. I'm out of here, my friend. It's been good talking to you. You make sure you have a nice day now.'

Niko wondered how T.S.A. would react. Once you were in, could you get out? What *had* happened to Operatives One, Two and Three? Niko doubted T.S.A. was funding a retirement home for lapsed assassins somewhere on the south coast. He decided, when his head was clearer, he would need to come up with some sort of exit strategy.

Niko fired up his recently acquired, state-of-the-art Mac — bought from the proceeds of his last successful crusade, the one before Martin Bead — and, as he waited for the screen to come to life, he wondered what little luxury he would afford himself with the payment for disposing of poor old Martin.

He knew the payment would be there, in the special account set up for him by T.S.A. He also knew the Swiss bank would be renowned for not asking any questions as to where their clients' money came from and for keeping any transactions completely and utterly to itself. They hadn't failed him yet.

Maybe he'd change his car. Another Mercedes, obviously. Couldn't fault the Germans when it came to engineering. Well, except for Zyklon B, perhaps. Maybe he'd go for something with a bit more room, something a little less sporty than the AMG Coupe he currently had. Jeeze, how old was he getting?

Niko entered his heavily passworded account. "Well, would you look at that, Mr M," he said. He moved his head closer to the screen, just in case his eyes were playing tricks like they sometimes did when he'd been smoking.

"Nope, there it is, Mr M. Yet another fifty k, just for squeezing a trigger. If only my old school teachers could see me now. Actually, if they were here now, I'd probably shoot the bastards"

Niko checked his e-mails, but knew there'd be nothing there.

Ever since he'd agreed to be Operative Four, the amount of social interaction he'd enjoyed, which had never been much to begin with, had dwindled to miniscule proportions. Somehow, T.S.A. had even put a stop to junk e-mails troubling his in-box, and, on their insistence, he'd cancelled all his social media accounts.

He switched off the computer and made his way back to the sofa. The cat immediately followed him.

"As normal, Mr M," Niko said. "Nobody really loves us. Do you know, I could count on the fingers of one hand the people who actually know you and I exist. We're like shadows, Mr M. Elusive by day and invisible by night. Even Cherie doesn't look at me when I… well, when I… you know? Just as well we have each other, eh, Mr M?"

Niko switched on his sixty-five-inch television. He tried to recall after which of his quarries he had treated himself to that particular extravagance, but failed to remember which it was. How could he not remember? There'd only been six.

"Hey, I think I know what this disc thing is, Mr M," Niko said, excitedly. "It's my own black hole. It's sucking away my memories like a… like a… well, something that sucks. A Dyson maybe! Yes, that's it. Sucking away my memories like an ultra-modern Dyson. I am no longer a substance of recalled moments, Mr M. Jeeze, nearly every human on this hell-hole of a planet we live on exists on past glories; retelling snippets of when they were exactly who they wanted to be, and oh, how they wish they could go back to those idyllic, salad-days, and do it all over again in the inane belief they were at their happiest back in the day. Just like when computers go tits-up and re-set to a time when everything was working fine and dumping all the shit that's happened since.

"Well, not I, Mr M. Not I, Nikolaus Andrianakis, also known as Niko the Greek, even though I was born in Shoreditch. The only son of an only son-of-a-bitch who left Mummy-dear and me in a rat-infested hovel in Bethnal Green and pissed off back to Greece, never to be seen again. I shall be like Alexander the Great, who liked to ignore the failings of his past and only bask in the undoubted glory of his future, albeit a future shortened by his failure to process copious amounts of red wine. Nevertheless, from now on, Mr M, with the help of my internal Dyson, we will not dwell on the past, but only look onward and upward."

The cat continued to blink slowly.

"What's that you ask?" Niko said. "What happened to Mummy-dear? Why, Mr M, thanks for being so curious. Now listen, I don't normally talk about it, okay, but seeing as you've asked nicely, I'll tell you. But be careful, Mr M, because we all know what curiosity did, don't we? Now, before I continue, you have to promise not to tell anyone, you hear me? Don't you dare go shouting off your feline mouth. I know what you cats are like. Thick as thieves. You'll be hanging about in The Cat's Whiskers, or wherever the hell you guys meet socially, and you'll be spilling your guts to all and sundry. Before I know it, every damned cat in the neighbourhood will be whispering as I walk past, nudging their partners, telling them, *'Hey, that's the geezer Mr M was going on about.'*

"Do you promise?" Niko squinted his eyes and stared at the cat. "Hang on a goddam minute," he said. "Are you sure I haven't told you this story before? I'm sure I've told you this story before. Actually, I'm sure I've told you several times."

The cat purred.

"Okay, okay. I'll take your word for it, although many wouldn't. Now, let's see. Where shall I begin?

"Well, Mummy-dear, like most people, needed money. No money equalled no rent, and, more importantly, no vodka. With no job, no qualifications, no man about the house, and a six-month baby squalling his way through life, what was a nineteen-year-old woman supposed to do?

"Now, fortunately, we were surrounded by Jews. It's no mistake, Mr M, that most Jews seem to have a knack for acquiring money. An old acquaintance of mine told me it's because they have a healthy respect for a quarter of one percent, and, whatever their trick is, it seems to work. Anyway, Mummy-dear decided to put her one and only talent — that of being able to get most things down her throat without choking to death — to good use. Fair play: it kept a roof over our heads and stopped us from starving to death. She was literally milking those Jews for whatever she could get."

The cat slowly made its way off Niko and meandered its way to the kitchen, where it drank deeply from its bowl.

"Yeah, I guess you're right," Niko said. "It's really not that interesting. Of course, by the time she was thirty, most of Mummy-dear's internal organs complained bitterly at the amount of vodka she was bathing them in and eventually her brain decided to bleed like a stuck pig. Let's just say the funeral was a small affair, and good old Nikolaus Andrianakis has pretty much fended for himself ever since."

The cat returned, suitably sated, and curled itself into its regular patch on Niko's stomach.

"Anyway," Niko said, gently playing with the cat's ears. "No more maudlin. What's done is done and nothing can change that shit. So, I shall let this Dyson disc do its stuff and devour the last thirty-plus years. From now on, my success and my future shall be synonymous. I will not have one without the other."

Niko let out a long whistle.

"Jeeze, Mr M," he said. "I should be writing all this crap down. I mean, it's bordering on philosophical genius. What am I? Like the modern-day Plato, or Aristotle or something? How about the father of them all, Socrates? Maybe I should get myself a corner table in Greasy Joe's and allow people to come to me for wisdom."

Niko finished his lager and winced at the heat from the last toke of his five-bar before stubbing it out. He salvaged a Star Wars-themed television remote from behind a cushion. “Now, let’s see if there’s anything worth watching on this overly priced box.”

Niko, as always, made sure the volume and the channel number were set at an even number before falling asleep to the sounds of some high-browed discussion about whether the country should reintroduce the death penalty.

WEDNESDAY

Stanley knew Assistant Chief Constable Patty Cleland wasn't listening.

If he'd been filling her in on a good old gangland killing, involving some of the East End's drug barons, or something racially motivated, or maybe even a case of someone removing the internal organs of prostitutes, she may have shown more interest. Hell, she would have shown more interest if he'd brought her a case of playground bullying. But the moment T.S.A. killings were on the agenda was the moment he knew he may as well have been talking to her about tiling his bathroom.

"Any eye-witnesses?" she asked, rearranging some papers on her desk. Stanley noticed that her wedding ring was missing from the appropriate finger.

Stanley took a deep breath. He'd already mentioned there were none. He glanced at the large wall clock: nine a.m. The chief had asked him to brief her at eight-thirty, but had kept him waiting due to, *'more pressing matters.'*

"No, Ma'am," Stanley said. "No eye-witnesses. Nobody saw anything. Nobody heard anything. Nobody really gives a wet fart about Martin Bead." Stanley considered adding, *'including you,'* but thought better of it.

"His family, what there is of it," he continued, "are not what you might call close. We have managed to find a distant cousin who's willing to come in and attempt to identify the body, but even she's said she hasn't seen Martin for around eighteen years. With half his head missing, I'm going to guess she may find it somewhat difficult. I suppose it doesn't really matter. We can always confirm who he is from fingerprints and other sources.

"Anyway, since his release from prison, he's been living on his own in a tiny one-room flat in Homerton. It's rented out by the probation service and used as a starting point for released prisoners with nowhere else to go. It looks like the only human interaction Martin Bead has had during that time has been with his parole officer, excluding the brief glimpse he may have had of whoever blew his brains out.

"I'm waiting for ballistics to confirm what type of weapon was used — it'll be a Glock — for forensics to tell me if anything was found on the body — there won't be — and for pathology to confirm cause and time of death, but you don't need to be a genius to—"

"Yes, yes," the chief interrupted. "I'm sure you're doing everything you can, Stanley, and keep up the good work. Just let me know if anything interesting crops up."

"And if it doesn't?"

"Sorry?"

"What if nothing *'interesting'* crops up? What then?" There were those damnable fingers again doing the speech-mark dance. Perhaps he'd chop them off. It was so annoying.

"Is something upsetting you, DCI Wood?" Patty asked, still moving papers pointlessly around her desk.

Stanley couldn't reconcile why he was feeling quite so angry. The chief's attitude to Martin Bead should not have come as any shock. It was the exact same attitude afforded to the last five investigations of T.S.A. victims he had conducted, and, as of now, Stanley had normally joined in the apathy. Maybe it was because Michelle had been asleep when he'd got home last night and he hadn't been there to help her to bed. Or perhaps it had something to do with the fact he'd missed the recycling day; again.

Recycling had always been Michelle's responsibility. Until it wasn't. Just like cooking, cleaning, washing, ironing and a whole host of other things. It had recently dawned on Stanley that prior to Michelle's illness, the only thing he used to do with any authority was remove spiders and put petrol in the car.

Maybe he just needed a holiday, Stanley thought. But not abroad! Stanley wasn't afraid of flying. He was afraid of crashing. He knew statistically it was the safest form of travel, but he also knew, in the event of a plane coming down, the chances of surviving were practically nil. Why put yourself at such risk? He felt the same about bungee jumping, rollercoasters, skiing and Indian takeaways. The odds were just too stacked.

Maybe he would take Michelle off to a cottage in the Lake District for a relaxing weekend. He was sure she'd once said something about liking it there.

"No, Ma'am," Stanley said. "Everything is just tickety-boo."

The chief looked up from her desk and peered at Stanley over the top of her glasses. Stanley noticed her eyes looked redder than normal. He couldn't recall if he knew how old Patty was, but whatever age she kept, Stanley believed she now looked older.

"Good. Like I said, just keep me informed," she said. "Oh, and by the way, I've had confirmation your request for retirement figures has been approved. You've done your thirty years. You should get them in the next week or two."

Stanley knew that, '*just keep me informed*' was Patty-speak for '*I couldn't give a damn. You're not getting any resources on this one so just leave me alone.*' He closed the door of the Assistant Chief's office just a little harder than necessary on his way out.

***

Stanley had purposely not yet looked at a morning newspaper nor listened to any television news. He didn't need to. He knew exactly the tone they would take. Martin Bead was a wrong-un, and, yet again,

T.S.A. had done every law-abiding citizen a favour by getting him off their streets. There'd been no torture; no long, lingering death. Just a quick bullet to the head. Martin Bead would have been dead before his body hit the ground: as humane a killing as a vet putting a sick animal to sleep.

Of course, the more anti-police media bosses would, yet again, suggest T.S.A. was doing the job the police constantly failed to do: keeping the people safe.

Verity was waiting by his desk, holding a cup of coffee. "A little extra sugar, as requested," she said, thrusting it towards him.

"You're late," Stanley retorted, snatching the coffee. "I had to go in and speak to Her Majesty myself. Could have done with some back-up, but then I guess you were too busy seeing to Mr Handsome's needs this morning." Stanley slumped into his chair.

Verity shook her head. "For your information," she said, slowly, "Mr Handsome was already gone when I finally got home last night, and I'm late because I queued for like forever for your bloody coffee." She marched off in the direction of the toilets.

"*For like forever*!" Stanley shouted at her back. "What sort of English is that?" He was aware people had started staring.

Stanley fired up his computer and called up the BBC website.

Sure enough, the report of Martin Bead's death had been given the treatment Stanley expected. It was nowhere near the primary headline, the privilege of which had gone to a young member of the Royal family who'd been seen at a party with a porn actress.

The report, what there was of it, informed their audience that Martin Bead, as a youth, had spent most of his days in and out of young offenders' institutes. There then followed a list of his many misdemeanours in adulthood, and concluded with the reasons for his latest time spent in prison. Their final flourish was:

The organisation known as T.S.A. has claimed responsibility for the death, once more deciding to take the law into its own capable hands.

"Is it safe to speak to you now?" Verity asked.

Stanley had not noticed her return. He wondered if he should apologise for his remark about Mr Handsome, but thought better of it. Apologising had never been a strong point of his. In any case, he believed Verity was probably made of stern enough stuff to handle a few choice words.

"Pull up a seat," he said, opening a new tab on the computer. "Let's see what Mr Fuckwit has to say."

Buck Witman's effort was on the front page of the Hackney Gazette.

THE SILENCING ASSOCIATION REMOVE MORE VERMIN FROM THE NEST

by

BUCK WITMAN

Last night, at 9.53 p.m., a male was found dead outside a lock-up in Jupiter Road, Homerton, right here in the heart of the East End. The man has been identified as 43-year-old Martin Bead.

Mr Bead, a local man, was well-known to the police, was unmarried, and leaves no children.

The organisation known as T.S.A. has claimed responsibility for Mr Bead's death.

Police were called to the scene by coded telephone message, and the body was found with a fatal single bullet wound to the head. Discovered on the body, inserted between the victim's lips, was one of T.S.A.'s simple calling cards: a white circle on a plain black background. Leading the investigation into the murder is DCI Stanley Arthur Peregrine Wood, who has confirmed the police have no leads as to the identity of any T.S.A. members, let alone who may have killed Martin Bead.

"The little prick," Stanley said.

This murder brings the total number of confirmed T.S.A. killings to twenty-three, with the last six being right here on our doorstep...

Attached to the bottom of the piece was a small head-shot photograph of Verity. The photograph had been cropped to show Verity's bare shoulders and a large portion of cleavage. On the face of it, it appeared she could easily be topless. Underneath the photograph, it simply read:

Helping with the enquiry, DI Verity Monique Chandler-Adebayo.

"What the hell!" Verity said. "I am going to bury that arsehole."

"Best of luck," Stanley replied. "He's pretty much indestructible." He pointed at the photograph. "Please tell me you were wearing clothes."

"Of course I was," Verity replied. "I'm not in the habit of having my photograph taken in the nude. I think that's from my twenty-first birthday. I was wearing a beautiful cocktail dress. Where the hell did he dig it up from?"

"I warned you," Stanley said. "Buck is a two-bit hack, but he can still be dangerous. Don't ever let him get inside your head."

"Do people actually read this rag?" Verity asked.

"Better believe it," Stanley replied. "In fact, the readership has widened in recent years thanks to the paper winning some fancy award from Private Eye for their investigation into Hackney's homeless problems."

"Oh great. So now most of the local populace is going to think I try to solve crimes naked."

"Yep. I'm guessing there's a large portion of them copying and pasting as we speak, ready to—"

"Please!" Verity said, closing her eyes. "Don't. Just don't." She reopened her eyes, leaned over Stanley, and cleared the screen from his computer. "Was the homeless thing one of Buck's pieces?"

"Good God, no! Way too good for his style. But it did stir the politicians into action."

"My father once told me not to believe anything I read and only half of what I see," Verity said.

"Isn't he a man of God?"

"Yes, well, I don't think he actually meant The Bible. Just everything else."

"Does he preach?" Stanley asked. "You know, in between fighting the good fight against disease."

"Well, he's not ordained," Verity said. "He's more like a religious after-dinner speaker, I suppose. But he does do a lot for the Church behind the scenes. Sits on all sorts of committees. Raises money. You know the type?"

Stanley believed he did know the type, and he was not in the mood to enter into an argument about how someone, who presumably believed in the words of the good book with its pregnant virgins; people who could cure the blind; turn water into wine; come back from the dead, and all that, could then tell his daughter not to believe anything she ever read.

Stanley had heard enough theologians argue their case in his time, and, in his opinion, which he firmly believed to be the right opinion, the good book was a crock of shit. Give him the Greek, Roman or Norse Gods any day of the week. They were still a crock of shit, but at least they were a more interesting crock of shit.

"Did you ever think about the priesthood?" he asked Verity. "Or medicine? You know, follow Daddy's footsteps."

Verity laughed. "Are you joking?" she said. "The priesthood? Me? Far too judgemental for my liking. I have no intention of marrying anybody, especially not God. I'd rather root out evil through police-work rather than fire and brimstone, thank you very much."

Stanley had never been a church-goer, but since Michelle had been taken ill, he'd occasionally found himself envying those with some form of blind faith. Under no circumstances had Stanley ever believed in the idea of an omnipotent God who had a hand in everything, but, periodically, he now wished he had something, or someone, to latch onto when the going got tough. Just a little helping-hand from some higher authority. A leg-up emerging from the ether like some super-hero in a Marvel comic.

Of course, he knew super-someones were the stuff of fiction, just like God himself, and Stanley, as always, would need to deal with whatever shit-storm came his way pretty much by himself. He'd been doing it all his life.

For now, the best he had was Verity.

"Yeah, well try not to root it out all in one go, there's a good girl," Stanley said. "Those evil people keep us in a job." Stanley stood up from his desk and put his hand on Verity's shoulder. "So, it's always handy to have a few of them milling about doing their thing."

Verity was wearing a blouse with cut-outs at the shoulders, and it was the first time, other than with Michelle, that Stanley had been in contact with a woman's bare flesh for as long as he could remember. Even though the contact was harmless, Stanley felt a surge of excitement run through him. He removed his hand quickly.

"I'll give it my best shot," Verity said, smiling. "But I'm not promising anything. Maybe we should put an extension on the building to house all the criminals I intend to apprehend."

"Maybe we'll start calling you Diana Prince," Stanley said, sitting back down. The thoughts of super-heroes were obviously still lurking. "That's the real name of Wonder Woman," he added, pleased to show off his knowledge.

"Actually, her real name was Princess Diana of Themyscira," Verity said, nonchalantly. "She used Diana Prince because—"

Stanley held up his hand and shook his head. "You need to stop right now," he said.

Verity acquiesced.

There followed a few minutes of silence which Verity eventually broke. "So, superhero duties to one side," she said, "what do we do next?"

“Simple,” Stanley replied. “We try and find out who took a disliking to Martin Bead’s brains. It’s what us detectives do. We detect. So, with that in mind, I want you to check with uniform. See if anything actually came out of the house-to-house.” Stanley knew the request was lame. He just needed some excuse to get Verity out of the way so he could gather his thoughts and stop being some sort of creepy, old man.

“Really?” Verity said. “Are you honestly expecting anyone to have seen or heard something? This is T.S.A. we’re talking about.”

Stanley gave out a solitary snort. “Okay,” he said, slowly. “Let’s establish the rules. There are only two. Rule One, I am always right. Rule Two, in the event of me being wrong, Rule One applies. So, whenever I ask your pert arse to do something, you simply smile, nod and go and do it. Understood?”

Stanley couldn’t believe he’d said the word *pert.* It hadn’t been a word he could ever remember using before. Maybe it wouldn’t have been so bad if he hadn’t used his fingers to bring attention to it. He really was going to have to chop them off. Fortunately, Verity seemed to take it in her stride. Stanley had the distinct feeling she was well used to overtly lewd adjectives being used to describe parts of her body. Stanley reminded himself it still wasn’t right, no matter how the recipient took it. He would need to be more careful. He could only imagine what Michelle would say.

***

Niko awoke with the usual fog in his head that followed a drinking and smoking session. He had not made it to bed and rolled off the sofa, still fully clothed, to find Mr M gently swiping its claws at a piece of paper on the floor.

"Morning, Mr M," Niko said. "What've you got there?"

The paper looked vaguely familiar. Niko gingerly got to his feet and made his way to the kitchen for a glass of iced water. As always, he poured two. He then drank one and poured the other away. The cat had followed him and now sat dutifully at Niko's heels.

"Right then," Niko said, crouching down to ruffle the cat's head. "Let's see what we've got for your breakfast. Don't know about you, Mr M, but I could do with a nice, big fry-up to sort my head out. Perhaps I'll pay Greasy Joe's a visit. What do you think?"

Niko fed the cat, showered, brushed his teeth — he was proud they were still as white as they'd ever been — and tidied himself up as best as was needed for a visit to Joe's café, renowned locally for its huge breakfasts at reasonable prices. Joe was second generation Italian and supposedly *connected,* although Niko doubted it.

"I think I'll be going all in today, Mr M," Niko said, picking up his keys with a flourish. "The full Joe's Special with extra everything. I'm sure I can just about afford it."

As Niko headed for the door, he registered the piece of paper Mr M had been playing with earlier.

"What the hell *is* this?" he said, picking it off the floor.

Written on the paper in Niko's handwriting were the numbers 2346.

Written on the reverse, in pencil, was:

YOU'RE SLIPPING FOUR. YOU LEFT THIS BEHIND. NO MORE MISTAKES!

Niko's appetite suddenly disappeared.

"Jesus Christ on a bike," he said. His legs just managed to support him enough for Niko to make it back to his sofa. He turned the paper over and over, hoping that somehow the information would be different. He waved the piece of paper at the cat.

"Any ideas when this arrived, Mr M?" Niko pleaded. "Come on, you're a bloody cat, you guys know everything. When did this arrive, eh? And who brought it? Please, Mr M, just give me something to work with here."

Mr M offered up no information, and Niko decided he needed some proper sleep in order to clear his mind. "I'm taking a rain-check on breakfast, Mr M," he said. "I'm going to get some shut-eye, but I really, really need you to keep your eyes peeled on that door." He pointed at the door to the apartment and noticed his hand was shaking badly. "And I need you to tell me if anybody comes within fifty yards of it, you understand?"

The cat made its way to its basket and curled up contentedly.

"Oh, great," Niko said, throwing his hands in the air. "That's just bloody marvellous. Why couldn't I have found a sodding great, big dog?"

Before Niko finally managed to sleep, he made two visits to the bathroom to be sick.

***

The bullet missed Martin Bead's head, putting a neat hole through the lock-up door. Martin Bead laughed loudly and pointed at Niko.

"You messed up big time," he said. "T.S.A. won't be happy about that."

He pulled his wallet out of a pocket and threw two ten-pound notes at Niko followed by some coins. As the money fluttered to Niko's feet, it turned into extra-strong mints.

"Hey, watch this," Martin Bead shouted. He pulled up his shirt and started belly dancing; his flab actually making slapping noises as it rolled. "I'm going home now," he said, starting to disappear from the feet up. "I'm going to give Isabella a good seeing-to."

Niko woke shivering and covered in sweat. He checked Martin Bead's wristwatch: three p.m.

He gave himself several minutes of deep breathing exercises to bring his body back under control before getting out of bed. After steadying himself with the help of the bedside table, Niko decided he needed some fresh air. Followed by a drink. Maybe several.

After tidying himself up, he made his way into the living room, where Mr M was still curled up, asleep. "I'm going to go for a walk via the pub, Mr M," Niko said as he picked up his keys. "And remember. Keep an eye on that door."

The cat didn't move.

***

Two hours later, sitting at a single table in a darkened recess of the local Wetherspoons, Niko was ear-wigging on a conversation, taking place in the next booth, between a local debt collector and a man who was trying to get his money back off a con-man who had sold him a dodgy timeshare. Niko finished his drink with a satisfying slurp and took his two empty pint glasses to the bar.

The alcohol had started to ease Niko's mind.

So, he'd dropped a piece of paper. So what? It only had some random numbers written on it. If the police had found it, they'd never know what the hell they meant, or whose writing it was. How could they? It had been a tiny, miniscule mistake. No biggy.

"Two more Fosters, please," Niko requested of the somewhat bored looking, but very pretty, young girl serving. Thankfully, she was not a talkative soul, and poured the drinks without any question as to why Niko was drinking two drinks at a time.

As soon as he was back at his table, Niko, once again, went through the thought process of who might have found the note. Obviously, someone connected to T.S.A. must have been at the scene after Niko had left, but before the police had arrived. A very tight window of time. Was T.S.A. watching him that closely? Could they be watching him right now? Niko scanned the handful of dead-beats in the pub and doubted it.

During the following two pints, a troubling image came to him. He hadn't noticed at the time, but the picture he now had in his mind's eye of Martin Bead's head showed the entry point of the bullet as just above the right eye. Niko tapped the middle of his forehead angrily.

"It should have been there," he whispered. "Right *between* the eyes."

Niko drained the remains of his drinks and decided he hadn't had anywhere near enough.

***

As Stanley had expected, Verity was able to confirm that uniform had uncovered nothing in their house-to-house enquiries.

The good people of the little corner of London where Martin Bead had been despatched had shown little interest in his existence. He had no friends to speak of, no drinking buddies, no lovers, no social circle — nothing. The tech boffins had managed to trace the occasional location of his phone over the last few days, but it had not thrown up anything of any interest.

Confirmation also came through that the time of death could be narrowed down to no earlier than nine-thirty p.m. Not too difficult to establish, Stanley thought, considering the coded call from T.S.A. had been received at nine-forty p.m. Also, when death had been pronounced at the scene, the body had still been reasonably warm and the blood from Martin Bead's head had still been fresh.

The cause of death was established as a single gunshot wound to the head, and death would have been almost instantaneous. For some reason, pathology decided to add the footnote that Martin Bead had an enlarged heart, high cholesterol, and was undoubtedly diabetic. Were they trying to insinuate Martin Bead didn't have long to go, anyway?

Ballistics had also wasted no time in substantiating that a single bullet from a 9mm Glock 19 had entered Martin Bead's head, just above his right eye, from close range. The bullet had pierced the victim's skull, travelled through his brain matter, taking a few curves here and there, and exited two inches above the nape of his neck, taking most of the back of his head with it. Despite being blunted by Martin Bead's head, the bullet still had enough velocity to punch a hole through the garage door behind him, and was eventually found on a rickety, empty work bench resting against the garage's back wall.

Stanley knew, that with the Glock 19 being one of the most popular handguns in the world, there'd be little-to-no chance of tracing where it came from.

"Ah, the good old Glock," Stanley said. "Favourite of police forces and criminals around the world and probably the only good thing to ever come out of Austria."

"Sigmund Freud was Austrian," Verity replied. "And some of the finest composers ever to have lived. Mozart, Schubert, Hayden, Strauss. Ferdinand Porsche was also Austrian, as was Niki Lauda and Arnold Schwarzenegger, and who could ever forget Eurovision song contest winner, Conchita Wurst?"

From the look on Stanley's face, Verity knew she'd made a mistake.

"I wish I had a Glock in my hand right now," Stanley said. "Do you not remember the rules? No one, and I mean no one, likes to be corrected by over-educated smart-arses who think they know it all. Now, if I don't see a perfectly made coffee in front of me within the next five minutes, I will forget my manners and beat you half to death with something very blunt."

As Verity moved through the department, Stanley noticed that a lot of eyes followed her.

"She certainly knows how to strut her stuff," Stanley whispered to himself.

By the time Verity returned, Stanley had received the expected news that no personal items had been found on the victim's body and there was no forensic evidence of any sort to go on. No hair fibres, no prints, no strange DNA that didn't belong to the victim; the conclusion being that the killing had been done by a professional assassin, and a very good professional assassin at that.

"Bloody hell, can't these guys just give us something?" Stanley muttered.

"What about the calling card?" Verity said, placing Stanley's coffee in front of him. Stanley noticed she'd gone to the trouble of adding two fingers of KitKat. "Can we at least find out where they're printed?"

"Been looked into many times before," Stanley replied, making sure he moved marginally in his chair to avoid any accidental contact with Verity as she placed the coffee and chocolate in front of him. "Nothing's ever materialised. The consensus is the assassins print them themselves. We believe every time T.S.A. move patch, they find themselves a different assassin. Now, what happens to the old assassins is anybody's guess. Perhaps they're sent off to live a life of luxury in Buenos Aries, or maybe they just wander into the mountains to die. Perhaps they have their own graveyards, like elephants. What we do know is the printing on the cards has been marginally different for each patch. The circle or the background a slightly different shade, or the size alters by a few millimetres."

"For T.S.A. that doesn't sound very professional," Verity said.

"Couldn't be further from the truth," Stanley said, unwrapping his KitKat. "T.S.A. obviously can't just go on the internet and order the goddam things from Mr Printy Prints printing firm, can they? If they're simply being printed off by random individuals on common types of printers, it's almost impossible, in fact, has been impossible, to trace."

"And is there never anything left on or around the victim?" Verity asked. "A paw-print; a muddy shoe outline; a discarded cigarette?"

"Nope," Stanley replied. "Not a thing. You would hope, as is the case with most serial killers, that they'd get a bit complacent the more victims they take out. At the very least you'd expect them to become bolder. Most killers through history like to tease the police every now and then; leave little clues lying around. But not these guys. Leave every crime scene as clean as a whistle. Except for the victim's blood, of course. That's normally splattered over a fair few square metres. By the way, if Michelle finds out you're supplying me with chocolate, she'll kill you. She reckons I need to lose a few pounds."

"Okay, duly noted," Verity said with a laugh. "But do we really have no idea who T.S.A. are?"

Stanley talked through his chewing. "The official line is always, '*We are following up on several lines of inquiry.*' The truth of the matter is we have no lines of inquiry to actually follow. There's been lots of speculation, of course. Especially in the press. And let's not forget we have the normal gaggle of misfits who claim it's them, but no concrete leads have ever surfaced. I'm sure whoever they may be are also fully aware that police resources are stretched so badly there's no real thirst from the top for discovering who is robbing society of its dross."

"What about social-profiling?" Verity asked. "Do we know the type of person we're looking for?"

"Ah, the good old psycho-babblers," Stanley replied, licking chocolate from his fingers. "Right, you're going to love this. Are you sitting comfortably?" Stanley cleared his throat. "More likely to be male, local, single, living on their own, aged anywhere between twenty-five and fifty-five, have no criminal record, no friends, no family to speak of, and will be inconspicuous in appearance and demeanour."

"Well now, isn't that helpful."

"Tell me about it. One thing we can be sure about is T.S.A. has money. Untraceable firearms do not come cheap and neither do the people who fire them. It's also a fair punt that the killers have had some sort of firearms training. Maybe even be ex-military or ex-coppers. It doesn't matter how close you are: it's extremely difficult to make a single bullet find its exact mark, every time, in the dark."

"I'm sure I read somewhere that they could be an elite, secret arm of the government, set up to alleviate the problem of over-crowded prisons and costly court cases," Verity said.

"And they just might be right. But look, whatever and whoever they are, they obviously have a sophisticated way of finding the people needed to carry out their bidding. They can't just pop an advert in The Gazette asking if anybody fancies shooting people in the head for a living. They evidently need to be one-hundred percent certain that whoever they approach will be willing and able to do the job."

"A bit like grooming," Verity said.

"Exactly," Stanley replied. "They must spend a lot of time researching. According to the babblists, the people they seek out will already have some sort of axe to grind. Something that's happened in their past to make them angry with society and therefore more willing to agree to remove total strangers from the land of the living."

"So couldn't we do the same?" Verity asked. "Couldn't we do the same sort of research? Maybe start by looking at all the ex-coppers or military in the area. Wouldn't that narrow our options down?"

Stanley cocked an eyebrow. "Do you realise how long that would take?" he said. "Don't forget, we're pretty much on our own on this one. Her Majesty will never give us the manpower we'd need to find the names in the first place, never mind follow them up. With just the two of us, it would take forever, and I intend to hang up my truncheon in the not-too-distant future, thank you very much."

Apart from Michelle and Patty, Stanley had not mentioned his potential retirement to anybody, and he wondered why he had felt the need to mention it now.

"Anyway," he added quickly, hoping to avert any conversation on the matter, "what if we did find a couple of fits? What then?"

Verity shrugged her shoulders like she was running out of ideas. "I don't know. Couldn't we bring them in for questioning?"

Stanley laughed. "And ask them what, exactly? Could you tell me, pretty please, are you a member of T.S.A? Did you put a bullet into Martin Bead's head on Tuesday night?"

"There must be something we can do," Verity said.

Stanley let out a sigh. "Listen," he said, "unless you've got some magic wand tucked up that rather tight-fitting top you're wearing, we're going to have to rely on a lucky break."

Stanley immediately rued mentioning Verity's top. What was happening to him? Was it that you automatically became a weird, sinister sex-pest once you'd passed a certain age?

"We're going to need a mistake," he continued, quickly. "A chance meeting. Somebody saying the right thing at the right time in the right place. Divine intervention. Hey, perhaps you could have a word with your father and see if he can ask the big man upstairs for a bit of help."

Verity looked down at her blouse. Maybe it was a little tight, she thought. The buttons over her breasts were gaping slightly. But it wasn't obscene; she certainly had tops that were more revealing. She pulled the blouse tighter, but it immediately sprang back to how it was. "What about CCTV?" she asked, giving up on her efforts. "With the number of killings these guys have carried out up and down the country, surely to God there's some footage somewhere?"

Stanley remained silent.

"What, nothing?"

Stanley shook his head. "I guess one of the fortunate things for T.S.A. is the fact the people they like to wipe out also prefer to stay in the shadows and don't exactly seek the limelight," he said. "So far, T.S.A. employees have been extremely competent at plying their trade in the darkest of corners. There's not one known single second of footage of these guys in action. It's why we believe the killers have to be local to the patch they're operating in. They must have local knowledge."

"But even local people can't know where *all* cameras are located," Verity said. "What about dash-cams, private security cameras, or even door-bell cameras. I mean, they've been doing this for ten years. You'd think there'd be a slip up somewhere."

"Yep, you'd think."

THURSDAY

Niko woke to the sound of movement. A quick scan of his surroundings told him he was in his own bed, but his brain wouldn't remind him how he'd actually got there. The last thing it was willing to picture was of him complimenting some woman at the bar in the Wetherspoons for her nice, sparkly top. He had no idea what time it was. He looked at his wrist, but the watch he'd taken off Martin Bead was missing. He tentatively swung his legs out of bed and noticed his clothes in a heap on the floor. Through the pain and fog in his head, Niko registered a low, conversational noise coming from his living room. It took several moments before it sank in: someone was in his flat.

"I thought I told that cat to keep an eye out," he whispered.

Niko continued to sit on the edge of his bed listening to the voice, simultaneously trying to persuade his heart-beat to slow and his mind to clear. He eventually settled on two options. One, he could remain sitting in his bedroom and wait for whoever was there to do whatever they were there to do. Two, he could open his bedroom door and confront the intruder.

After some deliberation, he settled on Option Two.

He looked around for something to arm himself with. His Glock, as always, was safely locked away in a drawer of the desk in his living room, and the only thing he could find was a small snow-globe containing a boy and a girl on either ends of a see-saw. Niko recalled he'd been under the influence of some Turkish weed when he'd bought the item. At the time, he'd thought the piece to be a thing of beauty, encapsulating the never-ending ups-and-downs of man's quintessential struggle with life. Right now, he thought it wholly inadequate for the possible job at hand.

Niko took several deep breaths, and then opened the bedroom door just enough to get a view of his living room. There was somebody sitting on his sofa. From the back of the person's head, Niko ascertained it was a woman. He could now also hear what she was saying more clearly. Was she talking to Mr M? That God-forsaken cat! He really would have to consider getting a dog. Niko stood on his toes and noticed the woman was wearing a sparkly top of some kind.

On the understanding that any would-be burglar intent on doing Niko harm probably wouldn't be sitting on his sofa in a sparkly top talking to his cat, Niko decided to make his presence known.

"Um, hello," he said, tossing the snow-globe behind him onto his bed.

The woman quickly turned her head and then stood up. "Well, hello there, sleepy head," she replied, smiling. A slight but noticeable hair-lip distorted her speech.

She made her way to Niko and gave him a peck on the cheek before returning to sit on the sofa. Niko noticed she was wearing a leather skirt which fell just above the knee, revealing varicosed calves, and the sparkly gold top he had vaguely remembered had the words, *You're never too old to sparkle!* emblazoned on its front. The woman was short — Niko estimated about five-three — extremely thin and had no figure to write home about.

"I hope you don't mind, but I've helped myself to some cereal," the woman said, picking up an empty bowl from the coffee table and waving it in the air to prove the point. "I'm afraid I've used the last of the milk to give Tiddles here a drink."

Niko noticed her nails were covered in bright, pink varnish with silver sparkles, all badly chipped.

Her long, thinning blonde hair, despite the pink streaks, was obviously greying, and the crows' feet around her eyes and mouth, together with slightly discoloured teeth, suggested Niko would not have to worry if he'd committed any crime as far as age was concerned. If he'd had the energy, he would have quite happily argued with the T-shirt's sentiment.

"I love your cat," the woman said. "He looks old and wise. Like me!"

"His name's not Tiddles. It's Mr M," Niko said, trying to rub the pain out of his head. "It's short for Mr Mephistopheles."

Niko, on seeing the bemused look of the woman, decided to elaborate. "Mephistopheles was the geezer who acted as the Devil's agent when Faust sold his soul in return for unlimited knowledge and worldly pleasures," he said. "It's from German folklore."

"Oh," the woman said. "He looks more like a Tiddles to me."

"Um, I'm sorry to ask," Niko said. "But are you… you know? And did we… have we… have you and I, you know, done anything with or to each other?"

The woman laughed. "No, I'm not," she replied. "And don't worry. I haven't rummaged the place for valuables. Unless, of course, you count the cereals. No, I came here completely of my own free will. No contract was needed. Unfortunately, heavy petting and a quick grope of my tits was as far as you got before you passed out. My, my, you were in a mess, especially after we'd smoked some of this stuff."

The woman waved her arm over the coffee table, which clearly showed the remnants of joint making items.

Niko noticed Martin Bead's watch amongst the debris.

"Don't look so worried," the woman said. "I didn't force myself on you. I found myself a spare blanket and slept here." The woman patted the sofa. "I must admit it's very comfortable. Expensive, I'm guessing. This is a very nice place you've got. Obviously done well for yourself, young man."

The woman picked up the wristwatch. "I mean, look at this. I bet this cost a packet." She replaced the watch back on the coffee table. "Now, according to that watch, I have half-an-hour before I need to be anywhere, so we could fuck now if you like. Obviously, I haven't had a chance to sort my face out this morning, so you can take me from behind if that helps. By the way, just in case you've forgotten, the name's Sylvia."

The woman stood up and slowly started making her way towards Niko. She lifted the front of her skirt to reveal she was travelling commando. "I find it saves fumbling about, and, let's face it, you're already naked."

In its confusion, Niko's brain had forgotten to remind him his clothes were in a heap behind him. He looked down at his naked form and was horrified at the sight of his manhood, which had obviously decided to retreat from the situation. He quickly covered his genitalia with his hands.

"Um… thanks for the offer," he said. "But I'm really not feeling my best right now, and I wouldn't want to disappoint you."

Niko disappeared into his bedroom, quickly closing the door behind him. "I'm really, really sorry," he shouted, pulling on his clothes. "Can we just blame the demon drink? Don't know about you, but I'd been on it all day. On an empty stomach as well. Not a good combination."

"Well, okay," Sylvia shouted back. "Have it your own way. I guess I'll be on my way then. Unless you want me to stick around for a bit just in case you change your mind."

"Um, don't think so," Niko said. "I'm really busy this morning. I have to visit my dying sister in Seven Oaks. Really should have left by now. It was nice meeting you, though."

"Well, if you're sure," Sylvia said, suddenly appearing at the bedroom door. "Just a word of advice before I go."

"What's that?"

"I'd get yourself a new back story if I was you. Telling impressionable, lonely, old women that you kill people for a living isn't what I would suggest in order to get their knickers off. Those that wear any. Perhaps tell them you're a pilot. Or a lumberjack. Or even an ex-leading goal-scorer for West Ham. Something like that. See you around."

Sylvia was well gone by the time Niko re-emerged from the bedroom. Had he really told her he killed people? He must have. Why would she mention it otherwise? What if T.S.A. had been in the vicinity? What if the next person he decided to boast to was actually a member of T.S.A? What then?

“Well, that’s an easy one to solve,” Niko said, aloud. “There won’t be a next time! For Christ’s sake, Nikolaus. Get a grip!”

Niko’s outburst had aroused Mr M’s interest.

Niko looked at the cat and was sure Mr M was looking back at him reproachfully.

“I know, I know,” Niko said. “I know exactly what you’re thinking. You’re thinking where the hell did the sister in Seven Oaks come from? But Jeeze, Mr M, did you see the state of her? I had to think of something. Anyway, I always thought it would be nice to have a sister. Preferably one who isn’t dying, granted, but if I’m going to invent her, why not make her from Sevenoaks? Oh, do stop looking at me like that, Mr M. You do know she called you Tiddles, right? Okay, enough of the small-talk, I’m off for breakfast. And this time I mean it.”

***

A few hours later, after being suitably fed by Greasy Joe, Niko was back at his flat playing chess against the computer. He had intended to perhaps while away more time at the café; maybe order more coffee and read the local rag, but he couldn’t get away from the feeling that customers were looking at him.

There were two old dears, in particular, who seemed to be settled in for the day, constantly watching him with obvious contempt in their eyes. They hadn’t just been watching, Niko thought: they'd been judging. It had seemed to Niko as if, somehow, they'd had knowledge of his treatment of poor old Sylvia; one of their own. Maybe, they were T.S.A keeping an eye on him, although he doubted it. Eventually, Niko had been unable to withstand any more scrutiny and left.

As always, Niko was playing white. He'd already lost two games and was well on his way to losing the third, being a bishop and a pawn down in the early exchanges. The computer had also just played a knight to check, pinning Niko's queen in the process.

"Ah, sod this," Niko said, pressing the resign button. "There's obviously something wrong with this computer today, Mr M. It's decided to play better."

Niko had been taught how to play by one of the Jews, and had immediately loved the symmetry. Thirty-two pieces in play, a perfectly acceptable number; sixty-four squares, an even better number; and only two choices of what colour to be. Okay, so the colours black and white may both have five letters in them, but if you added them together: ten. The supreme number.

Niko removed himself to the sofa and turned on the television. He tuned in to one of the twenty-four-hour news channels, half expecting the newsreader to be telling the nation that a certain thirty-three-year-old Niko *'The Greek'* Andrianakis of Stepney Way, London had been arrested for luring an unsuspecting, lonely, sex-starved woman in her sixties to his £799,000 boutique apartment by boasting that he killed people for a living. He then plied her with drugs, refused to cure her of her urges, and sent her on her way with nothing more inside her than a bowl of cereal.

Niko noticed even his imagination had not missed the fact the British were obsessed with how old people were and how much their properties were worth.

"God, Nikolaus, how can you be so bloody stupid?" he said to himself.

Maybe it would be a good idea if he reduced his intake of drugs and alcohol, he thought. He would, of course, also need to point out to the imaginary newsreader that he'd bartered the price of the flat to £800,000 as there was no way he could deal with the number seven hundred and ninety-nine. Perhaps he could ask him to lie about his age, as well, and tell the listeners he was either thirty-two or thirty-four. He hated being thirty-three.

As could have been expected, the real news carried no mention of how Niko had treated poor old Sylvia. It also carried no mention of the death of Martin Bead, despite occurring only two evenings ago.

Niko channel-hopped until he found himself scrolling through the soft-porn section. A well-fronted young woman, wearing thigh-high boots and balancing a mobile phone on her cleavage, took his fancy. According to the caption above her writhing body, her line was free, and her name was Chantel, but Niko doubted if that were true. Chantel, or whatever her name may be, was seductively gesturing Niko to come and do the most wonderful things to her. Of course, it hadn't been the first offer of the day, and a rogue thought formed, where Niko began to wonder what it would have been like if he'd actually done the deed with Sylvia when she'd invited it. He shook his head violently, attempting to send the thought away.

"Maybe it's time to give Cherie another call," he said. "What do you think, Mr M?"

The cat slowly licked its paws and took no notice.

***

Stanley and Verity had been summoned to Patty Cleland's office.

"I want you to take over this armed robbery from last Saturday," she said, passing over some sheets of paper. "Ahmadi's grocery store on the Essex Road. It was Caleb Smollenski's gig, but the stupid fecker's gone and broken his leg, playing with his daughter on a garden trampoline. Go and see Joanne. I'm sure she'll fill you in."

"So, what about Martin Bead?" Verity asked.

The chief peered over her glasses. "Who?"

"Martin Bead," Verity replied. "You know? The guy who—"

"No problem, Ma'am," Stanley interrupted. "We'll get right on it."

"Good," Patty said. "Normally, I wouldn't give a monkey's tit about Fred Ahmadi, or his store, but this robbery has left his poor old grandfather, Bijan, in hospital. On top of that, Fred's gone and spoken to that prick Witman at The Gazette and told him that, in future, he'll be safeguarding his shop with some *cousins*." It was Patty's turn to do the finger-dance. The list of fingers Stanley was going to have to remove was growing. "I don't want this boiling over into a war. Understand?"

***

Verity waited until Stanley was back at his desk before saying anything.

"So that's it, is it?" she said. "We forget Martin Bead. Drop him like a sack of potatoes."

Stanley sighed. "Listen," he said, "don't take it too personally. These T.S.A. killings are not exactly frowned upon by the populace. Mind you, neither are crimes against Fred Ahmadi normally. I suspect the chief is only moving on this one because of the grandfather's involvement."

"So, we just forget Martin Bead ever happened?"

"Not completely," Stanley said. "We just keep him on the back burner. There's still someone out there murdering people on my patch, and I don't like that. But arguing with Her Majesty isn't going to help, especially as she's having domestic problems at the moment."

"Domestic problems? What are you talking about? How do you know that?"

"Because I'm a top-class detective and have used my super-powers to notice she's suddenly missing her wedding ring." Stanley lowered his voice. "My guess is either she's met someone else, or he has, and the ring has ended up in a skip."

"Maybe she's just lost it," Verity said. "People do just lose things, you know?"

"Time will tell," Stanley said. "Anyway, time for me to pull rank and delegate. Go and ask Joanne if there's anything in particular we need to know about this robbery. And get me a coffee in the process."

"I would, but I don't even know who Joanne is."

"She's our oracle," Stanley said. "The all-seeing guru who knows pretty much everything there is to know about this part of the world and the people who live in it. She's a saint. She's the best community-liaison officer we have. Probably the best we've ever had or are ever likely to have. Better than any nark. So, go and hunt her down."

"Ah, nice one, Boss," Verity said, punching Stanley lightly on the arm. This time, the physical contact didn't quite have the same effect on Stanley as before. "I get it. Just call me Lewis Carroll, eh? I'm off to hunt the Nark. Nark — Snark. Very impressed. Excellent play on words."

Stanley didn't feel the time was right to tell Verity he had no idea what she was talking about. He knew Lewis Carroll had written some story about a girl falling down a rabbit hole or something, but he was unaware she had penned anything on police informers.

Verity suddenly started laughing. “Hang on — you said she was a saint, so perhaps we should call her Joanne of Nark. Do you get it?” she asked, noting Stanley’s lack of involvement in the merriment. “Joanne of Nark, instead of Joan of Arc.”

“Yes, I get it,” Stanley replied. “You don’t have to explain everything you say to me. I’m sure even my inferior male brain will occasionally understand your quick-witted, intelligent offerings. I will, of course, immediately let you know if your astute witticisms find themselves hovering well over my head, and politely ask you to sit me down on your knee and explain them to me in a manner in which even I, the village idiot, can comprehend. Now piss off and find Joanne. Oh, and best not tell her I sent you.”

***

Joanne Murray had a desk tucked away in a corner of the station. The desk was one of the tidiest Verity had ever seen, coming second only to her own father’s. Everything had its place, and all papers were neatly stacked with little post-it notes of differing colours poking out from between them. Joanne herself was as neat and tidy as her desk. Her dark hair was immaculately pinned up in a bob, and what little make-up she was wearing had been expertly applied. Verity spied a green drink of some kind in a clear, plastic bottle poking out of the top of a kit bag on the floor and deduced, from her healthy glow, that Joanne Murray's exercise regime and diet would put some Olympians to shame. At the very least, Verity believed Joanne would be vegetarian, maybe even vegan. Verity guessed Joanne to be in her early-to-mid thirties and thought her pretty enough to turn a few heads. Very kissable lips, Verity thought.

Having been in an all-girls' school, Verity wasn't unfamiliar with the sensation of kissing another girl, or even the odd fumble under the covers, but it had never *done* anything for her. The moment she'd got to Oxford and seen boys in all their glory, she'd immediately decided they were the way forward. It hadn't taken her long to realise she could use her abundant female assets to get pretty much anything she wanted in that respect.

"Hi, I assume you're Joanne," Verity said.

"You assume correctly." Joanne's voice was very petite and soothing. The sort of voice that would calm an angry dog, Verity thought. "And you're Verity Monique Chandler-Adebayo, Stanley's new partner."

"My, you do your homework," Verity said with a smile.

"I just like to know who's floating about," Joanne replied. "Now, what is it I can do for you, DI Chandler?"

"The chief has asked us to follow up on the robbery of Fred Ahmadi's convenience store on the Essex Road. Apparently, Mr Ahmadi is getting a bit disgruntled and has threatened to surround himself with some *cousins*. DCI Wood said you were the person to speak to for some local intel."

"Did he now?" Joanne said. "That's kind of him. Could he not have come and asked for himself, or is he still too scared to speak to me?"

"Why would he be scared to speak to you?" Verity asked. She hadn't known Stanley too long, but scared was not an adjective she'd have easily associated with Stanley's persona.

Joanne smiled. "It's okay, DI Chandler, I'm sure Stanley will fill you in, if and when he feels like it. He does most things as and when he feels like it. Now, what do you want to know?"

Joanne was indeed like an oracle. She informed Verity that Ahmadi's convenience store had been opened in the 1950s by the current incumbent's grandfather, Bijan Ahmadi. According to Joanne, Bijan was aged just twenty when he had been forced to flee Iran during the 1953 Anglo/American-led coup that saw Shah Pahlavi placed in control of the country.

Joanne didn't know why Bijan had been forced to leave Iran, but she advised Verity that the British authorities had apparently wasted no time in granting him all the assistance he needed to stay in the UK and open the store. When Bijan had retired in 1993, he passed the running of the store to his eldest son, Mahmoud, who had tragically died of pancreatic cancer in 2010.

The store, simply called Ahmadi's, was now in the sole control of Mahmoud's only child, Fahred Ahmadi, known locally as Fred, who, according to Joanne, was a complete arsehole, and it came as no surprise to her that his store had been turned over; again.

"This is the third time Ahmadi's has been done in the last twelve months," Joanne explained.

"I see. So do you think we can we rule out any thoughts of these robberies being racially motivated?" Verity asked. "Do you think they're simply because Fred is disliked?"

"Absolutely," Joanne replied. "The list of candidates who have some sort of vendetta with Fahred Ahmadi is quite a long one."

"Okay, so fill me in," Verity said. "How did these robberies go down?" Verity suddenly felt very hip at her use of language. She was, however, glad Stanley wasn't about to hear it. Somehow, she didn't think he'd find it quite so acceptable.

Joanne replied without the need for notes.

"The first robbery was committed at ten-thirty on a Tuesday night. One man, wearing a balaclava and dressed entirely in black, entered the store with a sawn-off, pointed it at the young girl behind the counter and demanded all the money in the till."

"Did she give it to him?"

"Of course she did. You're not going to find many people willing to put themselves on the line for Fred Ahmadi."

"How much did they get away with?"

"Very little. Fred had called into the store earlier in the evening and collected what had been taken up until then. Didn't stop him from telling us he was light of a few thousand pounds in his statement. However, when the insurance company asked for the till receipts, they only amounted to two hundred pounds. DI Smollenski wanted to arrest him for attempted insurance fraud, but the chief wouldn't sanction it."

"Has the store got CCTV?" Verity asked.

"More than you can shake a stick at," Joanne replied. "Inside and out. For the first robbery, it shows the man pulling up outside the store on a Kawasaki motorbike with the number plates blacked out with gaffer-tape. He was in and out in no more than forty-five seconds."

"Okay, so what about the others?"

"The second one involved two people, one of whom was definitely female. It was only a few months after the first one. This time, they got away with stock, as well as what was in the till. Alcohol mainly, but bizarrely a catering box of caramel Freddos went with them as well. They had their faces well covered with scarves, but were wearing pretty normal clothing otherwise. The male half of the partnership was carrying a baseball bat which he used to threaten the two members of staff with, whilst the female filled up a kit bag with the bounty.

"Again, the staff didn't put up much of a protest. The two thieves were last picked up on camera running down Packington Street, but then the trail goes cold. DI Smollenski did his best, which in his case is never going to be much, but nothing ever materialised."

"And this latest one?" Verity asked. She filed away Joanne's assessment of Smollenski.

"Last Saturday afternoon, in broad daylight, a stolen BMW pulled up and double parked outside the store. Three people got out. All male, their faces hidden with ski-masks. There was no need to hide the plates. The car wasn't reported stolen until well after the robbery. The owner was in work, and blissfully unaware his pride and joy was being used in a criminal act. The car hasn't been recovered yet, and I doubt it ever will be. Probably scrapped, or been sent abroad by now with a different identity.

"Anyway, from the CCTV images you can tell these guys are big, like heavyweight boxers, or at least people who really like to look after themselves. One was carrying a cricket bat. This time, they're not concerned with the till, or any type of stock.

"At the rear of the store, through a connecting door marked private, there's living quarters, small but comfortable, where eighty-seven-year-old Bijan has been peacefully living out whatever's left of his life. According to Fred, his grandfather spends most of his time sitting out there in an old armchair, listening to the radio. As two of the gang stood guard by the main door, the one with the cricket bat went through that door.

"I have no doubt it was Fred they were looking for, but it was Bijan they found. According to one of the staff, she heard the intruder continuously asking Bijan where Fahred was. Bijan's eighty-seven for Christ's sake. He simply didn't know.

"Anyway, after no more than a minute, the gang left. One of the staff then phoned Fred on his mobile to say they'd had some undesirables in, but because they confirm nothing has actually been taken, Fred doesn't rush to get there. When he does appear, about an hour later, he discovers Bijan unconscious in his armchair. We now know he'd had a heart attack. At first, it looked like Bijan was doing okay, but whilst he's been in hospital, he's had another one. The prognosis is not good. His chances of recovery are pretty much zero."

"Any ideas what the hell this Fred Ahmadi has done to make people this angry?" Verity asked.

Joanne laughed. "Where do we start?"

"Maybe at the beginning."

"Okay, you asked," Joanne said. "Fahred Ahmadi has been trouble all his life. His mother suffered a postpartum haemorrhage giving birth to him and died for her troubles; a rare occurrence made easier by her insistence on a home birth and an unprepared family member who liked to think of herself as a midwife. He was subsequently farmed around different relatives whilst his father, Mahmoud, concentrated on the family business.

"Fahred didn't cope well in school, getting himself a fearsome reputation as a bully. He also sold contraband goods, undoubtedly stolen from his father's store, to other pupils. We still have records of the school's liaison officer's reports if you'd like to see them. He did manage to scrape one GCSE in Business Studies, of all things. When he left school, with nothing better to do, he started serving at the store.

"As an adult, Fahred first came to our attention at the age of eighteen. There'd been reports of a gang of youths hanging around London Fields in Hackney, terrorising passers-by. Their modus operandi was to ride around on mountain-bikes, keeping an eye out for lone women with loosely draped handbags. Having selected a suitable victim, they would ride by as fast and as close as they could and one of them would snatch the bag.

"The gang was eventually rumbled when an undercover police-woman was sent to the park with a nice, big handbag strung over her shoulder. It just so happened, Fahred was the one doing the snatching that day. He was the only one of the gang who we managed to catch, but he was enough. Suffice to say, Fahred showed no loyalty to his fellow gang members and wasted no time in supplying their names and addresses in return for a less stringent punishment. He was given a twelve-month suspended sentence, whilst the others received some short-term jail-time. It was only a few days after the gang-leader's release that Fahred was found in an alleyway not far from the store. He'd been liberally beaten half to death with what turned out to be a piece of scaffolding pipe. Thanks to the event, Fahred still has a visible, ragged scar running from his upper lip to his right eye.

"When he was twenty, with his father Mahmoud on his deathbed, Fahred was arrested again; this time for his involvement in a ring of car-thieves. Fahred's role had been to launder the ill-gotten cash through Ahmadi's store. On this occasion, after he'd once again given detectives the three names they were looking for in return for a meagre six months in prison, the thieves decided a beating with a piece of scaffolding wasn't quite enough. One finger for each name was apparently the equation they'd decided to use. They managed to pass their mathematics through the prison system, and, two months into his time, Fahred found himself in a world of pain. He was found in the prison showers, bleeding profusely. When the bleeding was finally stemmed, it was discovered he'd been crudely deprived of two fingers on his right hand, and one on the left, courtesy of a stolen knife from the prison kitchen which probably wasn't the sharpest, or cleanest, tool in the box.

"Whilst Fahred nursed his wounds in a prison hospital, his father, Mahmoud, died. Fahred was given dispensation to attend the funeral.

“Fahred’s release from prison, having served only four of his six months, coincided with the finalising of his father’s affairs, which gave Fahred sole control of the store, as well as a large tranche of cash and belongings. In the eight years since, it’s a safe bet that most of the cash and belongings have disappeared, thanks to Fahred’s inability to select winning horses coupled with an unhealthy liking for cocaine. He’s also remained on our radar. Receiving stolen goods, VAT fraud, and a whole host of motoring offences have all since been added to his resume. He’s served several short terms of imprisonment.”

“Wow!” Verity said. “That is some serious knowledge, Joanne. I am mightily impressed.”

“Thanks,” Joanne replied.

“So, what about his marital status? Girlfriends? Boyfriends? Anything there?”

Joanne gave out a grunt. “The most sympathetic way I can describe Fahred is as unfortunate looking,” she said. “His complexion, whilst not as dark as Bijan’s or Mahmoud’s, is still swarthy, but his face is badly pock-marked. It displays the ravages undoubtedly brought about by years of imbibing illicit substances. Add to this the fact he’s at least fifty pounds overweight; only five-four on a good day; about as educated as a shoe-horn; missing a few digits, and is a serial pain-in-the-arse, and it should come as no surprise that he’s not had much success when it comes to attracting the opposite sex. Or even the same sex. Although, for certain favours, there was talk he'd been quite happy to relieve some of his prison inmates of their frustration."

"How do you manage to retain all this information?" Verity said. "You're more useful than any data base I've ever come across."

"All part of the job," Joanne replied. "I was born and bred here. I love the East End with a passion. I love the people, the smells, the history, the whole vibe. So, I decided what better way to make my living than to be at the heart of it? My partner says I'm just a nosey cow. Oh, and before you ask, my partner's name is Georgia, and, just like you, she's black and beautiful. If I was you, I'd be careful, DI Chandler. To some in the department you'll be just their type."

Was that a come-on? She may have only just met Joanne, but, on first impressions, Verity didn't think she seemed the type to fool around like that. Perhaps it was just friendly office banter.

"Thanks for the warning," Verity said. "So do we — sorry — do *you* have any idea who may be behind this latest robbery?"

"*Our* thought process," Joanne smiled, "is that it's the work of *The Islington Angels*."

"The Islington Angels? Who the hell are they?"

"Group of local young men, mainly third generation Windrushers, who've sprung up recently and like to take the law into their own hands when they feel justice isn't being done."

"Vigilantes?"

"If you like. We think they started operating out of a boxing club not far from Angel tube station, hence the aptly named title. We believe they've now moved their headquarters elsewhere. Somewhere less public, probably. I suspect you'll still find some of them keeping in shape at the club, though. Anyway, we're pretty certain they've been responsible for half-a-dozen or so broken bodies in the area over the last several months. So far, we haven't been able to get near them."

"And what makes you think it's them?"

"Well," Joanne lowered her voice almost to a whisper, and looked furtively from side-to-side. "The cricket bat," she said.

Verity followed Joanne's lead and lowered her own voice. "The cricket bat?"

"Yes, the cricket bat. If anybody with West Indian heritage is going to have a weapon, it's going to be a cricket bat. They do love their cricket." Joanne winked at Verity and smiled. "Georgia is from Port of Spain, Trinidad's capital. She tells me it's almost a religion out there."

Verity held in a laugh. Joanne may well be the font of all local knowledge, but deciding she'd cracked the case on the strength of a nation's love for cricket was probably one of the reasons she hadn't made it any further up the ranks.

"Okay, I'll keep the cricket bat in mind," Verity said, hoping she'd kept the amusement out of her voice.

"Now, who would we need to speak to if we paid the boxing club a visit?"

"Jack Norris," Joanne replied. "Or Jack 'Puncher' Norris to give him his full handle. He's highly praised by the local community who see him as a conduit for keeping troubled kids off the streets. The chief even added her own public compliments when Buck Witman did a piece on the club several months ago in The Gazette."

"Stupid question," Verity said. "But why is he called Puncher?"

Even though it was a stupid question, Joanne seemed happy to answer. "Norris used to be pretty handy in the ring in his day," she said. "Originally from Deptford, he became South-East London area middleweight champion. As he got older, he started struggling to make the weight and moved up to light heavyweight. Took a few bad beatings from guys who were naturally bigger than him. Eventually, he decided enough was enough, hung up his gloves, and opened his own club. He's a bit slow of speech and gait these days, but his mind is still sharp enough."

"You seem to know a bit about boxing, Joanne," Verity said. "I know you should never judge a book by its cover, but you don't strike me as the type to enjoy the noble art of pugilism."

"Can't stand it," Joanne replied. "Two sweaty men trying to punch each other's lights out is not my idea of sport. But I've learned something of it by association.

You see, Georgia's father was in the camp of Giselle Salandy."

Verity decided not to mention she found sweaty men trying to punch each other's lights out somewhat sexy. She did, however, confirm she'd never heard of Giselle Salandy.

"Giselle was a very famous Trinidadian boxer," Joanne explained. "She died, aged twenty-one, in a car accident: 2009, I think. They even gave her a state funeral. Georgia's father was one of her seconds and apparently wept for days after she died. I've been duty bound to show an interest ever since."

"So, do you think Norris will have any information about these Angels?"

"Without doubt. Unlikely he'll impart any of it, though. These are his boys. He's like their Fagin."

"And what about Fahred Ahmadi?" Verity asked. "Who's spoken to him so far?"

"DI Smollenski has dealt with all the Ahmadi robberies," Joanne said. "Everything's on file."

"Well, Joanne, you've been more than helpful," Verity said. "No doubt I'll be needing you again shortly." Verity turned to leave and then stopped. "Just a thought," she added. "Is there something I should know about DCI Wood's wife?"

***

The Islington Angels boxing club was open to all. The small, signed frontage belittled the long and spacious interior. Verity believed the building may well have once been two storeys, but any connecting ceiling had since been removed and the cavernous height gave the place a certain acoustic quality. Grunts, groans and shouts of encouragement echoed around like war-commands on an open field of battle. They could all be clearly heard, but none could be clearly understood, all mingling together to make one continuous wall of sound. The club was well-equipped with all the normal requirements of a gym and sported two full-size boxing rings. Stanley had already advised Verity that they'd undoubtedly be the centre of attraction as soon as they walked through the doors. He was not wrong.

The wall of sound quietened in stages with every step Stanley and Verity took further into the club. Within seconds, the club was eerily silent, and all activity had stopped.

"They could probably smell us from a quarter of a mile away," Stanley whispered. "These characters know filth when they see it."

"It's a wonder they can smell anything other than the stink in here," Verity replied. In certain circumstances, Verity found man-sweat very pleasant, but this wasn't one of them. This was overwhelmingly putrid.

Stanley and Verity made their way to the small office at the rear of the gym, where, through a large glass window, they could see Puncher Norris sitting at a desk. Like all of the patrons, Norris had spotted them, and, just like everybody else, he didn't look particularly pleased by their presence.

As they walked the gauntlet, an ebony-black, sweat-glistened boxer, who had been sparring in one of the two rings, leaned over the ropes and broke the silence with a voice that reverberated around the room.

"Hey girl," he shouted at Verity. "You mighty fine looking, so what you doing with shrivelled-up whitey there? Why don't you come up here and keep things in the family?" He grabbed his crotch as best someone can wearing boxing gloves. "You know us black boys is the best, and Leroy is in the groove. You hear me? Leroy is looking to keep you swee-eet. Do you wants it, girl? Coz Leroy will give you some big loving any goddamned way you want, ain't that the truth?"

A collective low murmur of agreement resonated amongst the clientele.

Verity opened her mouth, but was stopped from giving any reply by a knowing look from Stanley. "Leave it lie," he said. "We're here to see Norris, not get in a slanging match with the local wildlife."

"What?" Verity replied, quietly. "I was only going to give him my number. He's hot." She turned to the boxer and winked.

"Oh, do me a favour," Stanley said, grabbing Verity by the arm and marching her towards Norris's office.

"He's like the missing link. He can't even speak in proper sentences."

"You're breaking my heart, girl," Leroy shouted.

Stanley didn't wait for an invite to enter the office.

Puncher Norris wore the scars of an ex-boxer. His ears were badly cauliflowered, and there were many ragged scars above and below each eye. He was wearing the club's own branded, ill-fitting T-shirt which showed off Norris's barrel chest and thick, heavily tattooed arms. He may well have been in great shape in his day, but he had lost most, if not quite all, muscle definition. He also carried a tyre of fat around his stomach which, whilst not being huge, had gone past the definition of paunch.

Norris grudgingly indicated that Stanley and Verity were welcome to sit down. Stanley noticed Norris's eyes were firmly fixed on Verity.

"Before you ask, Darling," Norris said, "it took a lot of hard work to look this good." He laughed and circled his face. "Truth is I cut easy, see? My cut-man was as blind as a mole in the daylight as well, so that didn't help. Lost more fights from being cut than I ever did from staying on the canvas."

His speech, as Joanne had indicated, was slow and deliberate and his esses were slightly slurred, but his eyes themselves were bright, blue and clear. He smiled at Verity, revealing teeth that were too white to be his own.

"Now, in my day," Norris continued, "I reckon I could have turned your eye easy, see? I'd have had you in my arms and madly in love with me within an hour. Especially when I had all my own hair. Ooh, you should have seen my hair in those days, Darling." He rubbed a hand across his bald pate. "All black and shining it was. Yep, I was a catch, Darling, and no mistake. Saw myself plenty of action in and out of the ring if you get my drift. Not so lucky these days easy, see?"

"Oh, come now," Verity said. "I'm sure a man with your rugged appearance still gets plenty of action. If I was thirty years older, why I'd be all over you like a disease."

Norris laughed hard. "Okay," he said, "let's cut the bullshit." He turned his attention to Stanley, but pointed at Verity with a gnarled hand, badly clawed from arthritis. "Are you going to introduce me to this little darling, DCI Wood?" he said.

After Stanley had introduced Verity, and Norris had once again indicated how, in his younger days, he would have been more than happy to show her a good time, Stanley advised him they were investigating a robbery on Ahmadi's store, and their findings had led them to the possible involvement of a gang calling themselves *The Islington Angels.* Stanley asked Norris if he could throw any light on the subject.

"Never heard of the store, and never heard of The Islington Angels, neither," Norris replied. "Now, wasn't that nice and easy, see? You asked me a question, and I answered it all truthful like. I reckon that's why we get on so well. Anyway, it was nice talking to you both." He again smiled at Verity. "Especially you, Darling."

Norris leaned over his desk and cupped Verity's hands in his. "But a word of advice," he said. "On your way out, be gentle with young Leroy in the ring there. He's in training for a big fight next week. Quarter final of the Nationals. Not bad for a nineteen-year-old. In case you don't know, Darling, when a fighter is in training for a big fight like that, they're not allowed any fun outside the ring. You understand what I'm saying? The poor boy hasn't even smelled a female for the last two months. Seeing you, he's probably gone as hard as an oar. I wouldn't want him to be distracted."

"Listen," Stanley said, showing no interest in leaving. "We know the gang used to operate from here, and whilst their intentions may be honourable, their way of going about things are not. Personally, I couldn't give a flying poke if they want to teach Fred Ahmadi a lesson. He's an arsehole who deserves whatever he gets, but his innocent eighty-seven-year-old grandfather is now in hospital thanks to being intimidated by a thug in a ski-mask wielding a cricket bat. And that I do care about. So, any information you may have about possible members of The Angels would be really appreciated. If only so we can eliminate them from our enquiries. I'd also appreciate you taking your hands off my colleague." Stanley had no idea why he had added the last request.

Jack Norris released Verity's hands slowly and smiled. "Easy, tiger," he said. "We were only holding hands." He leaned back in his black, leather swivel chair which, like Norris, had seen better days. He sighed heavily. "So, it's true about Bijan?" he said.

"Heart attack," Verity replied. "And now he's had another one. Probably not going to pull through. I thought you said you hadn't heard of the store, so how come you know Bijan's name? We never mentioned his name."

Norris let out a snort. "You've got a lot to learn, Darling," he said. "It's easy, see? When I said I'd never heard of the store, what I meant was — now, how can I put this? — of course I've heard of the fucking store! Like me, it's been around these parts for like a hundred years. How can I not have heard of it? What I meant was — I couldn't recall having heard of it at the exact moment when I was asked. Easy, see?"

"And The Islington Angels?" Verity said. "Can we assume that when you said you'd never heard of them, what you meant was — of course you've fucking heard of them?"

"Oh, DCI Wood, I can see you really have got a lot to teach this fine specimen," Norris replied. "Look, let's make this simple so we can all go about our day. It's easy, see? Whether I've heard of this gang you talk about makes absolutely no difference because — and you can call me old fashioned, if you like — I wouldn't tell you in a month of Sundays. Take a look out there and tell me what you see."

Norris nodded to outside the office.

"There's what? Twenty or so young men without a pot to piss in. Hope, to them, is just another four-letter word. One they don't have access to. They're angry at a world they feel has let them down and believe their only way out is to put themselves in a ring up against another angry, young man with the same feelings, each with the intent of beating the absolute crap out of one another, and, if one of them dies in the process, then so be it. Why do you think they're not allowed any nooky, Darling? It's easy, see? If the guy standing in front of you is the reason you've not been able to swing your dick for months on end, then you're more likely to want to kill the son-of-a-bitch. Out there, my crime-fighting friends, is a bubbling volcano of aggression ready to explode all over someone's sorry arse. Every single one of those dead-beats is straining at the leash, just waiting to be let loose and do someone some real harm.

"Oh, and guess which section of society they feel particularly aggrieved with? That's right — you guys, the good old British police force. There's probably not one of those poor bastards out there hasn't got some sob story about being persecuted by the Bill, or how they get continuously stopped and searched simply because all black people look suspicious to you, or how his older brother was wrongly arrested, or how his father was shot dead in a case of mistaken identity.

"So, it's easy, see? If they think for one minute I'm giving you any information about any gang they may, or may not, be involved with, you'll be finding various parts of me turn up in all four corners of East London. Now, I feel particularly fond of my body parts, and I'd very much like to keep them, thank you very much."

Stanley noticed all work in the main body of the club was still silent. There were fighters simply holding on to punch bags; skipping ropes had stopped swirling; weights were floored; bench-presses were unpressed, and the four fighters in the two rings had not recommenced their sparring. One or two were on mobile phones but, in general, all eyes were trained on the office of Jack 'Puncher' Norris.

Leroy, the young man who had goaded Verity on arrival, smiled, winked and executed a crotch thrust. To Stanley's dismay, Verity winked and smiled back, and although she stopped short of thrusting, he noticed she couldn't help but let out a small sigh.

"Oh, for God's sake, you're going to make him explode," Norris said. "Leave him be!"

Verity ignored the remark and continued smiling in Leroy's direction. "You said he hasn't even smelled a female for two months," she said. "Why are there no female boxers here?"

"Not exactly the right setting for girls, Darling," Norris replied. "They're a bit too delicate for this line of work."

"Really?" Verity said. "What about Giselle Salandy?"

"Who the hell is she?" Norris said.

"A very famous female boxer," Verity replied. Out of the corner of her eye, she could spy Stanley looking at her. "Trinidadian. Gave her a state funeral after she tragically died in a car accident. She was only twenty-one."

"Yeah, well, good for her," Norris said. "If you ask me, the only women allowed in the ring should be those dollies who parade the round number about. Could tell you a few stories about them, I can tell you."

Norris stood up gingerly and made his way to the door. "Anyway, I think it's time you two were leaving," he said. "Give my regards to Bijan if you see him. He's a good guy and I'm genuinely sorry for his troubles."

"Before we leave," Stanley said, "is there any chance we can have the names and addresses of your members."

Norris laughed and opened his office door for them. "You know full well we lost all those records in that very nasty fire we had a month ago. Easy, see?"

***

"They had a fire?" Verity whispered as she and Stanley made their way back through the gauntlet.

"Of course they didn't," Stanley replied. "But they will do if we insist on seeing those records."

As Stanley and Verity passed the ring containing Leroy, he shouted, “So, what you say, Gorgeous? Are we going all Marvin and getting it on, or what?”

Verity stopped. “Wait for me in the car,” she said to Stanley. “I’ll only be a moment.”

Stanley watched Verity make her way over to Leroy. He let out a small laugh as Leroy instinctively took a step back. For all his bravado, he obviously wasn’t used to having females that were in Verity’s league walk towards him with a smile on their face.

***

Before starting the car, Stanley turned to Verity. “What the hell was all that about the female boxer?” he said. “You didn’t learn that at Oxford.”

Verity shrugged. “Joanne,” she said, as if that were enough explanation. “She’s better than any lecturer I ever had. She knows everything.”

“Which can sometimes be a burden,” Stanley said, turning the car key. “Anyway, what did you say to the missing link in there?”

“Just chit-chatting,” Verity said, smiling. “By the way, thanks for your concern.”

“Concern? About what?”

“Norris… touching me.” She blatantly made it sound sexy. “You were like a virile, white knight rushing to a distressed, virginous damsel on his huge, throbbing steed.”

"Oh, shut up, or I'll throw you out of this car and you can bloody well walk the rest of the way. And virginous? Really?"

Verity laughed long and hard.

***

"Do you think Leroy is an *Angel*?" Verity asked, settling herself back at her desk after following Stanley's instruction to supply him with a coffee.

"You spoke to him," Stanley replied. "What do you think?"

"I don't think he would have fronted us down like that if he was," Verity replied.

"I agree," Stanley said. "They're a bit too savvy for that type of behaviour. They haven't yet gone out of their way to make themselves known, especially to us. Also, he looked like a frightened puppy as soon as you started toward him. Not exactly what I would consider Angel material. But I'd bet a sizeable amount he knows people who are. Personally, I think our friend Leroy is just your typical gobby, young twat."

Without thinking, Verity said, "Mm, a big-muscled, good-looking one."

Stanley couldn't be sure, but he thought he heard Verity let out another sigh. "But still a twat," he said.

***

"Why don't you ever come to the apartment?" Niko asked Cherie. "Why do we always have to do it in the car?"

Cherie laughed. "Because, apart from this being a very nice car, in my experience, men often like to fall asleep after the event, especially if they feel comfortable."

"And what's wrong with that?"

"Do you really think it's safe to fall asleep with me in the building? Sweetheart, my type of business keeps a roof over my head, but it doesn't exactly keep me in the lap of luxury. Hell, by the time you woke up, I'd be away with anything shiny I could lay my hands on. For starters, that watch of yours would be in my swag-bag. No, I find it best not to put that sort of temptation in front of me, and so the car it is. You pick me up. We drive somewhere quiet. We do what needs to be done. You pay me. You drop me off. Everyone's a winner. What could be simpler?"

"I could help with money," Niko said, not really understanding where the sentiment was coming from. He felt like he was in freefall, as though he had started to confess to something and couldn't stop. "I'm not a millionaire or anything," he confirmed, quickly. "Far from it. But I'm not short of a few quid, either. If it makes you feel better, you could do things for me, and I'll pay you for them. You could cook or clean for me, something like that. You could meet my cat. His name's Mr M, which is short for—"

Cherie put her fingers to Niko's lips. The smell of his cum still lingered on them.

"Look, Sweetheart," she said. "In case it's escaped your attention, I just did do something for you, and you just paid me for it." She took a cursory glance at herself in the rear-view mirror and sighed. "Look, being lonely I get. Hell, if it wasn't for lonely men, I'd still be visiting food banks." Cherie took hold of Niko's hand. "In fact, purely from a business perspective, the lonelier the men out there, the better."

"You forgot fat," Niko said, tapping his stomach with his free hand. Niko was no more than half a stone over fighting weight, but it had started to play on his mind.

"Sorry?"

"I said you forgot fat. Lonely, fat men."

"You don't have to be fat to be lonely," Cherie said. Niko noticed she hadn't contradicted him. "Trust me, Sweetheart, there are plenty of thin ones out there, as well. Anyway, you're not fat — just cuddly. I like cuddly."

"Very diplomatic," Niko said.

"Anyway, like I was saying," Cherie continued. "Lonely I get. But — and I'll try to be as *diplomatic* as I can here — you're starting to come across a touch desperate, Sweetheart. Let me give you a bit of advice. There's a vast difference between a man with needs and a needy man, you hear what I'm saying? Women can handle a man with needs. Can thrive on it, in fact. Hell,

I make a living out of it. But a needy man, now that's a different basket of puppies. No woman in the world likes a needy man. You got it?"

"I get it," Niko said. The truth was, Niko didn't get it. In his opinion, he was the one trying to help someone with needs here. After all, who could be more needy than someone who sold their body for a living? "Have you ever thought about doing something else?" he asked. "You know, other than being a… being involved in the sex industry?"

"Now who's trying to be diplomatic? Like what?"

"I don't know. Anything." Niko settled himself in the seat as if he were in for a lengthy discussion. "What were you good at in school?"

Cherie laughed loudly. "I left school at fourteen, pregnant with a teacher's baby. Does that answer your question? Trust me, it's been downhill since then. Sweetheart, you need to get out and find yourself a nice woman. Or not a nice woman. That's up to you. But not a fucked-up woman like me, excuse the pun. Now, I have work to do." Cherie leaned over and gave Niko a kiss on the cheek before leaving the car.

***

Verity could turn heads without even trying, so on nights like this, where she'd gone to some lengths with her hair, face and outfit, the assembled patronage of the pub were having trouble not to come across as rude as she made her way back to the table from the bar.

"Orange juice for you," she said, placing the drink down. "And a gin and tonic for me. Just because you don't drink doesn't mean I can't enjoy myself."

"I do drink," Leroy said. "Just not when I'm in training."

"I understand there are other things you're not supposed to do when you're in training."

"I guess I could make an exception."

Verity lifted her drink up. "Well then," she said, winking at Leroy. "Let's make a toast to exceptions."

FRIDAY

Niko was drowning in a body of water full of odd numbers. He could see Cherie at the water's edge, semen dripping from the corner of her mouth. She was heavily pregnant and holding hands with one of Niko's old maths' teachers, whose name he couldn't quite remember. He knew he was Welsh, and his name was typical, like Evans, or Jones. He was holding one of Niko's exercise books and asking him, in a lilting voice of exasperation, why it was that Niko had only written on every other page. Niko could have easily explained that he was avoiding the odd numbered folios, but what did that matter at the moment? He had other things to worry about.

Cherie was shouting at him to stop being so needy and find a nice woman, or not a nice woman, just not a fucked-up woman. Niko was trying to reply that he would as soon as he could get out of the water, but every time he opened his mouth the number eleven floated into it. Niko hated the number eleven. It remained eleven whether you turned it upside down or reversed the digits. It was also the age he'd been when his mother had died. He spat it out with as much air as was left in his lungs and immediately started to sink. Was this the fabled third time?

Niko had always been a reasonable swimmer, so why the hell couldn't he stay afloat? He could hear his mother's voice coming from somewhere below him, but the only word he could make out was *'Schmuck.'* He looked down at his feet, and through the murk of the water could just make out the shape of Martin Bead hanging on to them, his weight too much for Niko to bear.

Despite the closing darkness, the bullet hole above Martin Bead's right eye was clearly visible, however, he was pointing at a bindi dot in the middle of his forehead.

"You messed up big time," he said. *"It should have been here, right between the eyes. T.S.A. won't be happy about this."* The words reached Niko in bubbles, which popped as they made contact with his ears.

As the last of Niko's air ran out, he could still hear his mother. *'Schmuck, Schmuck,'* she whispered, as if in some pleasure.

***

Niko awoke spluttering and gasping for breath, his body bathed in sweat. For a long time, he simply lay in bed shivering. When his breathing had returned to somewhere near normal, he made his way to the kitchen for a glass of water. Mr M offered him a passing glance out of one sleepy eye.

"Jeeze, maybe I shouldn't have had that second joint," Niko muttered, knowing full well he would never only have one. Without thinking, he was already pouring the second glass of water away.

"And what the hell happened to that Dyson disc thing hoovering away my memories? Maybe it needs a change of filter. Right, that's it, Mr M, no more drugs for me. From now on, it's the straight and narrow. I promise. Double promise."

Niko rarely made promises. He didn't really believe in them. In his experience, people who made promises were pathological liars. Politicians; teachers; bosses; parents. In particular, parents. More concisely, drunken parents. More concisely still, *his* drunken parent.

He couldn't speak for his father, of course. He only had his mother's say-so for what he had been like. And even that was sketchy. He'd been tall, a good dancer apparently, and spoke with an accent. He'd also been a bit of a dreamer, according to Mummy-dear.

'Always looking for the next big thing,' she had once told Niko. *'Spent whatever little money we had on the next grand scheme. Sometimes that grand scheme included young blondes. Basically, he was just an arsehole, Niko.'*

Niko had never been particularly keen to know much more. Having an absent father who was a tall, dreaming, philandering arsehole was good enough for him. He never really blamed his father for leaving, either, or held any specific hatred for him. Mummy-dear would tell him she only started drinking after the *'stupid Greek bastard'* had left, but given her propensity to lie through her arse, Niko could never be sure that was the case. In fact, he preferred to believe his mother's alcoholism was one of the reasons his father had left in the first place.

Jeeze, she'd been difficult for Niko to deal with in so many ways, but it was the empty promises that left the scars. An alcoholic's promises, Niko learned, were just unoccupied, barren sentences. The words were formed somewhere in a brain swimming, in his mother's case, in vodka and uttered by a mouth that had no comprehension of the pain it was causing. Niko would have preferred to have been like some of the other boys he knew, whose mothers would beat the living shit out of them in order to exorcise their frustrations, rather than live in a pea-souper of fabrication and exaggeration as he did.

Mummy-dear had once used the word *'sincere'* in one of her diatribes, and Niko had to look up what it meant in a dictionary he'd stolen from the school library.

Feelings free from deceit or pretence, the dictionary had told him. Niko hadn't really known what deceit or pretence meant either, but he understood the *feelings free* bit. His mother certainly knew how to let her feelings run free. They'd been released back into the fucking wild as far as Niko was concerned.

Niko had learned from television shows, films, documentaries, newspaper articles and song lyrics that there was supposed to be nothing greater than a mother's love for her children. What they all failed to tell you was that love gets superseded when there's a bottle of vodka in the mix.

'I promise this is the last, Niko. I'll stop tomorrow. Double promise. Super promise.' And then she'd hug him and cry and smother him with kisses. The sorts of hugs, cries and kisses that got forgotten the following morning. Dumped into the trash along with the promises and the empty bottles.

'Mummy-dear is just tired, Niko. I'm not drunk, I promise. Double promise. Super promise.' And then she'd hug and cry and kiss.

'I have no idea what happened to your birthday money, Niko. I promise. Double promise. Super promise.' Hug, cry, kiss.

'This is your Uncle... Um... Uncle Schmuck. Yes, Uncle Schmuck. He's going to stay with us and look after us for a while. He's going to be very good to us, Niko, I promise. Double promise. Super Promise.'

Uncle Schmuck had hung around for two months, far longer than most. He had a habit of wandering around the flat naked, except for his Kippah. Niko had been fascinated by the man's circumcised, and almost always erect, penis, which, even with Niko's limited knowledge at that time, looked quite large. The main problem with Uncle Schmuck was he liked to hug and kiss Niko as well. In those instances, it was Niko who did the crying.

"Jeeze, did I have to grow up quick, Mr M," Niko said. "But, onward and upward, remember? What say you and I buy something? Perhaps fire up the Mercedes website. What do you reckon?"

***

"Fecking hell, that was quick work," Patty Cleland said, casting her eye over the three names on the piece of paper Verity had just handed her. "Smollenski gave me not so much as a whisper. I give you the gig yesterday morning and here you are giving me names of suspects. What's your secret, DI Chandler?"

Stanley, who had not had time to speak to Verity properly before they had entered the chief's office, snapped his head. "Yes, what is your secret, DI Chandler?"

Patty Cleland chuckled and waved the piece of paper in the air. "You mean you haven't had anything to do with this, Stanley?"

"Not that I know of, Ma'am — no."

"Well, well, I'd keep your eye out for this one," the chief said, handing him the paper with the names on. "Looks like she's after your job."

"Or yours," Stanley said, just loud enough.

Patty Cleland shifted slightly in her seat. "Yes, well, anyway — how reliable is your source, DI Chandler?"

"Pretty reliable I think, Ma'am. Let's just say he came forth quite easily."

"Okay, well let's find some reason to drag these thugs in for questioning and see what they can tell us," the chief said. "Good work, Chandler. I can see you're going to be an asset to the team and a natural replacement for when Stanley calls it a day."

"Thank you, Ma'am." Verity could feel the heat coming from Stanley's face.

***

Back at their respective desks, it took a while before either of them spoke. Every time Verity glanced up from her computer screen, Stanley was staring at her hard.

Eventually, Verity broke. "Look," she said. "I know you're wondering how I got the names, but does it really matter? We've got them and—"

Stanley held his hand up. "You're mistaking me for someone who gives a damn," he said. "I couldn't give a panda's shit how you've managed to get these." He waved the paper with the names on it in the air.

"Then why are you so upset?"

"And what makes you think I'm upset?"

Verity laughed "Perhaps it's just the police officer coming out in me, but I'm sensing a touch of hostility. Call it a gut feeling if you like."

"I don't want to call it anything," Stanley said, scrunching the piece of paper into a ball and tossing it over to Verity. "I'm just wondering how it will look when it comes out our information has been achieved because one of the investigating officers slept with the informant. Can't see it going down too well with the CPS. And one can only imagine what Mr Fuckwit might write. Because, trust me, he will find out. Even if I have to tell him myself."

"How do you bloody well know I slept with anyone?" Verity barked. "How do you know that they didn't just volunteer the information?"

It was Stanley's turn to laugh. "Perhaps it's just the police officer coming out in me," he said. "Call it a gut feeling if you like. It was that Leroy, wasn't it? The missing link from Norris's place."

"No comment," Verity muttered. "Look, I just saw an opportunity and grabbed it."

"I don't want to know what you grabbed," Stanley shouted, just loud enough for most of the office to hear. "*You* can do all the work on this one. *You* can deal with any fallout on how we're obtaining information. And *you* can go and get me a coffee."

With Verity temporarily out of shot, Stanley rubbed his face vigorously and berated himself for his actions. Why the hell was he so irked? Okay, so she'd undoubtedly boned some low-life. Surely that was up to her. She was a free woman. Who she decided to spend her time with outside of work was nothing to do with him. She'd also managed to get information that, in normal circumstances, they may never have obtained. Caleb Smollenski never managed it. But then who the hell would want to sleep with Caleb Smollenski?

Maybe, instead of being angry, he should be praising her for — what did she say? *'Grabbing an opportunity.'* Despite his internal protestations, Stanley was finding the mental images of Verity writhing around with Leroy difficult to push from his brain.

"For Christ's sake, Stanley," he whispered to himself. "Get a grip."

***

"Right then," Verity said, placing Stanley's coffee in front of him. "One of us has work to do. You see, I have names of suspects to run. Names that I obtained by being a resourceful, diligent officer." She unfurled the piece of paper Stanley had thrown at her. "But, before I do, I'm going to give you the opportunity to tell me whether you've actually heard of any of them."

"Can't say I looked at them that hard," Stanley said, dismissively. The fact was, Stanley had looked at them and none of them rang any bells. "But I don't think so."

"I'm not that surprised," Verity said. "My informant reckons it's doubtful any of them have ever been in trouble with the police. Said it's an Angels' policy. Apparently, you can't get in if you have a record. Wouldn't let him in because he stole a car when he was sixteen."

Verity spent the next thirty minutes discovering that the information regarding acceptance to The Angels had been correct. There was nothing against any of the three names. She sighed heavily and leaned back in her chair.

Stanley had been watching. With each passing minute, he'd observed Verity's escalating frustration. He almost felt sorry for her, but then those images of her and Leroy resurfaced, and his pity quickly diminished.

"Nothing there, huh?" he said.

"Don't look so pleased," Verity said. "But no, not even a parking ticket."

"Maybe, the missing link gave you a few duds." Stanley noticed a touch of satisfaction in his voice. He inwardly reproached himself for using his fingers around the word *duds*. "Her Majesty will never let you bring these guys in just because their names have been given to you on a piece of paper."

"Will you please stop calling him the missing link?" Verity said. "He's a sweetheart. Deep down."

"Of course he is. I bet, in between stealing cars, he loves his mum, goes to church three times every Sunday, writes love-songs on a guitar, and adores the poetry of Byron."

"Well, now you're talking," Verity said. "I love Byron's poems. My favourite is, *She Walks in Beauty*. It's only short. Written in iambic tetrameter. Apparently, he wrote it about Anne Wilmot. She was the wife of Byron's first cousin and—"

"You need to shut up!" Stanley said. "Like immediately. In fact, before immediately. If I hear from you in the next five minutes, I'll—"

Whatever Stanley was about to threaten was interrupted by Patty shouting from her office door. "Oy, you two lovebirds. Get in here. Now!"

***

"What's the problem, Ma'am," Stanley asked as soon as he and Verity had taken their offered seats.

"Just heard from the hospital," Patty Cleland said. "Bijan Ahmadi died an hour ago."

"Ah, bollocks," Stanley said.

"So, I'm really fecking hoping those names are giving us something, DI Chandler," Patty said. "Come on, give me some good news."

Verity shifted in her seat.

"The names have yielded nothing, Ma'am," Stanley said. This time, he had managed to find some pity in his voice. "It's possible the informant was just yanking our chain." Stanley immediately wished he'd used some different words. Where the hell had those ones come from? They weren't even words he could ever remember using before. He wasn't even sure he knew exactly what they meant. But now all he could think of was Verity yanking Leroy's chain.

"Give them here," Patty said, holding out her hand.

Verity briefly looked at Stanley before handing over the piece of paper to Patty.

"Right, they've all got the same surname, so they're probably related, yes?" Patty said, tapping the piece of paper vigorously.

"Probably," Stanley said. "Although, it is a common surname, so it could just be coincidence."

"DI Chandler," Patty said. "Did you write these names down in the order your informant gave them to you?"

"I believe so, Ma'am, yes."

"So, the name Terrell Williams is at the top of the tree, and therefore the one your informant thinks is the most important. Find him and you find the others. Now get out of my sight!" Patty threw the piece of paper in Stanley's direction. "The pair of you!"

***

"What was all that about?" Verity asked when she and Stanley were back at their desks. "Is she normally like that?"

Stanley shook his head. "No. I think Bijan's death, albeit something that may have happened anyway, will naturally be blamed on the robbery. Bijan was a popular guy. There'll be a public clamour to find out who's responsible. A clamour that Her Majesty will have to fend off. Then, of course, there's whatever's going on in her personal life. The pressure is obviously getting to her."

"Talking of pressure. How the hell am I supposed to find this Terrell Williams?" Verity said. "I don't even know if he's local." Verity's eyes widened.

"What?" Stanley said. "What is it? You look like you've just discovered gravity."

"Local!" Verity said. "Local! If he's local, maybe Joanne has heard of him. What do you think?"

Stanley shrugged his shoulders. "It's a hell of a long shot," he said. "The East End is no country village. There's over a million people kicking about within a few miles radius of where we're sitting right now. Even Joanne doesn't know every single one of them."

"So, do you want me to ask her, or do you want to do it?"

Stanley squirmed slightly and gave out a small cough. "*You're* doing all the work on this one, remember?"

"What is it between you two?" Verity asked. "What the hell did you do to her?"

"What makes you think *I* did anything?"

"Perhaps it's the police officer coming out in me. Call it a gut feeling."

"Oh, piss off!"

***

Verity had been enthusiastically tapping away at her keyboard for some time after her return from visiting Joanne. Eventually, Stanley could contain himself no longer, and asked, "Well, are you going to tell me what Joanne said? Or are you keeping it all to yourself? It would have been a good idea to have brought a coffee back with you. A great idea, in fact."

Without looking away from her screen, Verity replied, "Joanne said she'd never heard of Terrell Williams."

"So, what the hell are you doing?"

"If you must know, I'm looking up cricket clubs in the area."

Stanley let out a laugh. "What? Why?"

"Because Joanne said — never mind, it's a long story."

"Right. Well, best of luck," Stanley said. "I still think your missing link is leading you a merry dance. You heard what Norris said. If The Angels thought for one minute he was feeding any information to us, they'd tear him limb-from-limb."

"Even so," Verity said, smiling broadly. "It's surprising what people will tell you given the right sorts of incentives."

"Oh, for Christ's sake," Stanley said. "I don't want to know anything about your bloody *incentives*." And there were the fingers again. Stanley considered he may need to lose the whole of his lower arms, not just the fingers. He noticed Verity's smile getting even wider. "And now what's put a look on your smug face like you've won the lottery?"

Verity spun her screen around for Stanley to see.

"Ta-da!" she said. "The rather handsome face you're looking at is none other than a certain Terrell Williams. Opening bat for The London Fields Cricket Club. It says he's got an average of sixty-one, whatever that means." Verity stood up and took a bow before sitting back down again.

Stanley shook his head. "It means he's pretty good," he said, turning the screen back around. "And there's no need to be so bloody self-congratulatory about it. We still can't bring people in just for being good batsmen. We're going to need something else."

"At least we now know what he looks like," Verity said. "That's more than we had half-an-hour ago. Think I'll go tell Her Majesty. See if it won't cheer her up a bit. According to the website, they've got a home fixture this Sunday against Tower Hamlets. It also says they like to meet after games at a place called, *The Pub on the Park*. Maybe, I'll just pop along and say hello. Want to come?"

"Certainly not," Stanley said. He stood up and retrieved his jacket from the back of his chair. "I don't know how many times I have to remind you, *you're* doing all the work on this one. Anyway, I'm busy Sunday."

"Doing what?"

"Mind your own business."

"At least we know one thing," Verity said, standing up from her desk.

"And what's that?"

Verity leaned into Stanley and whispered softly in his ear, "My informant wasn't yanking anybody's chain." She laughed loudly as she made her way to Patty's office.

***

"My, my, so this is our man," Patty said, looking at the image of Terrell Williams on her computer screen. "Good work, DI Chandler."

"It was more down to Joanne, Ma'am. She's the one who suggested I look at cricket clubs. She's a treasure if ever there was one."

"Okay, so when are you picking him up?"

Verity paused. "I think we need to tread carefully, Ma'am," she said. "As DCI Wood said, we can't just bring people in for being good batsmen."

"Oh, he did, did he?" Patty said. "And what does the perennial DCI Wood suggest? That we leave Williams alone? Slap him on his bottom and send him on his way? Of course we can bring the fecker in, DI Chandler. We can bring him in for whatever the hell reason we like. We hold the higher ground here. We're investigating an incident where somebody has threatened an innocent man with a cricket bat. Do not let this lead slip away, DI Chandler. If you do, I will have your head on a silver platter, do you understand?"

"Yes, Ma'am, but…"

"But what?" Patty thundered.

Verity cleared her throat nervously. "Well, as you know, Ma'am, there's practically a queue of lawyers outside our door just waiting for us to do something that isn't by the book. Like you said, I do not want to let Terrell Williams slip out of my grasp. If we bring him in without proper cause, we're going to open ourselves up to possibly losing him altogether."

Patty closed her eyes and rubbed her temples. "So, what do you suggest?" she said. "And it better be good."

"With your permission, Ma'am, I'd like to just conveniently bump into him after his cricket match on Sunday."

Patty Cleland still had her eyes closed. "For God's sake, bump into him to your heart's content, DI Chandler," she said. "Just get me some fecking results."

"Thank you, Ma'am." Verity stood to leave.

"One more thing," Patty said as Verity reached the door. She sounded deflated and out of energy. "Bijan's family, being the good Muslims they are, have already arranged his funeral. It's tomorrow afternoon. Lord knows what strings they had to pull to get him buried so quickly, and on a Saturday."

"It's called a Janazah," Verity said. "It's Muslim custom to wash and cleanse the body and then bury it within twenty-four hours so it remains pure. They don't actually need a funeral director, either. An Imam leads the proceedings."

"Whatever," Patty said, holding out a piece of paper. "I want you and Stanley to attend. Here's the details. I'd go myself, but I'm already committed to some shite awful seminar on modern leadership."

"Are you sure, Ma'am? Muslims don't normally like women attending their funerals. I'll stick out like a sore thumb."

"Yes, I'm fecking sure. Dress like a man if it makes you feel better."

"And are we going simply to pay our respects on behalf of the station, or is there some hidden agenda?"

"You're a police officer, DI Chandler," Patty said. "There's always a hidden agenda. Always."

SATURDAY

A steady fall of rain bounced off the one and only umbrella the station possessed. The occasional strong gust of wind drove the rain underneath the protection afforded by the ancient piece of equipment, straight into the faces of Stanley and Verity huddled beneath. If it hadn't been for the close proximity of Verity, Stanley, who was already miserable, believed he would be feeling a lot worse.

Stanley had made sure they were standing well back from the dejected and downcast throng following Bijan's coffin to the graveside. He had noticed that, despite any sorrow the mourners may be feeling, most of the crowd had taken a long, hard look at him and Verity at some point in the proceedings.

Or was it just Verity they were looking at? She certainly looked the epitome of the Femme Fatale, all dressed in black. Stanley found it difficult not to imagine her getting ready. Slipping into her black dress and heeled shoes; dabbing just enough perfume behind each ear…

"Wow," Verity said, breaking Stanley's image, "there must be three to four-hundred people here, despite this nonsense." She nodded up to somewhere indiscriminate. "If it was me, this would have to be the funeral of someone very, very close to get me out and about in this. He was certainly well respected, wasn't he?"

"Remind me why we're here," Stanley said. "Instead of doing some real work. Preferably, in a nice, dry, warm office. What did you say Her Majesty said?"

"Something about there always being a hidden agenda."

"Did that hidden agenda come with coffee?"

"I promise I'll get you one as soon as we're out of here. Now, I'm guessing that short, ugly one at the front is Fahred."

"Correctimundo," Stanley said. He winced as soon as the word was out of his mouth. What was he? Sixteen?

Verity gave out a small whistle. "Fancy waking up next to that!" she said. "I think I'd have to shoot him and then turn the gun on myself."

"Well, here's a thought," Stanley said. "How about not waking up next to him in the first place?"

Stanley realised he was either sounding like a jealous lover or a protective father, neither of which he'd had any experience of being. To Verity's credit, so Stanley thought, she just let it slide.

"Who are those soggy lumps either side of him?" Verity asked.

"Don't know," Stanley replied. "My guess would be they're those *cousins* Her Majesty was talking about. They don't look like they'd be much use if…"

Verity was vaguely aware that Stanley was talking, but her attention had been taken by something else. From this distance she couldn't be sure, but she nudged Stanley and nodded her head toward the funeral party. "Look," she whispered.

"What am I supposed to be looking at?" Stanley said. "And why the hell are you whispering?" Stanley waved his free arm about, the one that wasn't struggling to keep the umbrella above their heads. "We're a hundred feet away from the nearest pair of ears."

"There," Verity said, still with her voice lowered. She pointed towards the crowd. "That tall, hunky one at the back. If I'm not mistaken, that's Terrell bloody Williams."

Stanley concentrated his vision to where Verity had indicated. He found, these days, he had to squint to focus on anything further than twenty-feet away. Michelle had been nagging him for the best part of a year to see an optician, but the thought of someone reminding him he was getting old didn't fill him with desire.

The man was wearing a black hoody. He had his hands in the pockets, the hood up, and his head bowed, so his face was partially obscured.

"Can't really tell," Stanley said. "Oh, hang on, he's putting his hood down — bloody hell, is he staring at us?"

The hoodless Terrell Williams was indeed staring straight through the rain at Stanley and Verity. Very slowly, he raised a hand and waved. As he smiled, the sun momentarily broke through the rain and its rays caught a golden tooth at the front of his top row.

"The brazen bastard," Stanley muttered. "What the hell does he think he's doing?"

Verity started to raise her hand to wave back, but Stanley quickly grabbed her arm and lowered it. "What the hell do you think *you're* doing?" he said. "Jesus Christ, are you licking your lips?"

"Well, look at him," Verity said, smiling. "He's even better looking in the flesh, especially now he's all covered in rain. I bet he's well-ripped under that hoody, too."

"Oh, for God's sake," Stanley said, grabbing Verity around the waist and marching her away. "Come on, let's get out of here. I feel like a bloody goldfish. I'm about as wet as one, as well."

The act of grabbing Verity had brought their bodies even closer together, and Stanley fought hard with himself to stifle any signs of enjoyment. A rogue thought had even suggested lowering his hand to her backside. He shook his head vigorously. What the hell was happening to him?

"Are you all right?" Verity said.

"Yes," Stanley said, releasing his grip on Verity's waist. "Just shaking the rain off my face."

***

Niko was one of the last to arrive. He hadn't yet worked out the sat-nav system on the new Mercedes GLS he'd collected earlier in the day for a weekend's test-drive. Subsequently, he had originally turned up at the wrong graveyard.

Having been used to the coupe, it had also taken him some time to find a space large enough to park the SUV. In addition, his time at the dealership had been prolonged by trying to explain to the salesman that there was no way he would pay £75,000 for the vehicle. He would, however, be happy to pay either £74,000 or £76,000.

Before making his way to the dealership, Niko had called in Greasy Joe's for breakfast, where he'd overheard the two old dears — did they ever leave? — talking about the death of Bijan and his upcoming funeral arrangements later that day, of which, they seemed fully informed.

Niko, just like anybody who had lived in the neighbourhood long enough, knew Bijan. Not well, but well enough to know he was one of the good guys.

'A local character' was how the Gazette had put it in their report of the latest robbery on Ahmadi's store.

Niko recalled how angry he'd felt when he'd read the report. He knew the feeling had been contradictory and had spoken to Mr M about it at length.

What right did he have to be angry, given what he did for a living? Surely, if you killed complete strangers just because some underground organisation told you to, then you had no righteous reason to get angry about how someone else went about their business. Why was his way of meting out justice any better than those who had caused Bijan to suffer?

But, Niko had argued, Bijan was undeserving of such treatment, whereas he only despatched people who justified being removed from society. Mr M had countered with how could Niko know for sure that Bijan was underserving? Perhaps Bijan had been a wife-beater or cheated at cards. Perhaps he'd kept indecent photographs of children on his laptop or liked to strangle puppies. Perhaps he'd been the head of a terrorist cell. Perhaps he'd been the biggest heroin dealer in London.

In the end, despite Mr M's arguments, Niko didn't believe Bijan was anything other than what the Gazette had reported.

An innocent, hard-working man, who had never done anybody any wrong. An old man sitting in the wrong place at the wrong time, caught up in the cross-fire of someone else's argument.

And the unfairness had made him angry. So, having heard the old dears' conversation, Niko had decided to attend the funeral.

It was this same anger, Niko believed, that had steered him into the business of killing people in the first place.

***

The first approach had been a simple, glossy flier pushed through his door, asking if he'd like to earn more money by helping to clear the local community of its infelicitous sections.

Niko had needed to look up the word infelicitous.

Before becoming a hired murderer, Niko's home was a damp, run-down, one-roomer above a fast-food outlet in Selby Street, not far from Bethnal Green itself. Two days prior to the flier arriving, Niko had been dismissed from his casual, zero-hour job as a delivery driver for a well-known local supplier of electrical goods. There'd been some sort of audit for insurance purposes, and it transpired that Niko didn't hold the type of licence required to drive the vehicles he'd been using. In fact, Niko, at that time, had never even taken a driving test, let alone passed one. The employer had asked him to leave quietly, so as to avoid any fuss, just as the Royal Navy had done, many years previously.

After half-a-dozen cheap, but very strong, cans of lager — no Fosters in those days — coupled with two joints of sub-standard weed, Niko had decided it was too damned right he wanted to earn more money by clearing away *infelicitous* sections of the local community.

He'd contacted the number on the flier, firmly believing he was about to be armed with no more than a litter-picker and a hi-vis jacket.

Six weeks later, he'd found himself with an erection, standing over the body of a man who'd recently been acquitted of strangling his pregnant girlfriend to death on a legal technicality. The litter-picker had turned out to be a Glock, and the last thing he would have been wearing was a hi-vis jacket.

***

Despite being partially obscured by an umbrella, Niko easily recognised Stanley standing away from the crowd.

"Now, DCI Wood, what are you doing here?" he whispered to himself. "And who is that adorable creature you're sharing body heat with?"

Niko suddenly recalled the head-shot of Verity he'd seen in the Gazette's report of Martin Bead's death. "Ah, the new kid on the block," he mumbled. "Nice to see you with some clothes on."

In spite of his flippancy, Niko felt a tinge of nervousness at being this close to police officers.

It was no wonder, in Niko's mind, the police had never got close to finding any T.S.A. operatives. As he'd once explained to Mr M, committing crimes and getting away with them had been made infinitely easier thanks to budgetary cuts and the British love for paperwork. But, even so, the odd criminal was still occasionally found.

And it now appeared to Niko as if Wood and his colleague had suddenly started to show an interest in him. In fact, he was sure the woman had just pointed in his direction.

Niko felt a knot forming in his stomach. His head started swimming, and his knees suddenly felt like they were about to buckle. He looked around for something to sit on, but the nearest bench would have actually taken him closer to where the officers were standing. It was also drenched with rain.

Being discovered had never been discussed with T.S.A. Far from it. One of the unique selling points had been the knowledge that the police would never be too interested in discovering who was clearing away the *infelicitous* sections of its local community.

"Shit," Niko said, louder than he had intended. The sudden expletive produced a glance from the tall, hooded youth standing no more than two feet away. Niko felt he had to justify the sudden outburst.

"Would you look at that," he said, nodding to where Stanley and Verity were standing. "She is one mighty fine-looking specimen of a woman." He hoped he was speaking in a language the youth could understand. "I wouldn't mind having her keep me warm on a cold winter's morning. Or any morning, for that matter."

***

That night, Niko replayed several times what happened next.

"I just don't understand it, Mr M," he said, stroking between the cat's ears. "This guy, right. This… this… bloody boy, who, I tell you, could have been no more than twelve years of age—"

The cat purred.

"Well, okay, maybe in his mid-twenties. Anyway, he looks like he's come as the Grim Reaper, right. The only thing missing was the bloody scythe. Anyway, he turns to them, lowers his hood, and waves. Waves! Like they were best friends! Can you believe it? And get this, here's the real deal. If I'm not mistaken, Mr M, the woman copper — the one I said was sexy as all hell — she even looked like she was pleased to see him! Wood had to practically drag her away."

Niko tried to laugh as he pushed the cat off himself in order to roll a joint, but the incident still had Niko disturbed. For a small moment in time, he'd thought they were actually looking at him, and it had frightened him. Niko didn't like being frightened. He'd spent most of his childhood afraid. In particular of Jews like Schmuck, but of a whole host of other matters, as well.

Cowboys frightened him. They were something he couldn't look at without remembering how he'd lost his virginity to an act of statutory rape. The woman who'd bounced up and down on top of him had obviously taken part of her title of *'carer'* to mean dressing them both up in Wild-West garb and having her fun. She'd kept on her hat and boots and insisted Niko pointed the plastic gun she'd given him at her head, telling her to: *'Ride me like a whore or I'll shoot you in the head, bitch.'*

Niko guessed she'd been in her forties. He had just turned fifteen. Niko doubted if she could ever have guessed he'd end up *actually* shooting people in the head for real.

Rocking-horses frightened him. A bully had once placed him on one, backwards, at primary school and he'd fallen off, resulting in a concussion that seemed to last for weeks. Every headache he'd had since, he'd attributed to the incident.

Crying frightened him. Why hadn't evolution sorted this out? Why, when distressed, did we need to cry? Why did nature feel the need to give us a physical function that displayed to the world how we were feeling?

"Oh, stop crying, Niko, it's only a scratch. Double promise."

"Oh, stop crying, Niko, I'm sure Schmuck didn't mean it. Double promise."

"Oh, stop crying, Niko, I'll get you something nice for your birthday next year. Double promise."

"For God's sake, Niko, will you please just stop crying. You're giving me a headache. Honestly, if you cry one more time, I swear I'll give you something to cry about. Triple promise."

Eventually, the instruction must have stuck. Niko hadn't cried since the day of his mother's funeral. The closest he'd come since had been from the pain his lieutenant-commander inflicted on him as he went about his sordid business.

Niko smiled broadly as he recalled the moment of revenge.

"Oh, Mr M, you should have seen the look in the bastard's eyes as he realised the nice, quick hand-job he thought he was getting didn't feel quite right."

'*Feeling hot, Commander?*' Niko had asked.

The commander could only just speak. His voice coming out laboured and high. *'What the fuck — have you done?'*

'Thought I'd add some spice to the occasion, Commander. A Californian Reaper to be precise. The hottest chilli known to man.'

Niko's smile turned into a laugh. "It was worth getting turfed out for, Mr M," he said. "Apparently, the big bastard was soaking his dick in iced water for days."

Niko took a long drag of his joint and washed down the taste with the dregs of his can.

"Yes, yes, I know I said I was giving up, Mr M. But it's been a shit day."

He brought his thoughts back to the funeral.

"I was afraid there for a moment, Mr M," he said. "And do you know the first thought that went through my mind?" Niko caught hold of the cat's head and turned it to him. "I thought, who the hell is going to look after you if anything happens to me? That's what I thought."

He kissed the cat's head, and then allowed Mr M to slope towards the kitchen. Niko noticed the cat was markedly dragging one of its hind legs.

SUNDAY

"How did the funeral go yesterday?" Patty Cleland asked. "Did you get to speak to Fahred?"

"Sorry, did we do what?" Verity asked. "Ma'am, you never said anything about—"

"No, we didn't, Ma'am," Stanley interrupted. "Couldn't get anywhere near him. We tried our best, but there were just too many people about. Didn't feel like the right time. However, we did notice Fahred with those *cousins* you mentioned. Right pair of gormless looking goons. Safe to say, even I'd fancy my chances in a foot race with them. Or a maths test."

Verity and Stanley exchanged a glance.

"There was something else of interest, Ma'am," Verity said. "Or should I say — someone of interest."

"Go on," Patty said. "Don't keep me in suspense, DI Chandler."

"Terrell Williams was there, Ma'am," Verity said. "My guess would be, he wanted Fahred to know The Angels were still on his case."

"Hang on, Superwoman," Stanley said, turning to Verity. "Let's not try to base things on guesses, is it?" Prior to entering the chief's office, they had agreed to tell Patty about Terrell's attendance, but they hadn't discussed offering any reasons as to why he was there. "At this moment in time, we don't even know if The Angels are responsible. Even if they are, we don't know for certain that Terrell Williams is one of them. For all we know, he could have simply been there to pay his respects."

Patty Cleland took a deep breath. "So, let me try and get this straight," she said. "Terrell Williams, a prime suspect in our investigation, was within your reach, and neither of you even spoke to him. Am I right?" Her tone, Stanley thought, was surprisingly calm.

"Yes, Ma'am," Verity replied. "I was well up for a little chat, but DCI Wood thought it was the wrong time."

"Is that so," Patty said, still worryingly keeping things under control.

"Yes, Ma'am," Stanley said, glowering at Verity. "You see, I believe we'd lost the element of surprise."

"What exactly are you talking about, DCI Wood?" Patty asked.

"Well, Ma'am, Terrell Williams sort of…"

"Sort of what?" Patty said. The calmness was abating. "Come on, fecking spit it out."

"Well, he sort of… made himself known, Ma'am," Stanley said.

"But you just told me you didn't speak to the little gobshite."

Stanley shifted in his seat. “That’s right, we didn’t, but he sort of… waved at us. Sort of like this.” Stanley re-enacted the slow movement of Terrell’s arm and did his best to imitate Terrell’s mocking smile. He pointed to his mouth. “He’s a got a gold tooth,” he added, as if it were somehow important.

Patty shook her head slowly. “Jesus, save me,” she said. “We’re just a joke to these people, and I’m not surprised when we’ve got eejits like you two wandering loose. It’s the likes of you who make sure there’s no respect for the uniform anymore.”

“But we didn’t wear uniform, Ma’am,” Verity said. “In fact, I’d made quite an effort.”

Both Patty and Stanley stared at Verity hard.

“It’s a fecking figure of speech,” Patty said, gritting her teeth. “Right, DI Chandler, who doesn’t wear a uniform anymore, but will do if she doesn’t pull her finger out, I believe you’re off to a cricket match later today, correct?” She didn’t wait for a reply. “Now, I don’t care what you do with him, but I want this brazen idiot, Williams, squawking like a parrot by the end of the day. Understood?”

“I’ll do my very best, Ma’am,” Verity said.

Patty played with her ring-finger, where her wedding band once sat. “I’m going to be out for the rest of the day,” she said. “I have something I have to take care of. So, I’ll see you both in here bright and breezy, bearing me good news, first thing tomorrow morning.”

Stanley and Verity both nodded. “Yes, Ma’am,” they said in unison.

It dawned on Stanley that he didn’t know a great deal about his boss. He guessed her age at somewhere in her late forties and knew she was Irish. That much was obvious. He believed he’d once been told her husband’s name. It began with a B, or was it a D? Stanley had never heard her talk about children, or, more to the point, if she had, he obviously hadn’t been listening.

Of course, there was one person in the building who would know all there was to know about Patty Cleland. Maybe, it was time to bite the bullet and speak to her. Perhaps, time had dampened her anger. Perhaps, she would even offer some forgiveness. There was only one way to find out.

***

Stanley stood for several seconds at Joanne’s desk before she finally lifted her head. “My, my,” she said. “I am honoured. The great Stanley Wood has plucked up the courage to come and speak to me. For once, he’s not too busy being a knobhead.”

Obviously, Stanley had been wrong about time doing its thing.

“Look, Joanne,” Stanley said, quietly, “I don’t know how many times I have to apologise. I was drunk and just misread the signs.”

"What bloody signs?" Joanne growled. "And you apologised *once.* Even then you tried to laugh it off."

"Joanne, please," Stanley said. "You know full well that wasn't the real me. I honestly don't know what I was thinking. Are we really going to let one small incident spoil years of friendship? I mean, one minute we were all laughing and joking, the next, well, you know what happened next."

"Yes, I do. And the fact you've just referred to it as a *small* incident tells me everything I need to know. Now, what do you want? And make it quick. I have proper work to do."

Stanley wanted to scream at Joanne that, in his eyes, in fact, in any normal person's eyes, the incident would be considered *small*, and probably laughed off, by now, as a drunken misadventure, but he thought better of it. "It's about Patty," he said.

"What about Patty?"

"She's not quite herself," Stanley said. "I'm worried about her."

"Really? You, worried about someone? Wonders will never cease."

"Okay, never mind," Stanley said. "Forget I asked." He turned and walked away. He hoped Joanne was suitably shocked but didn't turn around to check.

***

Back at his desk, Stanley started throwing papers into a drawer, closing it with a slam.

Verity appeared with coffee in hand. "Here you go, Boss, just as you like it," she said, placing the coffee in front of Stanley.

"How the hell would you know what I like?" Stanley said, standing up and grabbing his jacket off the back of his chair. "I'm going home. Don't expect to see me for the rest of the day. And make sure you're in early in the morning to brief me about your cricket playing arsehole before we face Her Majesty. And don't you dare sleep with him!"

Verity stood open-mouthed and shrugged her shoulders to the watching office as Stanley left.

"What did I do?" she mouthed.

***

Michelle was equally perplexed. "Stanley, is that you?" she shouted from the living room. "What are you doing home?"

"I thought I'd just take a few hours off and come and keep you company," Stanley replied, placing his jacket on the hook in the hallway. He could hear the television spouting some lunch-time rubbish. "Perhaps we could finish watching Chariots of Fire. What do you think?" He made his way into the living room and gave Michelle a kiss on the cheek. He noticed she had not dressed. Obviously, a bad day.

"I've smashed a glass," she said. "In the kitchen. I tried to pick it up but—"

"It's okay," Stanley interrupted. "I'll sort it out later."

Stanley remembered how calm Michelle had been when, six months ago, the diagnosis had been delivered.

***

"Well, that answers a lot of questions," she'd said. "At least I know I'm not just clumsy."

Her reaction had been in stark contrast to the one, many years previously, when they'd been told Michelle could not have children.

When the doctor had said, *'Primary Ovarian Insufficiency,'* in a more than acceptable bedside manner, Michelle had been inconsolable and wouldn't stop apologising to Stanley for her body's malfunction.

Stanley could do nothing, other than continuously tell her everything would be okay, and, in some darkened corner of his mind, perfectly secreted away, Stanley had believed everything would be okay.

He'd never been keen to have children. He'd gone along with the whole, *'Let's get pregnant'* plan because it had made Michelle happy, but a childless life certainly held more appeal for Stanley. Ever since, he'd believed that Michelle's damaged ovaries had saved him a whole heap of drama and sleeplessness. Not to mention the money. Of course, he'd still shown, in his opinion, the necessary levels of disappointment at their devastating news.

But this time around, Stanley had not needed to simulate any distress.

It had started with a weakening grip, which Michelle had ignored until it got to the stage where she was struggling to hold a cup of tea. Since then, a host of other motor neurones had also decided their day was done, and more joined the list every day. She now dragged her right leg quite obviously, and her speech was starting to slur. For now, her swallowing and breathing were okay, but it was only a matter of time. The doctors had given her anything from a year to three. They had drugs which helped the symptoms, but none that held the cure. The doctors suggested they make the best of whatever time was left. She was forty-eight years old.

Stanley had offered the idea that they could do whatever Michelle wanted. She'd replied she wanted to just carry on as normal. No fuss or bother; just a quiet, dignified decline to the grave. She didn't even want him to tell his work colleagues.

"They'd look at you differently, Stanley," she'd said. "They'd be all sympathetic. It would drive you crazy. The only thing I want you to do is learn to cook so you don't starve when I'm gone. Don't worry, I'll point out where the kitchen is."

Michelle had handed in her resignation the day after the diagnosis. Her boss was genuinely upset to see her go and couldn't understand the suddenness of her decision. Michelle explained she didn't really need the money. After all, the salary of a part-time accountant's receptionist didn't exactly set the world on fire.

"Let's call it an early retirement," she'd said.

Her boss wished her a long and healthy life, the irony of which made Michelle laugh.

***

Stanley popped in the DVD and sat next to his wife on the sofa.

"You know, we're probably one of the few households left with a DVD player," he said. "It's all downloads and the like, these days. The guys in work keep telling me to get something called Netflix."

"What are you doing here?" Michelle asked.

"I told you," Stanley replied. "I thought I'd take a few hours off and we could finish watching—"

"No, I mean here." Michelle patted the sofa. "Your chair is over there." She pointed to the leather recliner Stanley normally sat on.

Stanley laughed. "Just fancied a change of scenery," he said, putting his arm around Michelle and pulling her closer. He gently removed her glasses and placed them on the arm of the sofa.

"Well, well," Michelle said. "Here I am pushing fifty and dying, and I've never had a booty call before."

"First time for everything," Stanley said, he then kissed his wife.

***

"Well, that was — quick," Michelle said, re-tightening her dressing-gown. "But fun," she quickly added.

Stanley re-buckled the belt on his trousers. "Yeah, sorry about that," he said. "I guess it's been a while and I was — you know — worked up."

"Really? That's your excuse?"

"Of course. What are you getting at?" Stanley attempted to intone as much misunderstanding into the question as possible, but he knew where Michelle was going. She may have been a lot of things over the last twenty-five years, but stupid had never been one of them.

"You were somewhere else," Michelle said. "I could see it in your eyes."

Stanley laughed, but it came out as nervous. "You're joking, right?"

"It's all right," Michelle continued. "I don't mind, honestly. I mean, you haven't touched me, at least not like that, since the diagnosis. And that's only to be expected, Stanley. Who the hell wants to be knowingly making love to a diseased woman? If it had been the other way around, I wouldn't be touching you with a bargepole. So, look, if you want to fantasise about other women when you're with me, then that's fine. I don't mind."

The truth had been somewhat the opposite. Stanley had been desperately trying *not* to fantasise about other women. One woman in particular.

"Now," Michelle said, "rewind that damned DVD. We missed all of five minutes." She jokingly ruffled her fingers through Stanley's hair. "Oh, and maybe it's time we dyed this lot again."

Stanley had inherited his father's colouring. It had never been much of a problem until he'd joined the army. There'd been some schoolmates who'd given him some banter, but for some reason, unknown to him, it was the first thing his army colleagues, in particular his superior officers, homed in on, and he had found himself having to defend its redness on a routine basis. Since leaving the army, he'd regularly dyed his hair black. Initially, even Michelle didn't know his real colouring. Not until she'd asked why he was a different colour *'down below.'*

Stanley's father had died in a car accident when he was only eighteen-months old, and he couldn't remember him at all. His only point of reference as to his father's appearance had been the photographs his mother had kept, all of which clearly showed him to have a fine head of red hair.

Maybe, Stanley thought, it was time to put his vanity to one side and allow his natural colour to come through. The problem was, his natural colour was now mainly white, and he didn't particularly like that idea. He'd once asked Michelle if she would like him white-haired. Just like George Clooney, he'd offered. Michelle's response was he'd probably look more like Helen Mirren than George Clooney.

Stanley wondered whether Verity liked white-haired men, after all wasn't it supposed to be distinguished? He then reminded himself he shouldn't be wondering what men she liked at all.

"Earth calling Stanley," Michelle said. "You've almost rewound the thing to the beginning. Give me that." She snatched the remote control from Stanley's hand. Stanley noticed her hand was shaking badly as she attempted to find the place in the film she was looking for.

"Sorry, I was just—"

"Look, I said I don't mind, okay?" Michelle said. "I often have to pretend you're Brad Pitt to get me going. It takes every ounce of my imagination, and I have to shut my eyes really, really tight, but—"

"Yeah, yeah," Stanley said, playfully punching Michelle on the arm. "Look, no matter what, you'll always be the only one for me, Shell, you know that, right?"

Stanley rarely shortened Michelle's name. He'd tried it once in her mother's company, to be met with a tirade of verbal abuse about her not being something you pick up off the beach. Since then, he'd almost always used her full name, but right now it felt okay to be more casual.

"By God!" Michelle laughed. "Is that your way of saying you love me, Stanley Arthur Peregrine Wood? I know you come out in a rash if you say the words directly, so I shall take it as a coded message."

Michelle leaned over and pecked Stanley lightly on the cheek. "Well, I love you too," she said. "Mind you, if I'd known your middle name was Peregrine when we met, I'd have run a mile."

"I'm surprised you didn't anyway," Stanley said.

***

Michelle had come into Stanley's life not long after he'd left the army. At only eighteen, she was four years younger than him, but infinitely more stable, seeing things through far clearer eyes. Their courtship had not been a particularly romantic affair. Stanley didn't go in for that sort of thing, but he'd certainly been the keener of the two to make things happen.

His first proposal had been only six months after they'd met. Michelle had refused, saying they hardly knew one another and were far too young. His second, a year later, had been after a particularly heavy weekend. That time, Michelle had turned him down on the basis they were both too drunk. Not just right at that moment, but in general.

It took another three years before, in a passing conversation, Stanley broached the subject again. To his astonishment, she'd said yes. The marriage had been a simple family affair at a local register office followed by a reception consisting of a buffet and disco in the upstairs function room of their favourite local.

Half-way through the evening, the DJ had found himself pretty much alone as the best man had organised a pool tournament downstairs, which, by judicial cheating, Michelle won.

Stanley had often wondered why Michelle hadn't insisted on a more lavish celebration. He'd always been led to believe all girls wanted their special day to be — well, special. He could only assume it had been another of Michelle's veiled statements to her over-protective parents.

Stanley had realised from early in their relationship that Michelle's parents had not been too keen on him. Nothing uncivil had ever been said, but then nothing particularly civil had ever been said either.

One night, on pointing out that, in his opinion, Michelle's parents had no qualms in hiding their coldness towards him, Michelle had told Stanley that, like all parents, they had probably hoped for something better for their only child. Stanley went along with the jibe, believing they undoubtedly had a point.

***

"Why do you think this is called Chariots of Fire?" Michelle's question brought Stanley back to the present. "I mean they're not hurtling about in chariots. They're not even Roman. They're just running about like normal."

Michelle's requirement to always see things clearly had sometimes been a cause of despair for Stanley.

"I think it's a quote from The Bible," Stanley replied. "Or a poem, maybe. Something like that."

"But this has nothing to do with The Bible. Or poetry. It's all about people running."

"I think it's a little bit more than that."

"Really? How come?"

Michelle had received a standard education, but had informed Stanley her reports mainly consisted of phrases such as, *could do better,* or, *Michelle doesn't work to her full potential.* She wasn't dumb — far from it — but when it came to thinking outside of any particular box, she struggled.

"Well, Liddell, even though he's running for the glory of God," Stanley explained, "has just informed the British Olympic Committee he refuses to run on a Sunday because of his religion. And the other one, Abrahams, is a Jew who's running to avoid prejudice."

Michelle yawned. "Still seems like a daft title," she said. She pulled her favourite sofa-blanket up to her neck and made herself as comfortable as she could.

Stanley guessed she'd be asleep in no more than five minutes.

***

"Are you following me?" Terrell Williams asked. He had removed himself from the noisy huddle of team-mates he'd been with and walked over to where Verity was sitting in the pub, alone. "First the funeral, then the match, and now here. Bit more than a coincidence, I think. Now, don't get me wrong, if I'm going to be followed by the filth, then I can think of worse people. Your colleague, Wood, for a start. He's been around these parts for a long time, but you — you're new. So why all the attention, Gorgeous? I'm guessing you're interested in a bit more than my rugged good looks, animal charm, and taught body."

"You played well," Verity said, raising her glass of wine in salute. "And no, I'm not following you. Not exactly. I'd just like to have a friendly chat if that's okay."

"About what?"

"Not here," Verity said. "Can we go somewhere quieter? Your friends over there are somewhat — how can I put this? — excitable."

Terrell's team-mates were shouting over with varying degrees of encouragement about how he should go about his business with Verity.

"Where do you have in mind?" Terrell asked.

MONDAY

Stanley was glad to see Verity had taken the instruction to come in early to heart. She'd also gone to the trouble of getting coffee. This time, it was accompanied with a Twix. He wondered whether he should apologise for the previous day's outburst, but quickly dismissed the idea. He'd never been a fan of apologies, either given or received. To Stanley, they just always felt false.

"So?" he said. "How did it go with Williams? Please tell me he's not currently having breakfast in your flat." Stanley immediately regretted the words. If only for the images it now conjured in his brain. Bloody idiot, he thought. Why can't you just keep your mouth shut around this woman?

"No such luck," Verity replied. "We went to a nice, quiet pub and had a drink, but he was far too street-wise for me. He did confirm he's got a couple of younger brothers, but apart from that, despite being as charming as I could be, I couldn't get a thing out of him. In fact, at one point, he mentioned contacting his solicitors and getting them to sue me for harassment. He was joking, of course. At least, I think he was."

"Which pub?" Stanley asked.

"Pardon?"

“Which pub? You said you went to a nice, quiet pub. I’m just wondering how you managed to find a quiet pub in East London on a Sunday evening.”

“I can’t remember the name of it,” Verity said, narrowing her eyes. “The something arms, I think. And of course, you’re right, it wasn’t quiet. What I meant was we managed to find a quiet table, that’s all. Am I under interrogation here, DCI Wood? Are you grilling me?”

Stanley laughed, but, even to him, it wasn’t a convincing laugh. What the hell was he doing? “Of course I’m not grilling you,” he said. “But Her Majesty will. I’m just trying to prepare you. So, exactly how did the conversation go?”

“Are you kidding me?” Verity said. “Why didn’t you just put a wire on me and save us all the trouble?”

“Look, Her Majesty is going to want to know everything from what he was wearing to how he smelled,” Stanley said, thinking the wire suggestion wouldn’t have been a bad idea. “We need to make sure we have our story straight.”

“I didn’t realise there was anything not straight about it. I asked a few questions of a man who we believe was possibly involved in a crime. Turns out he wasn’t too keen to speak to me. He left. I called a cab to take me home. End of.”

“How much did you have to drink?” Stanley winced as soon as the words had left his mouth. The next question also came out all wrong. “And how did you get the cab to know where you were? I thought you said you couldn't remember the name of the pub."

"Jesus Christ!" Verity said, getting off her chair. "Are you for real?" She pushed the Twix off Stanley's desk and started walking away. "I'll meet you outside the chief's office in five minutes," she shouted.

"Did you just say, 'End of?'" Stanley shouted after her. Stanley groaned as he bent down to pick up his Twix.

***

Patty looked from Stanley to Verity several times.

"Am I sensing something here?" she asked, waving a finger from one to the other. "Is there trouble at mill, as they say up north. Is everything not fecking rosy in Detectiveshire?"

"We're fine, Ma'am," Stanley said. The tone of his voice was unconvincing. "I'm just a little concerned that we sent DI Chandler to question a possible violent criminal with no back-up."

Verity snapped her head in Stanley's direction. "That's not what you're bloody concerned about," she said. "You're more worried that I—"

"Yes, yes, whatever," Patty Cleland interrupted. "Sort out your lover's tiff between yourselves. Now, hit me, DI Chandler. Tell me that Terrell Williams has confessed to every crime committed in these parts over the last ten years, including entering Ahmadi's store with a cricket bat, and that he's currently festering away in one of our cells. Go on, girl, give it to me." Patty closed her eyes, bowed her head, and held out her hands like a candelabra.

Verity looked to Stanley for help, but he just shrugged his shoulders. "Well, Ma'am, I can tell you that Terrell did confirm he's got two younger brothers, so you were right about them being related."

"Of course I was," Patty said. "Go on."

Verity gave out a single cough. "Well, that's about it, Ma'am. I tried everything, but—"

"Ah, fecking hell!" Patty screamed, banging her hands on the desk. "Right, get out. I've had it up to my neck with you two coming in here with nothing but bad news. I don't want to hear your voices for the rest of the day, unless it's to tell me I've won the fecking lottery."

***

"Wow," Verity said, once she and Stanley had returned to their desks. "She really is going mad. What was all that holding her hands out? She looked like a Buddhist monk."

"You really got nothing out of Williams? Nothing at all?" Stanley squinted his eyes and rubbed the bridge of his nose. "A woman armed with your particular assets has a relaxing drink with a low-life thug who may have thought, quite wrongly, of course, that there was something more rewarding on offer, and you're telling me he said nothing? Diddly squat?"

Verity gave out a snort. "The problem with all that, DCI Wood, is your assumption that Terrell Williams is a low-life thug. For your information, he was a charming, intelligent, young man. A very street-wise, charming, intelligent, young man. Any attempt to steer the conversation to The Angels, Bijan, Fahred, or anything to do with crime in general, was met with nothing but a smile. And I bloody well didn't offer him anything more rewarding!"

"So, what did you talk about?" Stanley shouted.

"We talked about how big his dick is!" Verity shouted louder.

Stanley attempted to make himself smaller in his chair. He was aware he was blushing, always obvious in people of his colouring. Why the hell had nature given him such an outward way of showing the world he was embarrassed and angry?

Eventually, mainly in order to get out of the station, Stanley said, "It's about time we paid Fahred Ahmadi a visit."

***

Niko woke on the settee, the television still tuned into some obscure, even-numbered channel. He reached down to his stomach where Mr M would normally have curled himself up throughout the night. The space was empty. A slight panic raised itself in Niko's head. "Mr M — where are you?" he shouted. He tried to rub the sleep from his eyes. "Mr M?"

Niko slowly made his way to the kitchen and let out a sigh of relief as he found the cat in its basket, its eyes blinking slowly.

"You had me worried for a minute there, Mr M," he said, the knot of panic subsiding. "What are you doing there? You're normally…" Then he noticed the blood slowly seeping from the cat's rear-end. "Oh, shit!"

***

The vet explained Mr M had suffered with an episode of dyschezia. "Severe constipation to you and me," she'd said. "A defective reflex in the anus that is extremely painful."

On hearing the words, Niko had felt relieved. Severe constipation didn't sound too serious, but something about the vet's demeanour told him there was something else. He didn't quite understand all the medical jargon but, *"...and we've found masses in the colon..."* was enough. The vet carried on in a well-rehearsed bedside manner with words she'd probably spoken a hundred times or more. Mr M's age had to be taken into account, along with the pain and suffering, etcetera et-fucking-cetera.

Niko chose the option to allow the surgery to dispose of the body. Where the hell did he have anywhere to bury a cat? They assured Niko it would be dignified. He could pay the invoice now if he wished.

***

Stanley parked the unmarked Volvo as close to the store as possible. The bad atmosphere in the car on the drive to Ahmadi's had been palpable, and conversation had been scant.

"I think we're in luck," Stanley said, killing the engine. "Fahred's delightful looking *cousins* are standing in the doorway. I reckon that means Fahred is in residence. So, you go and get us a ticket."

"Pardon?"

"A parking ticket," Stanley said. "The last thing we need is for some jobsworth warden to start sniffing around."

"You're joking, right?"

"Does it sound like I'm joking?" Stanley replied. "Just get the minimum amount. I don't think we'll be too long. Go on, off you go."

Stanley smiled as he watched Verity feed the nearest meter with coins.

"Five bloody quid that cost me," Verity said, re-entering the car and throwing the ticket on Stanley's lap. "We've got an hour."

“Daylight robbery,” Stanley said, inwardly still smiling as he placed the ticket on the dashboard. “But let’s call it due payment.”

“For what?”

“Oh, trust me, the list is growing.”

There was a pause before Verity asked, “Do you recognise either of those two?” She pointed to where the cousins were standing.

Stanley was not about to admit that he couldn’t make out too many features from where he was. “Can’t say I do,” he said.

“Do you think they’ll know you?”

“If they’re local I should imagine so,” Stanley replied. “I’m part of the fixtures and fittings in these parts. I’ve been around since Fred Flinstone had a property on The Mile End.”

“What, the cricketer? I didn’t know he mooched about these parts.”

“No, it was a joke. Fred Flinstone was a… oh, never mind. I’ve been around a long time, that’s all.”

“Right, so the minute those two lumps of lard see you lumber out of the car, they’ll probably send a message into the store to say the old-timer that is DCI Wood is on his way, and Fahred will be out the back door before we know it.”

“Possibly.”

“Definitely. But they won’t know me,” Verity said. “Unless, of course, they saw my picture in The Gazette, which I doubt. They don’t strike me as fans of reading.

So, why don't you stay here while I go and distract them. Once they're out of the way, we can go in and have a nice, friendly chat with Fred. Does that sound like a plan?" To Stanley's utter dismay, Verity used her fingers around *plan*.

"As long as there's no exchange of phone numbers," Stanley said. "And please don't do that thing with your fingers."

"What thing?"

"That inverting words thing. It's so annoying."

"But you do it all the time."

"So! If I went around mugging grannies all the time, would you do that as well?"

"Okay, okay," Verity said. "But when you spend lots of time with someone, you're bound to pick up the odd habit here and there."

"Well, try and pick up the good ones."

"Have you got good ones?" Verity said.

She undid the top two buttons of her blouse, showing her ample bosom, together with a hint of the lace bra holding things together.

"Uh, what the hell are you doing?" Stanley asked, unable to stop the heat, again, from reddening his face. He looked around the car, hoping for some help.

"I told you. I'm going to distract them," Verity replied. "Mother has always told me if you've got it, flaunt it. You ought to see some of the clothes she sells. Father is always saying he can't understand why women pay such large sums for such little clothing. Now, give me a minute. Even I can't get up to too much mischief in a minute. Anyway, they don't look like my type."

"You *have* a type?" Stanley said. "You surprise me."

"Ooh, DCI Stanley Wood, if I didn't know any better, I'd say you were jealous." Verity leaned over, affording Stanley an indecent glimpse down the front of her blouse, and kissed him lightly on the cheek.

"Piss off!" Stanley said, pushing Verity away. He wiped away the smudge of pink lipstick she'd left behind on his face with the back of his hand. "I know you can hardly resist me, but I'm a happily married man." Despite his best efforts at dismissing the situation as a joke, Stanley's body had actually quivered as Verity had kissed him. He daren't look, but he was also aware of his member hardening.

Verity laughed as she left the car.

"Jesus Christ," Stanley whispered to himself. "Get a grip."

Stanley watched as Verity started talking to the men. At one point, she threw her head back and laughed heartily. The goons were totally smitten: mere puppets in the hands of a master. "There's no way Williams said nothing," Stanley muttered.

After Verity's promised minute, the two men started walking away. Verity turned to the car and waved Stanley to her.

“Where the hell have they gone?” Stanley asked, reaching the store’s doorway. “And what the hell did you say to them?”

“Doesn’t matter,” Verity replied, doing up the buttons on her blouse. “But they won’t be gone for ever. Come on, let’s see the oil-painting that is Fahred Ahmadi.”

“He’s not here,” said the young girl standing behind the till. Her eyes darted to the rear of the store. The badge on her bright-yellow tunic informed Stanley her name was Esfir. Stanley thought the girl was only in her early teens if she was a day. But then he’d noticed anybody under the age of thirty looked pubescent to him these days.

“Is he out the back, Esfir?” Stanley whispered.

The miniscule nod of the girl’s head confirmed Fahred’s presence.

Stanley mouthed a thank you. He moved to an inner aisle and pretended to be interested in a range of cereals, whilst keeping his eyes firmly on the connecting door between the store and the living quarters.

“Boss, what are we doing?” Verity asked. “There’s plenty of cereals back at the station.”

“I’m going to wait for him to come out,” Stanley said. “I really want to surprise him.”

After a minute of rifling through cereal boxes, Stanley noticed the connecting door opening. Fahred had his eyes firmly fixed at his screen as he spoke to someone on his mobile, paying no regard to who may be in his store. He made his way towards the till area, facing it from the customer's side. Stanley moved quietly behind him, putting his fingers to his lips to request Esfir to say nothing.

Fahred finished his phone conversation with a promise to deliver something to someone, and then put his phone away. "Okay, keep the float, but give me the rest, innit?" he said to Esfir.

If he could have, Stanley would have arrested Fahred right there and then, educating him in the process that the English dictionary went straight from *innings* to *innkeeper*. There was no bloody *innit*.

"And for God's sake, girl, smile." Fahred banged the counter, making Esfir jump. "What my customers gonna think if they see you with face like you bin told your whole family bin gone and wiped out by axe-wielding murderer, eh?"

Fahred reached across the counter and grabbed Esfir under the chin. Tight enough, Stanley noted, to make Esfir gasp.

"And don't forget arrangement for weekend," he said. "You best be on time, girl, my peeps doesn't like to wait, innit? An' don't forget to bring one of the others like I said, you git me?"

Stanley and Verity stole a glance at one another. Stanley decided it was time to make himself known. He coughed. Apart from the noise, Fahred must have noticed some movement in Esfir's eyes. He quickly released her face and spun around. "Please, I can explain."

There was an instant look of relief on Fahred's face. "Ah, DCI Wood," he said, straightening out some non-existent crumples on his track-suit. "For a minute there I thought you was — well, never mind what I thought you was, innit?"

Stanley believed if he could have finished the sentence for him it would have been along the lines of *'for a minute there I thought you was carrying a cricket bat, innit?'* Stanley mentally started adding five years imprisonment for every use of the word *innit.*

"Anyway, to what do I owe the pleasure?" Fahred said. If he had meant to address the words to Stanley, his eyes asked them to Verity.

"Ah, yes, allow me to introduce my colleague," Stanley said. "This is DI Chandler." Stanley had raised his voice in order for the several customers who were in the store to hear. The resultant effect had the customers scurrying out without having made any purchases.

"Oh dear, it suddenly seems to have gone a bit quiet," Stanley continued.

"What can I do for you?" Fahred asked.

"We'd just like to ask you a few questions," Stanley replied. "It won't take long. Perhaps we could use those living quarters you've got out the back. Unless, of course, you'd rather answer them back at the station."

"Well, thing is, I'm in a bit of a rush right now, innit?" Fahred smiled as best he could, but the damage left from his scaffold pipe experience meant only one side of his mouth was capable of the exercise.

Verity thought he looked like one of those puppet-heads you stick your fingers in and manipulate into gross contortions.

"You know, things to do an' people to see an' all that, you git me?" Fahred turned to Esfir. "Now don't forget that party on the weekend," he said to the girl. "An' remember, bring a friend, innit?"

Esfir nodded.

Fahred may not be the brightest spark, Stanley thought, but he was obviously savvy enough to know Stanley had probably overheard his earlier conversation with Esfir. What better way to justify it as something innocent than to repeat it in front of him?

"Ooh, a party," Verity said. "That's nice. Where is it? A local cricket club, perhaps?"

Fahred turned back to Stanley and Verity. He stared at Verity, but she couldn't tell whether his lop-sided mouth was smiling or grimacing. "No," he said. "It's just a small fing, innit? Family only. Otherwise, I'd invite you along as well, you git me? You could have worn whatever you wasn't wearing in that photo I seen in The Gazette, innit?"

Fahred attempted to make his smile wider, which made his left eye squint. "Now, if we've finished, I've got to go an' get some supplies, an' I can't drive myself these days. Not since you lot took me licence, innit? So, gotta couple of my homeys waiting outside to—"

"Ah," Verity interrupted. "If you mean the two lovely gentlemen who *were* standing outside, I'm afraid they've gone to the Costa up the street to get me a coffee."

Stanley snapped his head. "A coffee?"

"Yes, a coffee," Verity replied. "They were arguing so much about which one of them would go that, in the end, I decided they could both go. I'm sure they'll be as quick as they can, but you know how busy these places are sometimes. And they're not exactly speedy, are they?"

Stanley wondered if she was talking about the cousins, neither of whom had looked exactly nimble, or the service of a normal Costa. He turned back to Fahred.

"Well, there you go," he said. "Looks like you're not in so much of a rush after all." For the briefest of moments, Stanley almost added the word *innit.* "If only they'd remembered you've actually got a coffee-making machine right here in store," he added, pointing to the machine.

"Look, if this is about them robberies," Fahred said, "I told that Polish geezer all I can, innit? He arksed me like a million questions, man. He made my head hurt. So, I got nothing else to say, you git me?"

"Mr Ahmadi," Verity said, in that tone Stanley knew only too well. She'd put her hands behind her back, pushed her chest out slightly, and was standing on the tips of her toes.

Jesus, he's got no chance, Stanley thought. Fred Ahmadi's eyes were already twice the size they had been, and Stanley was sure he could see spittle emerging from his crooked lip. Fahred used the three fingers he had on his right hand to smooth back his greasy, black hair.

"We're only here to help you," Verity continued, cocking her head to one side. "We know you've been the victim of some terrible, terrible crimes lately. On top of that, you've now lost your poor, beloved grandfather, who was much loved by everyone." Verity caught hold of Fahred's mangled hand and stroked it as gently as if he was a newborn.

Stanley thought Fahred was about to explode.

"We fully understand the pain you must be going through," Verity continued. "And we're throwing every resource we have at finding the animals who have caused you and your family such undeserved heartache. But we need your help. Will you help us, Fred? I can call you Fred, can't I?"

Fahred nodded his head. He used his free hand to wipe the dribble from his mouth.

"Excellent," Verity said. "So, Fred, why don't you and I go somewhere a bit more private? What about through there?" She nodded to the door marked private.

Fahred nodded his head quicker.

"Ah, excuse me," Stanley said. "Am I not included?"

Verity broke contact with Fahred and took Stanley to one side. "I'll be right back, Fred," she said over her shoulder. "Don't you go anywhere."

Fahred continued to nod. Stanley was reminded of those novelty toys you sometimes see on the back shelves of cars.

"Look," Verity whispered to Stanley. "When I'm in there wasting my time getting information we already know out of this ugly moron, why don't you have a quiet word with that young girl at the till and see if you can find something that actually might be useful?"

"If I'm not mistaken," Stanley said, "the last time I looked, I was the superior officer here. I call the shots, understood?"

"Yes, Boss," Verity said. There was the tone again. "So, what would you like me to do?"

Stanley looked at the ceiling and growled. "I'd like you to take Fahred out the back so I can have a quiet word with the young girl at the till," he said.

"Ooh, that's a good idea, Boss. I'll get right on it."

***

"Hello, Esfir," Stanley said, trying to adopt a tone he hoped sounded friendly enough. "My name is DCI Stanley Wood. Do you know what that means?"

Esfir shook her head.

"It means I'm a policeman," Stanley said. "And policemen are here to help people. You do know that, don't you?"

Esfir shrugged her shoulders and looked down at the floor. "That's not what Fred says," she whispered, just loud enough for Stanley to hear.

"Oh, and what does Fahred, I mean Fred, say?"

The girl shook her head. "I shouldn't be talking to you," she said. "I told the policeman who was here before all I could."

"DI Smollenski?"

Esfir nodded her head. "Fred said if I talked to the police again, he'd make sure me and my friends can't work here anymore."

Although her accent was cockney enough, Stanley thought it still carried a hint of Eastern European. From what he'd heard earlier between Esfir and Fahred, a certain image started to form in Stanley's mind. Despite the surround of that image being somewhat blurred, it was an image he didn't like.

"So, I'm not answering no more questions," Esfir said. "Please, leave me alone."

Stanley had to stop himself from correcting the grammar.

"Okay, Esfir," he said. "I won't bother you with questions, but perhaps we can just have a friendly chat? Just to kill the time whilst I'm waiting for my friend to come back. Surely even Fred won't mind us having a friendly chat, will he?" He didn't wait for a reply.

"Now, like I said, my name is Stanley, and I can see yours is Esfir. Where does that come from?"

Esfir lifted her face a little. "It's Iranian," she said. "It means star-like."

Stanley smiled his best smile. He hoped it looked genuine, but he had his doubts. Those bloody false teeth always made it slightly sinister. Michelle always said his smiles looked forced, even when they weren't.

"Well, isn't that a lovely name?" he said. "Far better than boring old Stanley. Do you know what my name means? It means *'dweller by a stone,'* or something like that. Nothing anywhere near as exciting as star-like." Bugger, he'd used his fingers around *dweller by a stone*.

"Have you come here to take Fred away?" Esfir pointed her face back to the floor.

The question took Stanley by surprise. "Why? Would you like me to?" he said. "Would you like me to take Fred away?"

Once again, Esfir just shrugged her shoulders.

"See, the thing is, Esfir, in order for me to take Fred away, I would have to have some reason. I would need someone to tell me that Fred has done something wrong. Something that's against the law. Do you understand?"

Esfir nodded slowly.

"So, has he done something wrong, Esfir? Has Fred done something wrong?" The blurred surround of the image Stanley hadn't liked began to clear. "Has he done something wrong to you?"

Esfir shook her head.

"Has he done something wrong to any of your friends?" Stanley let the question hang, but there was no reply. "Well then, I can't take him away, Esfir. If he's done nothing wrong, I'm going to have to leave him alone."

Esfir still said nothing and continued staring at the floor.

"How old are you, Esfir?" Stanley asked. "I know it's rude to ask a woman her age, but I've asked it now."

Stanley thought he caught the hint of a giggle.

"I'm not a woman," Esfir said. "I'm only fifteen."

Stanley winced and sucked in some air. He pinched the bridge of his nose. "Fifteen," he repeated. "So, you're still in school then?"

"Sort of," Esfir replied, quietly. "I don't go that much."

"And what do your parents say about that?"

Esfir giggled again. This time, Stanley thought it sounded more from nerves rather than anything particularly funny. "I haven't got parents," she said.

"So, who looks after you, Esfir?"

Esfir shook her head and said nothing.

Stanley was suddenly aware of a commotion behind him. He turned to find the cousins both trying to get through the shop doorway at the same time. They both had their hands on a take-out Costa Coffee mug and were arguing about who would be the ultimate deliverer.

"Oh, for Christ's sake," Stanley whispered.

He made his way to the door to the living quarters and knocked on it sharply. "Your coffee is here, DI Chandler," he shouted, taking great amusement out of the reaction of the cousins on hearing her title. They had both frozen, as if they'd been suddenly zapped by a laser from some super-hero.

Verity emerged from the living quarters, Fahred following her like a lapdog. She made her way to the open-mouthed, frozen cousins and prised the coffee mug from their hands.

"Thanks, guys," she said, immediately passing the coffee to Stanley. "Never touch the stuff myself, but DCI Wood here is quite partial."

Stanley accepted the coffee. "Yeah, thanks guys," he said. "Next time, a millionaire shortbread would be nice. Don't tell the wife though."

Stanley moved to Esfir and handed her his card. "If you ever need to talk about anything at all, you just give me a call, okay? Any time, day or night. I'll be there."

He turned to where Fahred was standing and stared at him for a long time. "And Esfir," he said, still looking at Fahred. "If you don't want to go to Fred's party, then you don't have to."

Fahred stared back and slowly, but surely, started to smile. Obviously, the trance Verity had put him under was starting to thaw.

"As much as I've enjoyed your visit," Fahred said, "I think it's time you and your partner left my store now, innit?" He looked at the cousins. "I'd like to have a quiet word with my employees." He then turned to Esfir. "All of them."

***

"Did you get anything?" Verity asked as soon as they were back in the car.

Stanley explained the conversation he'd had with Esfir. He also explained that, by his reckoning, Fahred owed him at least fifty years in prison for inappropriate use of language.

"I was just about to ask her what school she attended when those two goons reappeared," Stanley said. "She said she doesn't go much, but if we can find out which school it is maybe they can throw some light on her background. Don't know about you, but I'm getting a bad feeling. I really didn't like the sound of that conversation back there, and I'm starting to take a monumental disliking to that short, ugly moron."

"Oh, I hear you, Boss," Verity said. "Loud and clear."

"Okay, so what about you?" Stanley asked. Did Fahred come up with anything interesting when you were talking to him, or was he too smitten to speak?"

"No, nothing," Verity replied. "He pretty much stuck to the stories he'd given Smollenski. Although, he did look a bit shocked when I told him one of the *Angels* had been at Bijan's funeral. Wanted to know if we could offer him any protection." Verity laughed. "I asked him why he thought he needed our protection when he had his very menacing cousins to look after him?"

"I really, really hope we can get to him before any Angel does," Stanley said. "The thought of somebody else dishing out punishment to that imbecile doesn't sit well. That poor girl looked scared shitless. The sooner we can get her out of there, the better. Lord knows what he's making her do."

Stanley started the engine. "Right, I'm going to drop you off at the station," he said. "I need to go home and check on something."

***

Niko emptied the cupboard of cat food, throwing the tins in the bin. On the way home from the vet, he'd made a detour to Camden Market to visit the Lebanese stallholder and was currently enjoying the effects of some Acapulco Gold, which the man had told him was the best to help him, *'tatfu mae alsahub.'*

Niko had no idea what the man was trying to say, but he didn't really care. The man had also persuaded him to buy a large, new rug; currently still rolled up against Niko's bedroom wall. It had images of cats on it. For some reason, Niko had also bought a very expensive jacket.

Google translate had since told Niko the man had said, *'float with the clouds.'*

Niko looked at Mr M's basket. The blood on the blankets within had started to dry. He would need to dispose of them later, he thought. For now, he'd finish his five-bar and then pay a visit to the Wetherspoons, but first he needed to round up all the cat's toys and unite them with the cat food in the bin.

"Jeeze, I couldn't half do with killing someone," Niko whispered to himself. He made his way to his desk, unlocked the drawer containing the Glock, and removed the gun. He turned it over in his hands.

It had been made perfectly clear from the beginning: Niko was allowed to carry the gun on his person only whilst on crusade. No exceptions.

"I think I'll tidy up later, Mr M," Niko said. "What's the point of having a new, expensive jacket if I'm not going to show it off?"

Niko grabbed the jacket and his keys and left the flat.

***

"I need your help again, Joanne," Verity said. "I need anything you can find on a fifteen-year-old girl called Esfir. The name's Iranian but from her accent, DCI Wood reckons she's been in this country quite some time. She's one of Fahred Ahmadi's *'employees'* but I doubt whether she's on the books. She's apparently got no parents. Perhaps we could start with the notion she's in care." Verity used her fingers around the word *employees.*

"I see Stanley's still sending you to do his dirty work," Joanne replied. "And it looks like you've started to pick up some of his annoying *habits*." She inverted the final word with her fingers.

"Oh, God, I have, haven't I?"

"I'm afraid so."

Both women laughed.

"Okay, I know I haven't given you much to go on," Verity said. "But if you can find anything, anything at all, it would be really helpful."

Joanne continued to laugh and tapped a few keys on her computer. Within seconds, she turned the screen around so Verity could see. On the screen was a scanned image of a page from a notebook. The writing on the page was scrawled, as if it had been entered in a hurry. It read:

Esfir
Dom dziecka Three Rivers

"Bloody hell, Joanne. What am I looking at?" Verity asked.

"A page from Smollenski's notebook," Joanne replied. "That last bit translates as Three Rivers Children's Home. It's in Hornsey."

Verity stared at Joanne and slowly shook her head.

"What?" Joanne said, noticing Verity's stare.

"How? How do you do this? Are you magic?"

"Nothing quite so exotic, DI Chandler," Joanne replied. "Smollenski took an interest in her during one of his visits to Ahmadi's. He said she'd been on duty during all three robberies, and, according to him, he thought she'd looked *'shifty.'* His words, not mine. For once in his miserable life, he'd decided to do some good, old-fashioned police-work and actually found out where she lived. That's pretty much as far as he got. Jumped-up, arrogant, arsehole."

***

Since Verity's first conversation with Joanne, she'd learned Joanne's loathing of Smollenski was no secret at the station. He'd apparently tried it on at last year's Christmas party and found great difficulty accepting Joanne wasn't interested. She'd poured her drink over him when, according to those in earshot, he'd told her she was only gay because she'd never had a proper man. Apparently, he'd professed that Polish men knew how to make love properly and that the size of his dick would take Joanne's breath away. By all accounts, he even offered to send her a picture. He supposedly further suggested that because Polish men were so good in bed, there were no lesbians in Poland.

Over the next few days, so Verity had been told, the Chief had mediated and stopped Joanne's complaint from going official. Smollenski had subsequently received very little change out of Joanne and had therefore, in Verity's eyes, lost himself a valuable source of information.

***

"Anyway," Joanne continued. "Smollenski asked me to enter the details on Fahred's file. As soon as you mentioned the name, I remembered it. I mean, Esfir is not that common, is it?"

"Do we know anything else about this girl?" Verity asked.

"Nothing," Joanne replied. "Thanks to you, I can now add she's fifteen and of Iranian heritage with no known parents. By the way, if you could get DCI Wood to read a file every now and then, you may save yourself some time."

"I don't think it's his style," Verity said. "And I guess it can't hurt to occasionally see things with a different set of eyes."

"Maybe," Joanne said. "But I'd stay alert for where Stanley's eyes get drawn to if I was you."

Verity's mother had often taught her if she ever needed to know anything, anything at all, the best way was to ask.

'What's the point of wasting time, Verity? Just bloody ask. Somebody, somewhere will know the answer. And if you find yourself talking to someone who

doesn't, then ask to speak to someone who does. That's how I've got on in life. It's never failed.'

"Tell me to mind my own business, Joanne," Verity said. "But what is it with you and Stanley?"

Joanne took a deep breath.

***

Joanne explained that three months prior to Verity joining the unit, she had invited Stanley and Michelle to join her and Georgia for a celebratory '*new home'* meal at their recently acquired flat. Stanley and Joanne had always got on well, and their exchanges in work had been playful when the situation merited itself, and professional when needed. There had never been any hint the relationship was anything other than that of friendly work colleagues.

***

"I knew Michelle was ill," Joanne said. "And knowing Stanley, as I thought I did, I assumed he didn't often treat Michelle to a night out whether she was ill or not. I just thought it would be nice.

"The night had, in the main, gone well and had included a lot of wine. Too much wine. All of a sudden, half way through my famous crème brûlée, I see a look in Georgia's eyes that tells me something is not quite right.

"The atmosphere in the room suddenly changed, and I knew for definite something had happened when Georgia didn't finish her dessert. Georgia always finishes her dessert. What was even more surprising was that she got up from the table to go and start the washing up. Georgia never voluntarily does the washing up.

"Later, when Stanley and Michelle had left, Georgia, after some persuading, told me Stanley had placed his hand on her knee underneath the table, and had then started massaging her thigh."

"Bloody hell, the creepy old bastard," Verity said. "Who'd have thought it? DCI Wood a sex-pest. I'd have punched him where it really hurts, not got up to do the bloody washing up."

Verity was not entirely unused to having parts of her body suddenly molested, and, depending on who was doing the molesting, it was normally an unpleasant experience. She put herself in Georgia's position and came to the conclusion the episode would have been particularly disagreeable.

"Do you think Michelle noticed?" Verity asked.

"Don't know. It was obvious something had happened."

"Right, well, I can see I'm going to have to keep a close eye on him," Verity said. "But, once again, Joanne, you've been a Godsend. Tell you what, as a reward for all your help, let me buy you a drink. Are you doing anything tonight?"

***

"Twice in two days," Michelle said, re-buttoning her pyjama top. "I am a lucky girl."

"Yeah. Sorry I was bit — you know? Again. Not quite sure what happened. Did you — you know?"

"Don't you worry about me, Stanley Wood," Michelle said, smiling. "These days I'm grateful for whatever I can get. If it's quick, it's quick. Again."

Stanley rolled over and faced away from his wife. If he'd been alone, he would have smacked himself across the face.

Sleep came slowly. Every time he closed his eyes, the image of Verity's cleavage as she'd leaned over him in the car loomed in front of him. He could still feel the soft brush of her lips on his cheek; smell the scent of her perfume. He started to get hard again. He turned back to Michelle. She was fast asleep.

***

The man was bigger than Niko — much bigger. Niko was starting to wish he'd acted on his thoughts and brought his gun. At least he had a pool cue in his hands, which should even things out, he thought. What he hadn't bargained for was swinging the cue and missing the man altogether. The force of the swing into empty air, coupled with the many drinks he'd imbibed, not to mention the Acapulco Gold coursing through his veins, served to make Niko spin a full circle before stumbling several steps and falling, face first, into a table, sending drinks over the assembled punters.

"Right, you wanker," the man said, catching hold of Niko by the back of his collar and planting him on his feet. "I've tried to be patient, but you've asked for this."

Niko remembered the first blow. It had caught him high on the temple and made his head swim. He remembered nothing after that. Eye-witnesses informed the police there'd been several more blows delivered to Niko's head. The man had then dragged Niko outside and dumped him in the gutter, before going back inside the pub and resuming his evening. One of the more caring passers-by had dialled 999.

The first responder had insisted Niko go to hospital, if only to get some stitches. The police at the scene agreed he could go and get patched up but, on the testimony of the pub's clientele, which included two off-duty officers, they were arresting Niko for aggravated assault, their reasoning being the pool cue constituted a weapon. Taking everything into account, they'd agreed the man Niko had aggravated had been acting in self-defence, and, apart from taking his details, had allowed him to carry on with his evening. After all, it would save them on paperwork if they only had one arrest to worry about. They were already thinking the situation would mean not finishing their night-shift on time.

Niko was released from Accident and Emergency two hours later, straight into the arms of two waiting police officers. The stitches were crude but effective. The triage nurse who had administered them was used to closing the wounds of drunken revellers, but not so used to having two police officers time pressuring her so they could get about doing what needed to be done before going off-duty.

TUESDAY

Stanley parked the Volvo in the gravelled area of the well-manicured gardens of The Three Rivers Children's Home.

"Impressive-looking building," Verity said.

"Don't judge a book by its cover," Stanley said. "The façade is probably the best bit."

"Joanne told me it used to be a bustling community hospital."

"If Joanne said it used to be a bustling community hospital, then it used to be a bustling community hospital," Stanley said. "What that woman doesn't know about what goes on around here, you could write on the back of a stamp."

Verity smiled. "Yeah, there's not a lot gets past her. She certainly has a keen eye. I wouldn't want to be doing anything untoward when she's about."

Stanley sensed Verity was having some amusement at his expense but said nothing.

"Anyway," Verity continued, "Joanne says the place fell into disrepair when the hospital closed. Apparently, it was due for demolition before Three Rivers stepped in and bought it for a song."

***

Esfir Ardavan had been born in Iran, so the home's manager advised, but had come to the UK with her mother when Esfir was only eighteen-months old. The home had no details of who her father may have been. Esfir had been in the care of Three Rivers for only the last six months, but had been part of the care system since the age of six, just after her mother had died.

"She's been moved around quite a bit over the years," the home manager said.

The ancient radiator behind the manager's desk gurgled and groaned as if it was drowning. The manager picked up a stout stick from under her desk and hit the radiator with it. After several blows it stopped complaining.

"Sorry about that," she said. "We're trying to raise money to update the plumbing. The electrics could do with seeing to, as well. Don't suppose you'd consider a donation?" The radiator started grumbling again.

"Do we know how the mother died?" Verity asked, raising her voice over the noise of the radiator.

The manager explained that, to the best of her knowledge, there'd been a fire at the flat they were living in, something to do with faulty electrics. Esfir herself was at school at the time, otherwise she would have probably perished as well. The authorities had searched for anyone who might have been able to take her in but had drawn blanks. Esfir had been shunted around the system ever since.

"The poor little mite was entirely alone," the manager said, with what seemed like genuine sympathy. "Of course, she's now at a very difficult age and is a little — shall we say, disturbed? Yes, let's go with disturbed." The woman hit the radiator again.

"We understand she doesn't go to school much," Stanley said. "Isn't it your responsibility to make sure she attends?"

The manager, whose lanyard suggested her name was Kath, snorted. "She's a few weeks gone fifteen, Inspector," she said. "She leaves the home every morning and tells us she's going to school. We are aware that's not always the case. The school ring us every time she fails to show, but what do you expect us to do? We haven't got the resources or the manpower to hold her hand every second of every day. You know what fifteen-year-old girls are like."

"Not really," Stanley said.

The only experience he had of fifteen-year-old girls was when he'd been fifteen himself. At that age, with his bright-red hair; the gap in his teeth, and his form teacher insistent on calling out his full name for the register, his fifteen-year-old female classmates had generally stayed away. There had been a quick fumble during a school disco, but the poor girl in question had been as much of a catch as Stanley. The lasting memory

Stanley had of the incident was the metallic taste of the girl's braces.

With a hint of unfriendliness, he said, "Why don't you enlighten me?"

"Do you know she has a job?" Verity interjected quickly. "In a convenience store on Essex Road."

The manager shifted her not inconsiderable weight. "Of course," she said. "We always encourage our teenage charges to find work if possible. Gives them an independence they've probably never experienced. But it was supposed to be a weekend job so as not to interfere with school. After all, working during school hours is illegal at her age. It was meant to be just a nice little way to earn herself a bit of pocket money."

"Mm," Stanley said. "Hasn't quite worked out like that."

"Look," Verity said. "What my colleague is trying to say is we're a bit worried about this job she's got herself. Let's just say her employer is someone who we're keeping a very close eye on. You understand what I'm saying? But, we also don't have the resources or manpower to keep an eye on him twenty-four seven. In the meantime, it might be advisable for you to encourage Esfir to find an alternative way to earn her, as you say, pocket money."

"I understand it can be a big, bad world out there, Inspector," the manager said. "But we try to give the young people in our care the nearest experience possible to what might be considered normal. Our job is to support these youngsters the best we can. But we're not a prison, Inspector. We can't keep them wrapped in cotton wool all their life. They have to be released into the wild at some point.

"Look, Esfir has been on the radar of every youth agency you can think of. From a very early age she's been prodded and poked by so many people you'd need a hundred hands to count them all. If you want to wade through all the reports, then be my guest, but they all pretty much conclude the same thing. Esfir is *'at risk.'* Of course, identifying the risks is the easy part. Keeping her away from them is far more difficult. The only thing I can say to you is we do our best and will continue to do so. Right now, I think she's enjoying the extra freedom we've afforded her."

Kath pushed her ample bosoms out. "You have to understand that Esfir has some deep-rooted issues, especially when it comes to trusting adults, but she came to us like a frightened puppy and now, thanks to our nurturing, she's really finding her independence."

"Is that so?" Stanley said. "She still looked like a frightened puppy to me. Maybe she'd have been better off with the RSPCA. At least they would have had functioning central heating."

Kath's chest deflated and everyone remained silent for a while.

Verity finally broke the silence. "Is there anything else you can tell us about Esfir?" she asked. "Anything at all? Sometimes it's the smallest details that help the most."

"I suppose you could do worse than having a chat to a certain Miss Harford at her school," the manager said. The tone suggested she'd like this particular conversation to end. "She's the one who rings when Esfir doesn't turn up." The manager looked at a clock on the wall. "Now, if you don't mind, I have a meeting to attend."

"Thanks," Verity said. "Which school was it again?"

***

Miss Harford was a tiny, young creature with a voice that, if you could eat, Verity believed would taste like soft caramel.

Her petite face was framed by blonde hair, which, Stanley thought, looked like it had been modelled on a horse-shoe. The large, pink-framed glasses she wore had lenses which enlarged her eyes to cartoon proportions. To Stanley, she didn't look old enough to drive, let alone work in a school. She'd already explained she wasn't a teacher. She was head of pastoral support.

"Well, I say head," she said, laughing. "There's only two of us. Myself and Miss Kinney. Two for a school population of a thousand pupils. Keeps us very busy. They call us the Harford and Kinney show. There were six of us when I started two years ago, but, as people move on or retire, they don't get replaced."

Stanley told her he had no idea what pastoral support meant.

Miss Harford opened like a peacock. "We're here for any of those pupils who may be struggling," she explained. "Those with emotional, social or behavioural issues. Those who are finding life difficult for some reason. Maybe they've just lost a loved one. Maybe dad's in prison, or mum's an alcoholic. Perhaps they have to care for someone at home. Perhaps they've had issues with bullying. That type of thing. We're not here to necessarily help them academically; just to lend a sympathetic ear and point them in the right direction, so to speak. Of course, the safer they feel and the more settled they are in school, then academic achievement will grow organically. It's a difficult but very rewarding role."

"What about gambling?" Stanley said. He always took an instant dislike to anybody who felt the word *organically* should be used when referring to humans. At least Miss Harford had not used her fingers to emphasise the word; that would have been the last straw. "What about kids whose mothers gamble away their lunch money? Do those kids appear on your radar? Or do they *organically* fade into the background?" Stanley did use his fingers.

"I'm sorry," Miss Harford said. "I'm not sure I—"

"We're here to ask about one of your pupils," Verity said, shooting a glance at Stanley. "A girl named Esfir Ardavan. The manager at the care home she's in told us you could perhaps give us some information about her." She now looked hard at Stanley. "Isn't that right, DCI Wood?"

Stanley shuffled in his seat. "Yes," he said. "That's right. Any information you have about Esfir would be very useful."

Miss Harford explained they had become increasingly worried about Esfir due to the amount of school she was missing. She had joined their particular establishment only a year ago, as part of a managed move from a different school, where she was on the verge of being expelled for a whole range of misconduct.

"At first, she settled in well here," Miss Harford said. "But then, as is very often the case, like moths to a flame, she started bothering with the more delinquent element of the school. We've had to send her home on many occasions, and she's received many periods of exclusion. The head is at the end of his tether. He's threatening to permanently exclude her if things don't improve. He would have probably done it before now if it wasn't for the fact she comes with extra funding. The only lesson she will engage in is drama."

The description Miss Harford gave of Esfir being some sort of Beryl the Peril didn't really fit Stanley's own impression of her. "She just seemed like a timid, frightened teenager to me," he said. "She certainly didn't strike me as a trouble-maker. Are you sure we're talking about the same girl?"

Miss Harford smiled knowingly. "Like I said, the only subject she'll engage in is drama. She's a very good actor, apparently. In any case, everybody, including you, DCI Wood, acts differently in contrastive surroundings. It's human nature."

"Amen to that," Verity said. She turned to Stanley. "Don't know about you, DCI Wood, but when I've had my fair share of wine, I do all sorts of things I'd never dream of doing otherwise."

Stanley felt like reminding Verity that, in his eyes, there didn't appear to be much she wouldn't dream of doing whether she'd had a drink or not.

"What types of things has she done to get herself in so much trouble?" Stanley asked, putting his sentiment about Verity to one side.

"Ooh, pretty much everything she can," Miss Harford replied. "Drinking on the premises, smoking on the premises, fighting on the premises, damaging school property, truanting, general rudeness to staff, swearing, refusing to wear uniform. The whole nine yards really."

"Sounds like my time in the army," Stanley said. "The only thing that's missing is the marching. Unless, of course, you *do* make her march."

"I'm sorry," Miss Harford said, frowning. "Again, I'm not sure I—"

"As pastoral manager," Verity interrupted. "I assume Esfir talks to you. You know, about stuff. Personal stuff."

"Well," Miss Harford said, "yes, I suppose, sort of. Obviously, being pastoral, I can strike up a different type of relationship with our pupils to that of a teacher. More *organic*."

"And?" Verity said, before Stanley could say anything. She could feel the heat from his face. "What does she talk about? Does she give you any reasons for her poor behaviour?"

Miss Harford steepled her fingers. "Well, let's just say she's struggling with finding her place in life," she said. "She says she doesn't feel part of anything. She feels distant. She has no family to speak of. She does have some friends at the home, I think, but her friendship groups at school are not friends as such; simply pupils she bothers with. If she was a daughter of mine, they wouldn't be the pupils I'd want her hanging about with, if you know what I mean. They're certainly not the type who would be any help in a crisis."

"And what about sex?" Verity said.

Miss Harford coughed.

So did Stanley. He and Verity had not really confirmed what type of information they were searching for on Esfir, so Verity's question had come as a surprise.

"I'm sorry, what?" Miss Harford said.

"What about sex?" Verity repeated. "Has she said anything to you about being sexually active?"

Miss Harford twisted in her seat and looked at Stanley as if to ask if this was the sort of question that was acceptable.

Unfortunately for Miss Harford, Stanley looked equally ill at ease.

"Is that wholly appropriate?" Miss Harford said. "I'm not sure I should be…"

"It's very important," Verity said. "Isn't it, DCI Wood?"

"What?" Stanley said. "Oh, um, yes, very important." Stanley hadn't yet worked out how important it might or might not be. Did he really need to know? Verity had obviously decided it was something of interest. For now, that would have to be good enough.

Miss Harford straightened her back. She looked around the room as if trying to magically make someone appear who could help her out.

Eventually, she said, "Well, she hasn't gone into any specific details, you understand? But recently she asked me where she could get free," Miss Harford lowered her voice to a whisper, "condoms."

"And what did you tell her?" Verity asked.

"Well, I was shocked, Inspector, and I told her so," Miss Harford said. "I told her I might have expected it from some of the other girls, but not her."

Miss Harford brushed a stray strand of her horseshoe hair from her cheek and repositioned her glasses. Her face was noticeably blotching.

So was Stanley's.

Miss Harford carried on. "I told her having you-know-what at her age is illegal, even if she wanted to. I told her if Sean Adams was trying to pressurise her into doing you-know-what, then he was committing an illegal act. I told her she's far too young to be entering into that kind of relationship."

Stanley thought Miss Harford herself looked too young to be entering into that kind of relationship. She couldn't even say the word sex, never mind partake in it.

"Okay, so you mentioned a name there," Verity said. "Was it Sean Adams? Who's he? A boyfriend?"

Miss Harford looked to the ceiling and mumbled what sounded like a recap of what she'd just said. "Did I really mention his name?" she said.

"Yes," Verity confirmed. "You said that you had told Esfir that if Sean Adams was pressurising her into having sex, then he was committing an illegal act."

Miss Harford gave out a long sigh. "Sean Adams is in year twelve," she said, "and thinks he runs the school. Smug as smug can be. Acts like he's God's gift to women, which, for him, includes some of our younger female members of staff. He's horrid."

Stanley wondered whether he'd detected a hint of regret in Miss Harford's voice. Perhaps she wasn't on Sean Adams's hit-list."

"Anyway, I've seen him hovering around Esfir recently," Miss Harford said. "At break and lunch. I'm sure they've truanted together on the odd occasion as well. Miss Kinney said she found them practically fused together the other day out by the skips when they should have been in lessons. I don't think it can be a coincidence that the minute Sean Adams is on the scene, Esfir starts asking for," once again Miss Harford lowered her voice, "condoms."

Stanley shook his head slowly. He still hadn't worked out if any of this was relevant. "And have you reported Esfir's request for free condoms to anybody… anybody… senior?" he asked. What he'd really wanted to say was *older*.

Miss Harford continued to shift uncomfortably in her seat. "Yes, as is protocol, I immediately informed our Child Protection Officer," she said.

"And what did she say?" Stanley asked.

"It's a *him*, Inspector," Miss Harford said, triumphantly. "Mr Ford."

"Okay, so what did *he* say?" Stanley corrected.

"*He* said he'd have a word with Esfir."

"And did he?"

"Yes, but Esfir denied any such conversation with me. Said I was nothing but a liar and was making her life a misery. According to Mr Ford, she then went off on one about how everybody hated her, and she might as well kill herself."

"She threatened suicide?" Verity said.

Miss Harford giggled, nervously. "Yes," she said, "and you have to understand that, under normal circumstances, we would take the threat very seriously. Very seriously indeed. But…"

"But what?" Stanley said.

"Well, let's just say Esfir has used the threat on more than one occasion," Miss Harford said. "It crops up regularly when she wants to get out of a situation she doesn't particularly like."

Stanley thought about reminding Miss Harford that pretty much every suicide is committed because victims want to get out of situations they don't particularly like.

Stanley had only ever attended one successful suicide in all his time on the force. A local postman, Stanley recalled, who'd hung himself because his wife had been having an affair. It had obviously been a situation the postman didn't like. Stanley hadn't been too keen on it, either.

"So, you did nothing?" Stanley said. "A young girl who you are partly responsible for threatens to kill herself, and you did nothing."

Miss Harford opened her mouth to answer, but Verity interjected.

"I think that's all, for now," she said. "Thank you for your time, Miss Harford. We'll be in touch if we need anything further." She stood up and gestured for Stanley to do the same.

Stanley stopped at the door as he was leaving. He turned to Miss Harford. "The next time you see Esfir," he said. "Tell her I can't make people go away unless I have good reason to do so. Can you at least do that?"

“Of course,” Miss Harford said, re-arranging her clown glasses.

***

Back in the car, Verity asked, “What is your problem today?”

“I have no idea what you’re talking about,” Stanley replied.

“Really? I’ve had to play good cop to your bad cop all day. You snapped at Kath in the home, then Miss Harford. Is this the Stanley Wood way of getting information now?”

“Don’t you dare!” Stanley snapped. “Don’t you dare bloody lecture me about how I operate. I’ve been at this game since before you were born, and in my opinion, which is undoubtedly correct, I’ve given both women the relevant level of my respect. At least I haven’t used the Verity Chandler method and shagged the information out of them.”

The journey back to the station was spent with Verity staring out of the passenger side window. Neither of them spoke.

On their return, Stanley, in an effort to show he was still annoyed, slammed the car door and practically sprinted up the steps to the station. In truth, he just wanted to avoid any contact with Verity, verbal or otherwise. He couldn’t believe what he’d said about her using sex to get information. That had been way out of order. Even if it was true.

Verity took her time, allowing Stanley to disappear into the station. She didn't feel much like speaking, either. As she pulled open the main door to the station, a man, who was struggling to put on his jacket, bumped into her. The impact knocked her small handbag to the floor, spilling out its few contents. The man mumbled something as he quickly walked away.

"Arsehole," Verity shouted, bending down to retrieve the items. "Why don't you sodding look where you're going?" She looked up, but the man had disappeared.

***

Niko woke to the sounds of distant voices. He felt in considerable pain from several sources and raised a finger to one of them, just above his left eye, which he hadn't managed to open yet. He winced at the touch and decided not to explore any further. He swung his legs off the low, small bed and sat up. The sudden movement made him nauseous, and he managed to crawl to the toilet in the corner of the room just in time. Every movement brought stabs of pain, particularly to his eyes and mouth, and, along with whatever else was being ejected from him, there was blood.

When his body had emptied as much rubbish as it could, he leaned against one of the bare walls and attempted to take in his surroundings. The watch he had taken from Martin Bead was missing, so he had no idea of time. He was still fully clothed, he noted, apart from his jacket, which was a worry, and his shirt was covered in dry blood.

The argument with the man in the pub began to vaguely form in his mind, and he therefore surmised the blood was probably his own. His mind also brought a memory of being in the presence of several people in uniform: he even believed one of them had been friendly. A nurse, maybe. However, this was definitely no hospital. Niko crawled back to the bed, covered himself with the one coarse blanket, and tried to go back to sleep. For a brief moment, he worried about who would feed Mr M. But then he remembered.

***

Niko was unsure how long he'd remained under the coarse blanket before the cell door opened and a voice said, "Hope you've slept it all off now, son? Follow me, please."

The fat, plain-clothed officer interviewing him had the air of someone who would rather be doing something else. Probably eating, Niko thought. He had introduced himself as DS Delaney. He re-read Niko his rights. Even though the arresting officer had done so, he explained, he was taking the assumption Niko may not remember.

"Right, Mr Nikolaus Andrianakis, why did you give the arresting officer a false name?" Delaney asked, emphasising Niko's real name. He checked some notes laid out on the desk in front of him.

"Did I?" Niko winced at the pain that forming words produced.

"Yes," Delaney said. "You did. Let's see..." He ruffled through the notes. "Here you go. You initially told our officers you were someone called Martin Bead. Then, at the hospital, you told the triage nurse your name was Mr…" he picked up the notes and held them closer to his face. "What the hell does that say? Mop His Heels?"

"Mephistopheles," Niko mumbled. "It's the name of my cat. Or at least was. He's dead now."

"Sorry to hear that, son. I'm a dog man myself. Can't stand cats. They always think they're bloody superior. Now, a dog you can train to do whatever you want, but a cat — a cat will just do whatever the sodding hell it likes." Delaney replaced the notes on the desk. "So, Nikolaus, any ideas why you decided to use the name of your dead cat?"

Niko shrugged his shoulders. He knew the action was what would be expected of a stroppy teenager, but he was in no mood to talk. Talking hurt.

Delaney laughed. "All right, so what about Martin Bead? Who's he? A dead hamster, perhaps?"

Niko's head was pounding, like somebody was in there excavating tin. He desperately wanted to just go home, sit in a hot bath and sleep. He didn't want to think, didn't believe himself capable of putting the process together in his current condition, but he knew he needed to find some morsel of cognisance if he was going to get out of here. Why *had* he given the name Martin Bead? He took some solace in the officer obviously not having heard of him. There'd also been no mention of Niko's jacket and its contents yet either, which was promising. Niko knew he was in trouble. Delaney's use of his full name confirmed that, but perhaps he wasn't in as much trouble as he could have been.

Niko moved his lips into the best possible position he believed would give him less pain. "I think I read about him in the paper," he said.

"Really?" Delaney said. "Do you know, son, I've had all sorts in here. I've had David Beckham, Prince Charles, The Queen, Simon Cowell, Alan Sugar, even Jesus Christ himself. You wouldn't believe who people say they are. Especially when they're pissed. I had one woman who told me she was the spirit of Lucrezia Borgia. Do you know who that is, son?" Delaney didn't wait for a reply. "No, neither did I. Had to look it up on my phone. Anyway, this woman poisoned her husband by putting arsenic in his food! Bloody stupid when you think about it. Not for poisoning her husband. She had plenty of reasons for that. But stupid for giving us a false name. Face facts, son, we're always going to find out who you are eventually, aren't we?"

Delaney waved his hand in the direction of Niko's face. "Little bit of advice. Next time you want to pick a fight, pick on someone who's not twice your size and a member of a boxing club." Delaney laughed loudly. "Lordy, Lordy, the things you drunken arseholes get up to, eh?"

Niko tried to smile in comradeship but failed. He took some solace in the knowledge there'd still been no mention of his jacket or its contents.

When Delaney had brought his enjoyment under control, he continued, "Anyway, I've looked at the arresting officer's report and have decided aggravated assault is pushing it." Delaney sighed with some disappointment. "Okay, so you did arm yourself with a pool cue, but, let's face it, you missed. Missed by quite some distance, apparently. Now, I've run your *proper* name through our fancy, dancey computer, and, fortunately for you, there's nothing there. Of course, there will be from now on. Also, judging by your clobber and what with living in Stepney Way, you've obviously got a quid or two. So, I'm guessing you could afford some smarmy lawyer who would successfully argue you missed on purpose."

Niko felt a tinge of panic at the mention of his clothes. Was Delaney referring to his jacket?

"So, we're going for drunk and disorderly," Delaney said. "Basically, just being a twat."

Niko felt the panic diminish.

“We’re going to pop you back in that nice, comfy cell when I finish the paperwork, and then we’ll send you back out into the wild.” Delaney collected all the notes off the desk. “Unless, of course, you want to confess to anything else.”

Niko tried to laugh, but it hurt. He simply shook his head, which also hurt. “What will I get?” he managed.

“You’ll be unconditionally bailed on the promise you’ll attend court when summonsed. It’ll be up to the judge to decide the penalty. I’m guessing a nice, juicy fine and some condition to keep the peace for a year or two. Now, why you’re supposed to only keep the peace for a short time is beyond me. Surely, you’re supposed to keep the peace for ever. Anyway, in the meantime, I’d try and stay out of trouble, son. I don’t want to see you in here again, okay?”

Niko was of the opinion that in order to keep the peace, it would need to be in your possession in the first place. How could you keep something you’d never had? If he’d been in the right frame of mind, Niko would have also pointed out that if every idiot in the world suddenly decided to be peaceful, there’d be no need for the likes of Delaney. He decided not to share these attitudes with the officer. After all, the copper didn’t strike him as a listener. Not like Mr M.

***

"So, Nikolaus And-ria-nakis," the desk sergeant said, struggling with the surname. "What is that, Greek?"

Niko nodded and mumbled in the affirmative.

"Not feeling very talkative?" the desk sergeant said. Niko noted the man's accent as Geordie. "Well, I'm not surprised. My colleagues tell me you were in a right royal state last night. *'Arry,'* they said, *'you should see the state of the geezer in number two. Right royal state and no mistake. Got himself pissed as a parrot and picked a rumble with a juggernaut of a chap.'* I would ask how the other guy looks, but I'm guessing, in the right light, he could still win a beauty contest."

Niko took some comfort in the fact he'd been in cell number two.

"Anyway, just sign here and you can be on your way." The desk sergeant passed over a charge sheet. "Normally, we'd have got you to sign it last night, but apparently you flaked out as soon as we put you on that nice, comfy bed." The sergeant let out a laugh. "If I was you, I'd go home and spend a few days lying low. Don't suppose you've had chance to look in a mirror yet, have you? To be honest, you look like you've gone fifteen rounds with that boxer, what's his name? You know the one? British. Black. Gold at the Olympics. Went a few pennies short of a pound. I tell you, my bloody memory is terrible."

"Audley Harrison?" Niko said. His swollen and cut lips made Harrison come out as Hasshon.

"That's the one!" the sergeant said. "Audley bloody Harrison. Honestly, my memory. The wife says she's thinking of having me seen by one of those head doctors."

Niko signed the sheet with a hand that was shaking badly.

"Okay," the sergeant said. "Now, let's see what we've got?"

The items held, and subsequently returned to Niko, included Niko's jacket. According to the desk sergeant, the officers at the scene had been told that Niko had removed it before taking on the man in the pub. "Apparently, you told the big bastard you didn't want to get any of his blood on it. You're a funny guy, you know that?"

Niko joined the dots. It was from the jacket the police had obviously found Niko's wallet, and it was from the wallet they had found his driving licence carrying his proper name and address. But it was what they hadn't found that interested Niko.

"That's a very canny jacket," the sergeant said, handing it over. "You're lucky it didn't walk. I guess it's nice to know there's still some law-abiding citizens kicking about. Probably a tourist. The local wildlife would have been away with it in the blink of an eye. Hell, even I'd have thought twice about keeping it."

When it came time for the sergeant to hand over Martin Bead's watch, he whistled and waved it in the air. “This looks like it cost a bob or two,” he said. “Didn’t nick it, did you?”

“Present,” Niko said, taking it off the sergeant and quickly putting it on his wrist. He noticed there was a new scratch on the face, probably from where he’d been tossed into the gutter. “Off a dead friend.”

“Wish I had friends like that,” the sergeant said. “Not dead,” he added. “Just rich.”

Niko grimaced as he attempted to put on his jacket and allowed a few groans of pain to leave him. He eventually got one arm in but was struggling with the other.

“Easy, tiger,” the sergeant laughed. “Here, let me come round and help you.”

Niko raised a hand and shook his head. The action created another wince of pain.

“I’ll manage,” he said, making his way quickly to the main door, the jacket still flapping.

The collision with the woman, albeit no more than a bump, sent waves of pain to Niko’s head.

“Sorry,” he mumbled.

“Arsehole,” the woman replied.

Niko walked away as quickly as possible.

The woman shouted something else at him as he turned a corner.

The walk from Bishopsgate to Stepney Way was thankfully short. If Niko had been incarcerated further away, he perceived there may have been problems with any bus or taxi driver wanting him to step into their vehicles. Of course, if necessary, there was always the tube. The tube was indiscriminate. It didn't judge. Any number of bloodied, stitched-up, drunken bums could ride the tube to their hearts' content.

During the walk, Niko managed to attract the odd look, plus a comment or two from the more talkative amongst the populace. Even a man sitting in a doorway with a sign in front of him, saying *'Hungry, Homeless, Hippy,'* had whistled as Niko passed and said, *'Hey man, you look like you could do with some love.'*

***

The apartment was quiet. It was too modern to give the creaks and groans of age. Niko had never realised how much noise the pretty-much-silent Mr M had made.

He poured himself two glasses of water and immediately drank one. The other, he poured away. Niko struggled out of his jacket and checked the pockets one last time. He'd already fumbled every pocket several times during the journey home. He wondered how he had not noticed the jacket had five pockets. As soon as he could, he would get rid of it.

There was not much about the night before he could remember, but he knew the three bags of Acapulco Gold he'd purchased from his Lebanese market trader had definitely been within one of those pockets when he'd left the apartment. He also knew they weren't there now.

If any of the police personnel who'd been involved in his adventure, so far, had found the packets, then surely he'd still be at the station answering a whole host of awkward questions. Unless, of course, they were partial to a smoke themselves and considered the find a pleasant bonus. But, the more likely scenario playing in Niko's head, was that the person who had handed in his jacket, even though having some moral compass, didn't have the heart to allow three bags of premium marijuana to be lost to the authorities.

Niko stripped off with some difficulty and threw his shirt in the bin. He then ran himself a bath. Niko had always liked his baths as *'hot as hell.'* Mummy-dear used to wonder aloud if he was made of asbestos, as he cried out for *'more hot'* as a child.

The bath helped. Niko started to relax. He sunk his face under the water and allowed the heat to permeate the pain. It hurt. It hurt a lot. In the back of his mind there was some instruction from the nurse about not getting the stitches wet, but he didn't care. The pain felt good. He remained under the water until his lungs were screaming for air.

Niko closed his eyes, rested his head on his luxury bath-pillow, and tried to make sense of what had happened over the last twenty-four hours.

He'd made mistakes, he was fully aware of that. He was also fully aware T.S.A. was not a fan of mistakes. That had been made plainly obvious from the start.

DO NOT, UNDER ANY CIRCUMSTANCES, DRAW ATTENTION TO YOURSELF.

Until now, Niko had managed to comply with the order. But what had really happened here?

One — his cat had died, so he'd got stoned and had himself a drink. Perfectly understandable.

Two — he'd picked a fight with a man who was bigging it up in the pub. Niko now recalled the man had been showing off in front of some women, and Niko had got annoyed. Sort of understandable.

Three — he'd got arrested for, how had Delaney put it? Being a twat. Just about understandable.

Four — some opportunist had nicked his three ounces of Acapulco Gold. Fully bloody understandable.

Adding everything together, maybe, just maybe, there'd been a slight element of drawing attention to himself. But nothing that would end up as front-page news. In due course, when his court-case for *being a twat* was heard, he may get a mention in the *'look who's been in court'* section of the Gazette, but surely T.S.A. took no notice of that.

Niko emerged from the steamed-up bathroom feeling hungry. He tried to recall the last time he'd eaten. It had been a while. He knew Greasy Joe's would still be open; Greasy Joe's was always open. He entered his bedroom and started to pick out some clothes; nothing too fancy for Greasy Joe's. A branded T-shirt and some dark jeans would be ample. He looked at the items he'd thrown on the bed and didn't relish the pain he knew would come from putting them on. He turned and looked at himself in the wardrobe mirror. His face was bad. Very bad.

Maybe, he thought, I'll just phone in a pizza. Niko didn't welcome the idea of having any of Greasy Joe's clientele, especially the two old dears, who would surely be there, scrutinising and judging what he might have been up to. Yes, he decided, pizza it is. Nothing vegetarian. He needed meat. He just hoped eating would not be too painful. Of course, he'd also make sure the pizza was of an even number of inches in diameter and insist the maker slice it into an even number of pieces. He put his clothes back in the wardrobe and took his Dior dressing gown off the hook on the back of the bedroom door.

At some point, Niko fell asleep on the sofa. He woke with the remnants of a noise in his head and an empty space on his stomach where Mr M would normally have been. As if to remind him of the emptiness, his stomach rumbled. Niko recalled his hunger and the subsequent phone request for pizza. Had that been the noise that had awoken him? Had there been someone at the door?

Niko absent-mindedly rubbed his eyes. The sudden pain made him shout, both in pain and anger. He used the arm of the sofa to help him stand up, and he started making his way groggily to the door. Every step brought the three small plastic bags lying on the floor more sharply into focus. Even without close inspection, Niko could tell the bags contained the same amount of Acapulco Gold they had when he'd last seen them.

Amongst the bags was a note. Niko bent down gingerly and picked it up. Written on the note, in pencil, were three words:

OH DEAR, NIKO!

Niko flung open his door, startling the small, crash-helmeted person about to knock on it. Niko grabbed the person by the collar of their flimsy motor-cycle jacket.

"Did you put this note through my door?" he demanded, waving the note at the person's visor.

The small person shook his head vehemently and said, "I just deliver pizza." By way of attempting to prove the statement, the person held up a pizza box. "Please, I just deliver pizza. Very good pizza." The person behind the helmet sounded no more than a boy.

"Did you see anybody?" Niko said, pulling the boy closer, squashing the pizza box between them. "Did you see anybody hanging around my door?"

"Please, I just deliver pizza. I no see anyone. I just deliver pizza. Very good pizza."

Niko released the boy's collar, grabbed the box containing his very good pizza, and slammed the door. He could hear the boy's footsteps waning as he ran away from the apartment.

"Shit!" Niko said, banging the back of his head repeatedly on his door. The action brought almost unbearable stabs of pain to his face, especially to the area above his left eye. Droplets of blood started to appear on Niko's dressing gown. The stitches had broken.

It took some time before Niko also realised that hot molten cheese was seeping out of the misshapen pizza box and burning his hand.

"Shit!" he repeated, throwing the box to the floor.

WEDNESDAY

Patty Cleland's reading glasses were discarded on her desk, and her eyes were red and swollen. Verity deduced she'd been crying. Verity glanced over to Stanley, who simply shrugged his shoulders.

"How's the investigation going?" Patty asked. She had to cough to clear a little squeak in her voice. "Have we got anything I can make public? The community hard-hitters are giving me grief. Reckon we're not moving fast enough to find who's going around threatening one of their beloved elders with a cricket bat. That idiot Witman is still stirring things up, too. Did you read his piece in The Gazette about Bijan? Painted him out to be Mother fecking Theresa, which has only made matters worse. I wouldn't mind getting his smug head on a plate. Trilby attached."

"And I'd be happy to deliver it, Ma'am," Stanley said, smiling. "But I'm afraid we've got nothing concrete. We firmly believe *The Angels* were involved, but we haven't got any evidence. Since DI Chandler's little chat with Terrell Williams, we've seen neither sight nor sound of him. Guess she must have frightened him off."

Patty Cleland leaned back in her chair and looked at the ceiling. "So, we have nothing? Not a fecking morsel. Not a single crumb I can feed to the people baying at my door. You know, sometimes I wonder why I do this job. I also wonder why you two are still getting paid. Jesus Christ!"

Stanley waited several moments before speaking. "We have had a report of a nasty brawl between two people in a local pub on Monday night, Ma'am," he said. "One of the names given matches one of the names on DI Chandler's list."

"Excellent!" Patty said, rubbing her hands together. "We've brought him in and questioned him, right? And now he's festering away in one of our holding cells, having confessed to being at Ahmadi's with a cricket bat."

"Afraid not, Ma'am," Stanley said.

"Of course you're afraid fecking not. Why?"

"By all accounts," Stanley said, "he was simply defending himself from a drunken lunatic with a pool cue. Delaney said the officers at the scene were satisfied he'd acted purely in self-defence and allowed him to go on with his evening."

Patty sighed, long and hard. The sigh turned into a growl. "Get out!" she screamed. "And don't come back until you've got something interesting to tell me. And by interesting, I mean like mind-blowingly interesting. Like you've unarguably discovered who Jack the Ripper was. Or you've found the body of Lord Lucan.

Or you've found Jesus Christ himself living in a bed-sit in Bermondsey. That type of interesting."

Stanley and Verity got up to leave, but Stanley hesitated at the door. "There is one thing, Ma'am," he said, without turning around. "There's a girl. Iranian. Works at Ahmadi's. Name of Esfir Ardavan."

"What about her?" Patty asked. "Is she a descendent of Nostradamus? Is she going to predict when you're actually going to solve a crime? Because, DCI Wood, that would be fecking fantastic."

"Not quite, Ma'am," Stanley said, now turning to face Patty. He knew she wouldn't like what he had to say, but he felt he had to say it anyway. "She's only fifteen, Ma'am, and well…"

"Oh, for God's sake, DCI Wood — well, what?"

Stanley sat back down at Patty's desk and indicated for Verity to do the same. "This latest attack on Ahmadi's was obviously conducted with the express aim of doing Fahred some harm. I mean, they took no money, no stock, nothing."

"So far, DCI Wood," Patty said. "You are not furnishing me with anything I did not already gather for myself."

"Of course. Sorry, Ma'am. But we therefore have to ask ourselves, what is it that Fahred is doing to make people want to smack him about with a cricket bat?"

Patty drummed her fingers on the desk. "That is sort of what I've been asking you to do, DCI Wood," she said. "And, so far, and please correct me if I'm wrong, you've come up with… oh, that's right… nothing!"

Stanley ignored Patty's obvious disappointment. "What if Fahred has got himself involved in something — something different to his normal stuff?" he said.

"Just for the sake of getting this conversation finished so we can all go about some proper business," Patty said. "What type of different are we looking at?"

"Not quite sure, Ma'am," Stanley replied. "At least not yet. But, when we were in Ahmadi's, we overheard a conversation between Fahred and this girl, Esfir. It really sounded off, Ma'am. He was telling Esfir she had to attend some party, and that she had to make sure she was on time because his people didn't like waiting. Oh, and he told her she had to bring one of the others, whatever that meant. He tried to pass it all off as—"

"Just let me stop you there," Patty said, holding up her hand. "That's it! That's what you're giving me? A snippet of an overheard fecking conversation that sounded a bit off." Patty whistled. "Fair play, this really takes the biscuit, DCI Wood. Why don't I call a press conference right now? I'll stand on the steps of the station, puff out my chest, and say, with a twinkle in my eye, that I'm proud to be the leader of such a hard-working, diligent, creative, dedicated team, who have just brought me a snippet of a conversation that sounded a bit off. Now, both of you, do me a favour and get out of my office!"

Stanley and Verity stood to leave.

Patty Cleland played with her ringless finger. “Look, just do what the hell you have to do,” she said to their backs. “The whole of Christendom knows there’s something not quite right with the fecking idiot that is Fred Ahmadi. Like I said, just do what you have to do. I don’t care anymore.”

“If you don’t mind, Ma’am,” Verity said, stopping at the door. “Could I stay for a moment and have a word?” She turned to Stanley. “Alone,” she added.

***

Verity sat down at her desk opposite Stanley and waited. She pressed a few buttons on her computer keyboard, simply to make a noise. Stanley’s silence worried her. She’d have felt better if he’d started screaming at her, ordering her to go and get him a coffee.

After a minute, Verity could take no more. “Look,” she said. “I just needed to speak to her about—”

“Stop!” Stanley said, without looking up from his computer keyboard. “I don’t need you, or want you, to fill me in. If you and Her Majesty want to have a cosy, girlie chat, be my guest. Nothing to do with me. I’ll just go about my merry business by myself.”

“It was just—”

“I said stop! If you want to talk about me behind my back, don’t let me stop you.”

“For Christ’s sake, Stanley. Not everything is about you,” Verity said. “The woman is on the verge of a nervous breakdown. Can't you see that? I just thought she looked like she needed someone to talk to, that's all. A shoulder to cry on."

Stanley laughed. "And you're the right person for that, are you? A twenty-nine-year-old who has had everything handed to her on a plate, including men. What the hell makes you think you're qualified enough to offer advice. On anything!"

This was better, Verity thought. Better than silence. She was aware people in the office had stopped what they were doing and were listening in, but it was still better.

"Now go and get me a coffee!" Stanley screamed. "And then make yourself scarce for an hour or two. I'm fed up of looking at that goddamned ugly face of yours."

"Gladly," Verity replied.

***

Verity pulled the car onto the gravel drive of the family home in Towers Road, Pinner, parking next to her mother's new Range Rover. She knew her mother would be home; her mother was always home, but she had phoned in advance to check, anyway.

Verity's mother opened the front door as soon as Verity emerged from the car. She smiled, showing teeth that would induce snow-blindness if one got too close, and opened her arms wide.

"Verity, come and give Mamma a big hug," she said. "I've got some cocktails and nibbles set out on the patio."

Despite the early hour of the day, Verity's mother was dressed as if she were going out for a good time. Verity would have expected nothing less. For as long as she could remember, her mother always looked like she could attend a party at a moment's notice. The tight leopard-print top she was currently sporting did nothing to camouflage certain assets.

"Have you had work done again?" Verity asked releasing herself from the bear-hug. "Those things feel like rocks."

"Just a small lift," Verity's mother replied, lifting her breasts with her hands to illustrate the fact. "Please don't tell your father though. You know how he goes on. I really don't think I could stand one of his sanctimonious sermons about changing what God has given us and all that."

"I think he'll notice, Mum," Verity said. "I mean, they're not exactly hidden, are they? And I assume you still — you know — get naked in his presence every now and then."

"Oh, I could dance around him starkers with a rose between my teeth, Verity, and he wouldn't notice," her mother said. "Your father's eyes are far too busy putting the world to rights to worry about what I'm doing. Now, come on, those cocktails won't drink themselves." She grabbed Verity by the hand and started pulling her through the house to the rear garden.

Verity had noticed a slightly glazed look in her mother's eyes, and even though the sun wasn't yet over the yard arm, she wondered how many cocktails her mother might have already enjoyed.

"I can't have a drink, Mum," Verity protested, still being dragged by the hand. "I'm working. My boss has only given me an hour or so."

"Oh, don't be a boring, old moo," her mother replied. "Nobody likes a boring, old moo. One won't hurt you. Come and tell Mamma all about life in uniform."

"I don't wear a uniform anymore, Mum. I'm a detective now, remember?"

"Oh, that's right. Well, I hope you still kept the uniform. You know, for those special moments." Verity's mother turned and winked, then continued to march through the house, tottering slightly on her Louboutin heels.

"Bloody hell! Have you had your arse done as well?" Verity asked, noticing how her mother's behind was accentuated by the tightness of the leather trousers she was wearing. "I'm sure I could balance an Atlas on that."

Verity's mother stopped and laughed. She faced Verity. "Shush," she said, putting her fingers to her lips. "There's no need to tell the whole world."

"But there was nothing wrong with your arse, Mum," Verity said. "Or your tits, for that matter."

Verity's mother tossed her head and snorted. The action made a few strands of her peroxide-blonde hair enter her mouth. "Oh, that's easy for you to say, Verity," she said. "You just wait until you get to my age and everything starts travelling to Brighton. Then you'll have a different opinion, I can tell you."

"Travelling to Brighton?"

"South, dear. Everything starts travelling south. Oh, do keep up." Verity's mother turned and dragged Verity the final few yards to the patio, where she released Verity's hand and slumped into a large cottage-style sofa.

Verity seated herself on one of the three wicker armchairs that also formed part of the patio furniture. "Dad at work?" she asked.

"Of course Dad's at work," her mother sneered. "When have you ever known the great Tayo Adebayo not to be at work? It's a wonder he found time enough to conceive you. If he isn't at his practice, or at the hospital, he's off to seminars and fancy dinners with his equally fancy friends. Or off playing golf with Lord somebody or another. Even when he is at home, he spends his time in that monstrosity of an office of his, speaking to God-knows-who." Verity's mother nodded her head to somewhere generic within the house.

***

Verity knew the office well. She used to sneak in there regularly as a child. She loved the smell of the highly polished desk, the treated-leather chairs, the hint of aniseed and juniper coming from the opened-up globe containing bottles of alcohol; the hundreds of books neatly stacked on oak bookshelves with titles by all the great authors, each set having its own place and its own distinct aroma. The Dickens collection actually smelled Victorian; the Hardys and the Brontes of the countryside; the Fitzgeralds and the Hemingways of decadence; the Joyces even smelled — well, Irish.

But her favourite smell was that of the cigars. As all small children know, any box is an invitation for exploring its contents. However, the ornate wooden box with its brass clasps sitting on her father's desk screamed *'open me'* much louder than any box Verity had encountered before or since. On the box-lid was the fanciest writing Verity had ever seen, and inside there were always ten individually wrapped, fat, brown sausages that smelled divine.

Whilst studying at Oxford, Verity had picked up a copy of the novel *The Count of Monte Cristo* and had spent several days wondering why the title looked so familiar. It eventually dawned on her that the fancy writing she had seen on the cigar box in her father's study, all those years ago, had said *Montecristo Cigars.*

Every Christmas since, Verity had bought her father a range of Montecristos.

The only item in the office that had ever made Verity feel uncomfortable was the overly-large Bible sitting on its own wooden stand on a handmade African-blackwood table a few feet away from her father's desk. Verity always got the feeling the Bible knew she was in there without permission, and it would somehow make sure she paid for her crimes at some later date.

The Bible was always opened to the same page — Galatians 6:7

Do not be deceived,
God is not mocked,
For what a man sows,
that will also reap.

These were the words her father would say to her whenever she'd performed any sort of misdemeanour. Even now.

Verity had never shared her father's religious vigour. The idea of having to account for everything you did to some higher power never seemed to her like an acceptable concept. Particularly as she got older, Verity preferred to believe she could do a lot of sowing without worrying about the reaping. However, whenever her mind wandered to her father's office and that open Bible, she would momentarily wonder if someone was keeping some sort of tally. She hoped not.

Verity was brought back to the present by her mother's voice.

***

"I'm sure he must be seeing somebody else, Verity," her mother blurted, reaching for a tissue from a box on the ornate glass table in front of them. She started to dab at her eyes. Verity could see no tears.

"Of course he's not seeing anybody else, Mum," Verity said, though she had no evidence to support the theory either way. "This is Tayo Adebayo we're talking about. He's far too busy to be having an affair."

"Well then, maybe I should have one," her mother said. "Maybe I should go out and find myself a man who would actually acknowledge my existence. Maybe I should start talking to that footballer who lives next door — what's his name again? Used to play for Watford. I bet he would treat me like a proper woman; not just someone who's here to cook and clean."

"I doubt it, Mum. He's living with his boyfriend. Anyway, haven't you got a cleaner?" Verity asked. "And doesn't Dad do most of the cooking?"

Her mother dabbed her eyes again. "Well, yes, but it's me who has to organise the cleaner's rota. And I do all the food shopping. It's not easy pressing those buttons, Verity. Oh, you just wouldn't understand what it's like to be me. You really don't know how difficult it is to be married to a powerful man."

"Well, they do say behind every great man, there's a great woman," Verity said. She kept the tone light, but her mother didn't seem to notice.

"Exactly my point, Verity," her mother said. "You have no idea the sacrifices I've had to make in order for your father to shine. Who knows what I could have been if he hadn't had his wicked way and got me pregnant?" She leant over and grasped Verity's hands in hers. "Oh, now don't get me wrong, Verity, you've been the best thing in my world, and I love you with every inch of my body." She released Verity's hands and leaned back in the sofa. "But, if my mother had gone to a different doctor when she was having her treatment, I have no doubt I would have gone on to be a household name. The name Sienna Chandler was going places, Verity, and make no mistake. I had top-notch modelling agencies fighting over me. Of course, they all dropped me faster than a lead balloon as soon as I started showing…"

***

It was a story her mother had told many times, each time with some minor embellishment. But, no matter how her mother spun it, not much of the story stacked up under scrutiny. Verity had once run the name Sienna Chandler through Google but had found no mention of her mother's supposed burgeoning early career. In fact, the search had been more interested in sending her towards the model of a new Toyota car.

Verity had not been surprised.

There were plenty of photos dotted around the house of Verity's mother in her so-called heyday — although, none in her father's office — and Verity would certainly never describe her mother, then or now, as a beautiful woman. Sexy, yes. Sexy as hell. But beautiful, no. It was easy for Verity to envisage how her father, ten years older than her mother, would have reacted when the twenty-one-year-old Sienna Chandler walked into his clinic with her own cancer-laden mother on her arm. It would have been the same reaction, Verity thought, that men greeted her with most times she herself walked into a room.

Verity knew her parents had married six months after they'd met, with Sienna already four-months pregnant. She also knew her father's father had been devastated at the news.

'He believed I had made some pact with the Devil,' her father had told her after she'd asked why her grandfather had never wanted to know them. *'I was born in Sapele, a town in the south of Nigeria, hence my middle name. Sapele is a very traditional place and my father, who had made money in the gas and oil trade, always told me that my mother, God rest her soul, had her heart set on me becoming a doctor. My father therefore sent me to a top boarding school here in the UK to get a proper education. I was eleven years of age.*

'Tayo, in my language, means 'boy of happiness,' but trust me when I tell you, I was not a happy boy at that boarding school. I shall spare you the details, but I

am sure you can understand the types of hardships I had to endure. However, I had a mission in life. I strived to please my father and honour the wishes of my dead mother. I worked hard, and when I finally left that awful school, I attended university. I continued to work hard. I did not party or involve myself in sordid activities, as did some of my fellows. I did not drink or take any form of drug. I concentrated entirely on my mission.

'When I finally became a doctor, my father paid for the whole family to fly from Nigeria to join in my celebrations. It was a happy time. My father said very little as he was a man of few words, especially those of sentimentality, but I could see in his eyes that a prouder father could not have been found anywhere on God's good earth.

'The day I told him I was doing the honourable thing and marrying your mother, he became a man of many words. None of which were pleasant. From that day to the day he died, he was a man of no words.'

The story of her paternal grandfather's reaction to the marriage was in stark contrast to Verity's grandparents on her mother's side.

Elsie, a supermarket worker — who saw Tayo as her saviour — and Derek, a dock labourer, were simple folk with simple means. Growing up, Verity had found Elsie, in particular, full of tales that bordered on the bizarre. She'd once told the then fourteen-year-old Verity that she'd wanted to call her mother Sandy, because she'd been conceived in a bunker on the fourteenth green at the local golf club. Apparently, Derek had argued vehemently against it, pointing out he wasn't even a member.

The name Sienna was therefore chosen because Elsie and Derek had once passed through there on a coach trip to Italy and Elsie thought it sounded nice.

By all accounts, when Verity's mother had announced she was carrying Dr Adebayo's child and he had proposed marriage, Elsie and Derek celebrated wildly.

Verity liked to convince herself her consummation only brought her parents' marriage forward: that they would have married at some point anyway. She had no way of proving the belief, but she was sure there must have been, and still was, some love in the marriage — after all, they'd stayed together for thirty years without a hint of parting.

However, Verity was aware that if there was a pie-chart of her mother's love for her father, a large section of it would be taken up with the money and kudos that came with her marriage to an eminent consultant. These days, she didn't have to rely on her husband for money thanks to her online fashion business doing so well, but that hadn't always been the case. Everybody knew the business would not have got off the ground if it had not been for Tayo's financial help and his acquaintanceship with the right people.

In Verity's eyes, her mother was a lucky woman. Her father was still a handsome man. Apart from the ever-increasing number of grey hairs appearing whenever Verity saw him, there was very little else to suggest he was a man in his sixties. He carried no fat and displayed no lines or wrinkles on his face. He still walked militarily upright, showing off every inch of his six-foot frame, and still played sports with the competitiveness of the young; squash and golf being his first choices.

If that were not enough, when Verity was barely a teenager, she'd overheard her mother talking to a friend on the phone. *'That God he likes to thank everything for has given him a todger the size of a baby's arm, and boy, have I taught him how to use it.'*

Yes, her mother was a very lucky woman indeed.

***

"…So, use me as an example, Verity, and if you want to keep all your bits and pieces in the right place, don't get yourself pregnant. I mean, look at the state of me!" Verity's mother scanned her hands up and down her body. "My body never recovered from the pounding it got bringing you into the world. Overnight, I went from being a young woman heading for the stars to being a wife and mother rooted to the ground. Fast forward thirty years and here I am. Just past fif-fif-forty. Stuck in this rambling house by myself when your father is out schmoozing with the great and mighty."

"You're not stuck, Mum," Verity said. "Dad doesn't keep you locked up in handcuffs. You can go and do whatever you want."

Sienna Chandler took a sip of her cocktail, leaving bright-red lipstick on the straw. "I wish he would use handcuffs every now and then," she said, winking at Verity. "He's just not interested in danger anymore. At least not with me. Oh, Verity, we used to do it everywhere." She put the cocktail down and giggled. "Did I tell you about the time we were in Waitrose—"

"No!" Verity said. "God, Mum, you are incorrigible. Stop it! I do not want to know about you and Dad's sordid sex-life."

"There's nothing sordid about it these days," her mother said. She took the straw out of her drink and enjoyed a large measure. "It's all safe and sound now. Every Tuesday, like clockwork. The closest thing to spontaneity your father has got recently was a quick grope under the tablecloth at dinner on that cruise we went on last month."

Verity smiled. "For your four-four-fiftieth!"

"Oh, do shut up, Verity."

Both women laughed.

Verity pretended to take a sip of the drink her mother had insisted she have. She placed it back on the table and stood up. "I have to go, Mum. Like I said, my boss only gave me an hour or two and you know what the traffic can be like." She took an envelope out of her pocket. "I'm just going to leave this on Dad's desk. It's just some business I need him to take a look at."

Sienna had to use the arm of the sofa to steady herself as she stood, also. "So, you didn't come to see your mother after all, then. You and your bloody father, eh? Always been thick as thieves."

***

"Where the hell have you been?" Stanley said.

Verity sensed some excitement in Stanley's voice. "To see my mother," she replied, placing her jacket on the back of her chair. "Why?"

"Her Majesty has played a time-out card," Stanley said. "Came out of her office just after you left and announced she was taking some down-time in order to put her personal life back in order. Said she'd been granted compassionate leave. Didn't specify for how long."

"Glad to hear it," Verity said, sitting down.

Stanley squinted his eyes. "What the hell did you say to her this morning?"

"I told her how lucky I was to be working with such a wonderful, charming man as DCI Wood. Coffee?"

Stanley's desk-phone rang. Stanley had noted, over time, that phones had different rings for divergent scenarios. To the untrained ear, the distinction would probably be unnoticeable, but thanks to Stanley's years of accepting phone calls for all sorts of reasons, to him, the contrast was conspicuous. Stanley could guess with an alarming success rate what the call may contain simply by the ring alone. Danger; comfort; anger; protest; waste of time; costly: they all had their own peculiar shade. Stanley allowed the phone to ring a few times in order to fully ascertain its implication. After the fourth ring, he got it: hope.

The officer on the front desk told Stanley there was a young female asking for him. She'd told him to tell Stanley her name was *star-like.*

"Right, a definite yes to that coffee," Stanley said, replacing the receiver. "Get a Coke to go with it and meet me outside interview three."

***

Stanley thought Esfir looked even younger than when he'd last seen her. Perhaps it was because she was in her school uniform, instead of the yellow tunic of Ahmadi's.

"Hello again, Esfir," Stanley said, sitting down opposite her. "You remember my partner, DI Chandler. She was with me when we called at the store the other day." Stanley slid the can of Coke over the table towards Esfir.

Esfir ignored the drink. She hadn't yet looked up from her shoes. "You said she was your friend," Esfir said.

"Pardon?"

"When you called in the shop. You said, could you and I have a chat when you waited for your friend to come back."

"Well, yes," Stanley said. "DI Chandler is my friend. But we also work together."

A magazine article that Michelle had read aloud to him a while back surfaced in Stanley's mind. According to the article, you had to know someone for seven days to form a casual friendship, fourteen days for a real friendship, and thirty days for a close friendship. A quick calculation told Stanley he had known Verity for thirteen days. So, seventeen more and they'd be close. He'd look forward to it.

"Does anyone know you're here, Esfir?" Verity asked. "Have you told anyone that you were coming to see us?"

Esfir lifted her head slightly. Stanley thought he could make out the makings of a bruise on her cheekbone. "I didn't want to see both of you," she said. "I just wanted to see him." She nodded her head in Stanley's direction. "I think this was a mistake. I want to go now."

"Tell you what," Stanley said. "Why don't we send DI Chandler to get you something to eat? How about a MacDonald's? What do you say?"

Esfir paused. "I'll have a Big Mac meal. Large."

Stanley turned to Verity. "Okay," he said. "Big Mac meal it is."

"With a strawberry milkshake," Esfir added.

"With a strawberry milkshake," Stanley repeated.

"Right on it," Verity said. "Another coffee while I'm at it, Boss?"

Stanley nodded.

"Right," Stanley said, as soon as Verity had left. "Now it's just the two of us, perhaps we can have a nice chat. But, I have to mention, Esfir, that if you want to tell me something important, then I really am going to need another adult in the room. And I'm going to have to put this machine on that you can see." Stanley pointed at the recording machine on the table. "It records what we say to one another."

"Why do you need to record what we say?"

"Because people may not believe us, otherwise."

"So, Fred is right," Esfir said. "He's always saying people won't believe me."

"Believe you about what, Esfir?"

"Why did she call you, Boss?" Esfir asked from underneath her eyes, her voice barely discernible.

Stanley didn't like the fact Esfir had changed the subject but hoped they could get back to Fahred Ahmadi soon. "Because I hold a higher rank than her," he said. "And, even though she's my friend, that technically means I'm her boss. Just like Fred is your boss. Now, I really think it's time to get another adult in here, don't you? Don't worry, it doesn't have to be another police officer, if you don't want it to be. It can be someone you know. What about Kath from the home, or Miss Harford from school? I'm sure if we gave either of them a call they could be here in double-quick time. What do you say?"

Esfir slowly lifted her head. With Esfir's face now in full view, the bruise was more apparent. Furthermore, Esfir was smiling broadly. Her shoulders straightened and her eyes cleared. "I think it's time we cut the bullshit, don't you?" she said.

Stanley felt as if he, or someone, had altered the situation by simply clicking their fingers. Like a genie out of a bottle, Esfir's demeanour had gone from a shy, frightened little girl to that of a seriously pissed-off teenager.

Stanley realised he had little experience of dealing with pissed-off teenagers. Pissed-off adults he'd dealt with all his life, but for reasons best known to his superiors, he could count on one hand the times he'd been asked to interview anyone under the age of sixteen. The sudden change in Esfir caught him off-guard, and he struggled to find what his next words should be.

"Oh, I'm sorry," Esfir said. "Have I surprised you?"

"A little," Stanley said, trying to regain his composure. He was aware that the mood-swings of teenagers were notoriously volatile, but he didn't think this had been a mood-swing; this had been play-acting from the beginning. Maybe even from when he had first entered Ahmadi's. Drama was, after all, Stanley recalled, the only thing Esfir would engage in.

"Yeah, well, sorry about that," Esfir said. "Not a lot sorry, but a little. Now, here's the deal. We're not going to record anything, and I certainly do not want some other pathetic adult in the room. Especially not Harford! It was her who forced me to come here in the first place."

"Okay, okay, hang on," Stanley said. "Are you telling me Miss Harford knows you're here?"

"Of course she knows."

"She knows you're here right now?"

"Keep up, will you?"

"And she's allowed you to come here by yourself? She didn't offer to come with you?"

Esfir laughed. "You don't get it, do you?" she said. "Harford *has* come with me. Or at least she brought me. Against my will, I might add. You should be arresting the goggle-eyed bitch."

Stanley rubbed his face vigorously. This wasn't how he had envisaged the conversation panning out. "Sorry, I'm totally confused," he said. "You say Miss Harford brought you here?"

"Like I said, against my will."

"Then where the hell is she?"

"She's parked outside," Esfir said, nodding her head towards the door. "Said she couldn't come in because she's parked on doubles. Said she'd need to make a quick getaway if a traffic warden came along."

Stanley took a dep breath. "All right," he said, slowly. "Let me just sort this out in my head. At this precise moment in time, you're confirming that Miss Harford, the pastoral manager at your school, brought you here and is now sitting outside in her car but hasn't deemed it worthwhile to accompany you into the station because she's worried about getting a sodding parking ticket?"

"Not exactly Sherlock, are you?" Esfir said. "You left out the part where I'm here against my will. If she hadn't been watching me like a hawk through those stupid glasses of hers, I'd have done a runner as soon as I got out of the car. Have you seen Sherlock? It's mint. I think the guy who plays the baddie is really fit."

"His name is Moriarty," Stanley said, looking at the ceiling.

"I thought it was Andrew something," Esfir said.

"No, not the bloody actor," Stanley replied. "The actual name of the baddie was — oh, never mind. Look, why did Miss Harford bring you here, Esfir? What is it that she expects you to do?"

Esfir shifted in her seat. "I bloody hate her!" she said. "She's out to ruin my life just like everybody else. I told you, it's her you should be arresting, not me or Sean. She's nothing but another idiot I have to deal with. She said I either come here and tell you about it, or she'd come in and do it herself. Well, I couldn't let her do it, could I? God knows what the stupid bitch would have said."

Stanley sighed heavily. "Come here and tell me what, Esfir?"

"She's a creep," Esfir said. "If she was a man, she'd be a paedo. Always snooping about. Always got her witch's nose in my business. I mean, what was she doing coming into the girls' toilets, anyway. Reckon she's just jealous coz she's too ugly to get any."

Stanley's mind registered the mention of another name. Sean. He vaguely remembered the name from his visit to the school. "What were you doing in the girls' toilets, Esfir?" he asked. "I assume it was something you weren't supposed to be doing." Stanley didn't really relish being told what Esfir might have been doing, but he was duty bound to listen.

"We were just messing about," Esfir said. "That stupid bitch hates Sean and everyone like him. She went shitting mental."

Stanley closed his eyes. "What does *'messing about'* mean?" he said. There were those infuriating fingers again. Perhaps he'd see a hypnotist.

"What do you think it means?" Esfir said. "Don't worry, we were being careful. We're always careful. I did slip and bump my cheek on the cistern, but other than that, we were careful."

Stanley groaned. "Always careful?" he said. "You said you were *always* careful. Does that mean this sort of messing about has happened before?"

"Of course it's happened before," Esfir said. "Have you seen Sean Adams? He's got a real boss body since he started going to that boxing place out by Angel."

Stanley put his head in his hands. "So that's it, is it?" he said. "Miss Harford, the parking ticket worrier, has sent you in here, by yourself, to confess to messing about with some boy?"

"Not just some boy," Esfir said. "Sean Adams, no less."

"I stand corrected," Stanley said. "Miss Harford has sent you in here, and I repeat, by yourself, to confess to messing about with Sean Adams? The boy with the boss body."

"Hooray, now you're getting it."

Stanley removed his head from his hands. "And what does the wonderful Miss Harford expect me to do with this information?" he asked. "Has she told you that?"

"What can you do?" Esfir said. "It's like I told Harford, me and Sean are not doing anything wrong. It's not like he's forcing me to mess about. I want him to do it. She's probably a lezzo and fancies me or something."

"Bloody hell, Esfir," Stanley said. He leaned back in his chair and put his hands behind his head. "This really isn't what I thought you'd come here to tell me."

"Really?" Esfir replied. "What did you think I'd come here for?"

"Well, I thought it might be something to do with… something… somebody else. I thought it might be to do with that party Fred mentioned." Stanley couldn't be sure, but he thought he noticed a slight change in Esfir: spotted a quick look of panic in her eyes.

"You're not going to arrest Sean, are you?" Esfir said, once again changing the topic away from Fahred Ahmadi.

"I really don't know what I'm going to do," Stanley said, thinking he'd really like to retire, right this very minute, and sail off into the sunset.

"You can't arrest him," Esfir protested. "I wanted him to do it. Anyway, there's no other adult in the room and nothing's been recorded, so you can't arrest him. Now, I've done what that bag of dog-shit Harford wanted me to do and now I want to go."

"But what about your food?" Stanley said, now in some desperation. "Your Big Mac and strawberry milkshake."

"You have it," Esfir replied. She dropped her head and looked at her shoes. Barely audibly, she said, "Please, DCI Wood, I've been a good girl, so can I go now?"

***

"Uh, correct me if I'm wrong," Verity said. She looked around the interview room, quizzically. "But there was a young girl called Esfir in here the last time I looked."

"She's gone," Stanley said.

"Gone?" Verity placed the takeaway goods on the table. "What do you mean gone?"

Stanley picked up the coffee and indicated for Verity to sit down.

They shared the gastronomic delights of Verity's purchase — Stanley ate the burger, Verity had the chips with copious amounts of ketchup — as Stanley explained how the conversation with Esfir had panned out.

"Well, well, the crafty little minx," Verity said, licking her fingers. "Not as frightened and demure as we first thought, then."

"I should have known really," Stanley said, eyeing a globule of mayonnaise that had landed on his shoe. "I guess you don't spend most of your life in the care system without picking up tricks about how to play adults along the way."

"So did she say anything at all about Fahred, or was it all about this Sean Adams?"

"There was one thing," Stanley said, using one of the paper napkins to wipe the offending mayonnaise from his shoe. "She said Fred had told her nobody would believe her."

"Nobody would believe her. About what?"

Stanley groaned as he straightened. "I dread to think," he said.

"So, what do you reckon about this Sean Adams character?" Verity asked, dipping her last chip in the ketchup and throwing her head back, devouring it like a sword-swallower. "Do you think we should pick him up? He has broken the law, after all."

Stanley couldn't understand how Verity had made eating a chip look so bloody sexy. He shook his head, partly to shake the image from his brain, and partly to confirm his answer. “I don’t really want to waste our time picking up a seventeen-year-old gigolo,” he replied. “As much as it would satisfy the wonderful Miss Harford, I don’t think anybody else would really care. Except Esfir, who I think would care very much. At the moment, I’d rather keep her on our side as much as we can. For all her acting skills, she couldn’t hide that fragment of hope in her voice when she asked if I was going to take Fred away when we were at the store. Earlier, she also baulked when I mentioned the party. I’m absolutely convinced he’s dragging that young girl into a terrible situation, and I’d like to stop it, if I can.”

“What do you suggest we do about Miss Harford?” Verity asked.

“What about her?”

“Well, she knows we’ve been told that a seventeen-year-old boy is having sex with a vulnerable fifteen-year-old girl. If we do nothing, she might decide to make waves. Especially if Esfir is right and she’s out to fry Sean Adams.”

“I hate to admit it, but you’re probably right,” Stanley said.

“Wow, can I have that in writing,” Verity said. “Quick! Somebody grab a calendar. Let’s mark the date that Stanley Arthur Peregrine Wood admitted someone else was right.”

Stanley pretended annoyance. “Right,” he said. “For that, you can go and pay Miss Harford a visit all by your little lonesome. It was pretty evident she didn't like me, anyway. I'm sure you can use your boundless charms to smooth the water."

"And tell her what, exactly?"

"Tell her we're following up on what Esfir has told us, but things as sensitive as under-age sex take time to go through the relevant procedures. Something like that." Stanley stood to leave the interview room. "Ooh, hang on, Esfir said Miss Harford might even be a lesbian, so ask her out on a date if that's what it takes to keep her sweet." Stanley left the room laughing.

"The last time I used that tactic you chewed my head off," Verity said under her breath.

THURSDAY

Despite the darkness of the slim tunnel, and the dripping sweat from his forehead stinging his eyes, Niko could clearly see Mr M a few yards in front of him.

'Come on, Schmuck, keep up,' the cat said, dancing on its hind legs.

Niko concentrated every sinew he had on trying to run, but there was something wrong with his legs. They felt as if they'd been filled with a liquid of some kind and wouldn't move where he wanted them to.

'T.S.A. don't like to be kept waiting and we're already late,' Mr M added as he got further and further away. Eventually, he disappeared.

Martin Bead suddenly ran past Niko. He was looking at a scratched watch on his wrist. *'He's right,'* he shouted, also disappearing into the darkness ahead. *'You're already late.'*

The exertions of attempting to get his legs to work was taking all of Niko's breath from his lungs. He bent over, put his hands on his leaden thighs and took huge gulps of air. The air smelled like cold pizza.

As he tried to figure out where the smell was coming from, his ears picked up a sound from behind him. He didn't have the energy to raise his head and look, but as the sound got closer, Niko defined it as the high-pitched whine of a motor scooter. Within seconds, the scooter had passed him and disappeared down the tunnel. A voice echoed back, *'I just deliver good pizza.'*

Niko straightened up. "Look out for my cat, you arsehole!" he shouted. "He's down there somewhere. If you hit him, I'll rip your head off. There's a dead bloke down there somewhere, as well. I couldn't give a shit if you hit him."

Niko's stomach suddenly lurched. His body felt hollow, like it had been excavated. He attempted, in vain, to get his legs moving again, but he could only manage to lurch from side to side, bumping into the walls of the tunnel. "Wait for me!" he screamed. "I don't want to be down here on my own." The emptiness in front of him remained silent. "I don't know where I'm supposed to go. I can't see. It's too dark." He sat down and started to cry.

Niko had no idea what passage of time had elapsed before he heard his mother's voice. *'That's because you have to make your own light, Niko,'* she whispered, helping Niko to his feet. *'Not all tunnels have light at the end.'*

"Does this tunnel even have an end, Mummy-dear?" Niko asked, wiping the tears from his eyes. "I've been in it for a very long time, I think. You see, my legs don't seem to work."

Niko's mother laughed. He felt her hands on his shoulders. *'Oh, Niko, you silly Schmuck. Even though there's no light, all tunnels still have an end.'*

Niko noted his mother was smiling broadly. She looked happy. Happier than Niko could ever remember. Oddly, she was wearing a Kippah. Niko smiled back.

Niko's smile slowly disappeared as, now that his eyes were adjusting, he noticed Uncle Schmuck standing not too far away. Holding Uncle Schmuck's hand was Cherie. Both were completely naked.

Niko could not recall ever having seen Cherie entirely unclothed. His eyes were drawn to three ragged welts across her stomach. She released Uncle Schmuck's hand and stepped in close to Niko. She placed her hand under his chin and lifted his head.

'Eyes up, Niko,' she said. *'You don't want to look down there.'* With her free hand she started massaging Niko's crotch.

Uncle Schmuck moved behind Niko and put his head on Niko's shoulder. He put his hands on Niko's hips and pulled Niko towards him. Niko could feel Schmuck's hardness. Niko began to cry again. The tears stung.

Niko's mother gently moved Cherie out of the way and caught hold of Niko's hand. She dug her fingernails into the burned flesh left there by the pizza. Niko screamed.

'Oh, stop crying, Niko,' his mother said. *'You're going to give everyone a headache. It's only a scratch.*

Schmuck didn't mean it. I'll get you something nice for your birthday. Double promise. Super promise.' She released Niko's hand and pecked him on the cheek. *'We're going now, okay?'* She turned, and with her arms around the shoulders of Schmuck and Cherie, the three of them danced away down the tunnel.

Before his mother and her little entourage had fully disappeared, a new voice landed on Niko's ears.

'I'm going to make sure you pay for this, you degenerate little prick!' the voice shouted.

Niko turned to find his old lieutenant-commander a few feet away. The commander was hopping from foot to foot and his genitals were encased in an ice-pack. The sight brought a smile to Niko's face.

'Right, you wanker, you've asked for this,' the commander screamed. He ran at Niko. He had a pool cue in his hand. He lifted the cue above his head and swung.

***

Niko made it to the toilet bowl just in time. Each spasm of his stomach hurt, and he wondered how his body thought it could still carry out the process of vomiting. He'd put very little of anything solid inside himself since he'd salvaged what was left of his pizza. When was that? Had it been Tuesday? Since then, he'd existed on alcohol and Acapulco Gold.

Maybe, he thought, it would be a good idea to eat something. Also, he was down to the last of the Gold. Maybe he'd combine a trip to Camden Market with a novel visit to a supermarket for a food-shopping sortie.

He flushed away the mainly liquid bile he'd thrown up and used the toilet bowl to help him to his feet. He looked at himself in the bathroom mirror, gingerly prodding the wide gash above his right eye. It hurt like a bitch. A small trickle of liquid oozed from the corner of the wound. The discharge carried a hue of pink. "What the fuck?" Niko whispered. "Pink?"

Niko wondered if the scar the wound would undoubtedly leave would look cool. There were certain scars, he believed, that added to a person's style. Gave them a groove, so to speak. Not on women, of course. Heaven forbid! In Niko's view, any scar on a woman's face screamed abuse and nothing else. He recalled the occasional wound on his mother's face. *'Sometimes they get over-exuberant, Niko. Honestly, it's just a scratch. Promise.'*

But a scar on a man's face — now that was a different thing. A scar on a man's face indicated any number of dangerous and exciting journeys in his life. Just look at Harry Potter, for Christ's sake. Niko remembered reading somewhere that Prince William had a similar scar to that of the boy wizard after having been hit with a golf club. And he'd landed himself that sexy bird Middleton, so scars *must* be cool.

After making two cups of strong, black coffee, Niko fired up his computer.

Thirty minutes later, having exhausted his list of favourite porn stars, it was obvious nothing was stirring.

"Shit," Niko mumbled, shaking his hand to relieve the cramp. He contemplated ringing Cherie, but didn't relish the idea of showering, shaving and getting dressed, all of which had the promise of pain. He also considered Cherie may not be best pleased to see him in his current condition, although, he was sure her professionalism would not allow too many signs of disgust. She'd probably seen a lot worse. In any event, he decided he'd leave her alone for now and spare her the sight. He also decided to spare the general public the pleasure of his current appearance and browsed his way to a supermarket site. It was just as he was about to finalise the purchase that he remembered to delete the cat food.

Niko left the computer and made his way to the sofa. He picked up the Star Wars remote from the coffee table and surveyed the detritus of the night before. In amongst the papers, matches, tobacco, empty Fosters cans, and what was left of his Acapulco Gold, was a half-empty bottle of cheap brandy. It had Martin Bead's watch draped around the neck.

Niko squinted at the bottle. It brought an image of Niko rummaging around in the back of a kitchen cupboard. Niko now remembered searching for it after he'd run out of Fosters.

"For Christ's sake, Nikolaus," he said, flicking on the television. "You don't even like brandy. No wonder you were sick."

Niko sank into the comfort of the sofa and closed his eyes. Maybe he'd try and get some more sleep before visiting his Lebanese friend.

Sleep wouldn't come.

***

Adrian Mahoney had been his name. Niko's first.

It had been raining heavily, Niko recalled, and everything smelled damp. He'd taken great care to keep his Glock dry, wrapping it in clingfilm before leaving. He'd spent three days deciding on the best spot and had arrived at the chosen location far earlier than necessary. He knew Mahoney wouldn't be there for another half-hour. Niko's research had unearthed that Mahoney, despite being a raging alcoholic, was a creature of habit, his daily movements always identical.

In that half-hour of waiting, Niko had played the forthcoming scene over and over. Several times he'd practiced removing the gun from his pocket and pointing it to where he believed Mahoney's head would be. He knew how tall he was — he'd checked — but he also knew Mahoney tended to walk with his head down. At that time of night, he also knew his intended victim struggled to move in a straight line. T.S.A. had been insistent it needed to be a single shot, close range, straight between the eyes.

Niko remembered trying to explain that his firearms training had been limited. '*In the navy, they don't expect the catering corps to shoot too many people,*' he'd said. '*What if I miss? What if I can't pull the trigger?*'

T.S.A., as Niko recalled, had indicated that missing was not an option. They gave him one last chance to change his mind, although Niko didn't really believe he had any choice left; he was already in too deep.

As soon as Mahoney had appeared, Niko quickly discovered he *could* pull the trigger. And he didn't miss. He also discovered his manhood enjoyed the experience; an affliction that had continued with time.

Surprisingly, the cheap bottle of brandy Adrian Mahoney had been carrying survived his backwards fall into a puddle and rolled harmlessly into a nearby grass verge. It had been residing in Niko's kitchen cupboard ever since. Until now.

***

Niko opened his eyes and decided there was just enough Gold left for one last joint. He didn't like the fact he had left enough for only one, but out of all the odd numbers, one was almost acceptable. It was odd, certainly, but Niko had the feeling it had aspirations to do better.

Whilst collecting the required items to make the joint, Niko noticed a small plastic tube of superglue on the table which had a globular bubble of pink glue around the tip of its nozzle. Niko stared at it in confusion for several seconds.

"What the hell is this?" he said, rolling the tube around with his finger.

Slowly, another image presented itself. The image explained why his eye-wound had seeped pink. He vaguely remembered having the idea of the glue to seal the wound when he couldn't find a stapler.

Niko started rolling papers.

He decided he might as well finish what was left of the brandy as well.

"Jeeze, there's some stupid twats about, Mr M," Niko said, extinguishing the joint and taking a large slug of brandy straight from the bottle. He shook his head as the heat burned his throat. "Hee-haw," he screamed. "That is some nasty stuff, Mr M." He took another large slug. "Mr M, where are you?" He looked around the room. "Oh, that's right. You're not here anymore, are you? You're dead. Sorry, I forgot. Anyway, as I was saying, there's some stupid twats about. I mean, look at this wanker." Niko waved the brandy bottle in the direction of the television screen. "All he's got to do to win eleven grand — eleven fucking grand, mind you — is name the first ten states of America in alphabetitical order, and his first effort is Texas."

Niko started laughing. “Did I just say alphabetitical?” He repeated the word several times, which got him laughing so much his stomach hurt. It brought tears to his eyes, which also hurt. The pain made Niko laugh louder. “Ooh, man, that hurts,” he said, trying to bring the laughter under control. He rolled off the sofa onto the floor. He was laughing so hard he thought he might lose control of his bladder. Through the laughing and the pain, Niko sensed another noise. It had initially registered as distant and unimportant, but was slowly getting clearer and of more consequence. It was beginning to sweep the laughter out of him. Eventually, the only thing Niko could concentrate on was the noise: the noise of someone knocking on his door.

Niko gave out a yelp and quickly crawled underneath his desk, where he sat cross-legged on his evenly dimensioned rug.

“T.S.A.” he muttered. “Shit, shit, shit.” He put his hands over his ears to stop the noise from getting to them. It didn’t work. He counted the knocks. They were coming in rhythms of five at a time. For Christ’s sake, at least add an extra one, Niko thought.

Niko pictured his Glock sitting in the drawer of his desk, just above his head. Would he be able to get to it in time if T.S.A. broke down his door. How many of them would he need to deal with? He couldn’t remember if the gun was even loaded. And now there was another noise to deal with.

"Hello," shouted a voice. "Is anybody home? Hello, hello. Are you all right in there? I can hear the television."

Niko looked at the television and willed it to be quiet, but the host of the programme had just asked the audience to show their appreciation for the wanker who'd offered up Vermont as his second possible answer, hence losing the eleven grand. No wonder he was leaving with nothing, Niko thought. It was no more than he deserved.

"Hello," the voice repeated. "Mr Andrianakis? My name is Buck Witman. I'm from the Hackney Gazette. You may have heard of me."

Was that just a ruse to get him to open the door? Niko crawled from under the desk and used it to help him stand up. He felt a trickle of sweat run down his back. He tried to shake himself into some cognisant thought. Surely T.S.A. wouldn't pretend to be someone else. It wasn't their style. If T.S.A. really had come for him, there would have been no announcements. They would have simply arrived and gone about their business. No mess. No fuss.

Niko picked up the remote on his way to the door and paused the television. He peered out through the spy-hole and caught a glimpse of the man calling himself Buck Witman, whose name did seem vaguely familiar. "What do you want?" Niko asked. He noticed his voice was slurring badly.

There was a pause before Buck replied. "I'd just like a word about the events of a couple of nights ago," he said. "The fight you got into. The police have given me their version, but I'd really like to hear your side of things."

Niko's relief that the menace at his door was becoming increasingly obvious it was not T.S.A., coupled with having topped up his blood-stream with Gold and cheap brandy, started to take its toll. His head felt like it was far too light for the rest of his body, and he started laughing again. He suddenly felt euphoric.

"What about it?" he said. "I lost."

There was another pause. "Would it be better if we talked without speaking through a locked door?" the man calling himself Buck Witman asked.

Niko had an idea brewing. What if he went and got his gun and just blew this idiot's brains out? What if he went and got his gun and just blew *every* idiot's brains out? Uncle Schmuck, Lieutenant-Commander, the wanker on the television, this arsehole at the door. The whole bloody lot. Hey, why didn't he go and get his gun and blow his own stupid brains out?

When Niko had been eight, he'd walked in on his mother and three Jews. He'd never been so surprised. Until now.

"Wow," he whispered, as the mental picture presented itself. "Blow my own stupid brains out. What the hell would that look like, Nikolaus?"

He looked over to his desk. There he was, sitting on his swivel-chair, which was still slowly spinning, staring open-eyed at the ceiling. The back of his head lay several feet away.

However, it wasn't blood or brains seeping from the hole in Niko's head: it was people. They came out in pairs, as if Niko's head had been some version of the Ark. They emerged as tiny miniatures of themselves, landing on his wooden floor like lemmings off a cliff. From there, they immediately grew to their full form, pulling themselves upright like some scale of man's evolution. After a brief rub down of their naked bodies, they all marched past him, snapping their heads in his direction and nodding once, as if he was some military dictator, before disappearing through the door of his flat which Niko now held open for them.

There went Mummy-dear, and there was Uncle Schmuck; Martin Bead put in an appearance, as did Adrian Mahoney, Lieutenant-Commander, the two old dears, and the wanker on the television. They were interspersed with people Niko had to squint at to try and identify. Minor characters in his life whom he barely recognised. Was that stereotypical Greek guy, smashing plates, meant to be his father, and who the hell was the blonde woman next to him? And why was she wearing a cowboy hat? Who was that with Greasy Joe? Could it be Delores? There were car salesmen, shop workers, bank clerks, Niko's Welsh maths teacher, and several navy colleagues. Even Alexander the Great — who was riding a rocking-horse — and the Grim Reaper filed past him. Finally, out came Cherie and Mr M. Cherie was sporting a military-style drum strapped across one shoulder, which hid the worst of the scars on her stomach. She was beating it methodically, much to Mr M's enjoyment, who was dancing along on his hind legs, leaving a trail of blood from his anus behind him.

Niko suddenly became aware that someone had past him in the wrong direction. They'd come in through his door, not gone out. Was someone trying to find their way *into* his head?

Niko looked back towards his desk, but the Niko who had been sitting there with the back of his head detached had disappeared.

As far as Niko could tell, the only Niko left in the room was the one who had opened the door to let his visitors out, hence giving the man who called himself Buck Witman the impression he was welcome to come in.

"Thanks," Buck said. "That's very kind of you."

Niko poked his head out of his open door and looked up and down. He half-expected to see the backs of his head-visitors disappearing into the distance, but there was nothing. Niko turned to confront the blur of cream standing in his apartment. Whoever or whatever it was, it was also wearing a stupid hat.

Buck tried not to stare too long at Niko's coffee table.

"Do you mind if I take notes?" Buck asked, removing his notebook from one of the many pockets in his trademark coat and waving it in the air. He pushed his trilby further back on his head. "Just so I don't forget anything. My memory these days isn't what it used to be. Must be an age thing."

Buck attempted to keep the tone light. In his experience, people talked far more openly if they felt at ease. He removed a small pencil from a loop of fabric on the notebook, licked the end of it, and flourished the pencil in front of him as if it were a magic wand.

Niko cocked his head to one side and squinted, giving the wound above his eye its own dance. He took a step closer to Buck, and, being slightly shorter, looked up into his eyes. The two men stared at one another until Buck coughed.

"Do you mind if I ask you a few questions? I won't be long, promise."

Niko took a sudden intake of breath through his closed teeth. He poked Buck in the shoulder, harder than Buck would have liked. Hard enough to make Buck's trilby fall off his head.

"Now is that a single promise, a double promise, a triple promise or a super promise?" Niko asked. He did not wait for an answer before poking Buck in the shoulder again. "Are you a Jew? Is your name Schmuck? Have you ever been in the navy?"

Buck opened his mouth, but suddenly closed it again. He had the feeling there were right answers to

Niko's questions. Problem was, he didn't know what they were. He was, however, damned sure there were wrong answers.

"You look like a Jew," Niko added, quickly. "I shall call you Schmuck. So, Schmuck, do you know the first ten American states alphabetitically?" Niko hunched his shoulders and started giggling. "Look, I said it again."

"I'm sorry, Mr Andrianakis," Buck said. "I'm not quite with you. You've lost me, I'm afraid." Buck had lost the tone of enlightenment and a slight quiver had entered his speech.

This wasn't how Buck had envisaged the interview going. Like all well-prepared people, Buck had given himself a picture of what would happen when he met Niko Andrianakis; a mental order of things so he could keep on track and not waste any precious time. Buck had learned that if you decided beforehand what *might* happen, then in all likelihood it's what *would* happen. The strategy worked nine times out of ten.

Buck got the distinct impression this was going to be the one time where it didn't.

Niko stopped giggling and put both his hands on Buck's shoulders. "I bet you'd know Vermont and Texas are not in that list, right?" He tapped Buck lightly on the cheek. "You'd know that much, right?" He repeated the tap but on the other cheek. "Please tell me you'd know Vermont and Texas are not in the top ten states," Niko took a deep breath. "Alphabetit...

alphabetit… alphabetit." Niko started giggling again. The giggling turned into full blown laughter.

It had been a slow-news week at the Gazette. The only two local matters of any interest Delaney had given Buck was this, and the case of an old woman getting deliberately run over by a four-by-four in Asda's car-park in an argument over a disabled parking space. Buck was now wishing he'd taken on the old woman. He made a mental note to put more pressure on Delaney for something juicier in future. After all, the fat idiot wouldn't want all that nonsense about his sister coming out in the papers.

Niko released Buck's shoulder and doubled over. "I'm — dying — here," he said, between the snorts of laughter. "My ribs — are — killing me. Man — this hurts." Niko started to laugh-cry.

Perhaps, Buck thought, now would be a good time to leave. Just slip out whilst Mr Andrianakis was so indisposed. Put the whole episode down to experience and go and find the old woman who'd been run over.

Buck started to make tentative steps towards the door, but then remembered his hat. He couldn't leave without his hat. His hat, just like his coat, formed the being that was Buck Witman. Without them, he'd be plain-old Lionel again, and who the hell would want to read anything written by plain-old Lionel? Nobody, that's who. Nope, he definitely needed his hat.

Buck turned and made his way quietly to where he could see his hat lying on the floor. Upon re-donning the trilby, he immediately felt more like the intrepid reporter, Buck Witman: the finest journalist the Hackney Gazette had ever seen. He looked at Niko, who was still doubled over, his arms flailing around for something to hold on to.

Finding only thin air, Niko sank to his knees. He started crawling across the floor. "Schmuck, I — just want — you to stay there — okay?" he said. "See that — desk over there? I'm just — going to get something — to show you. Trust me — it'll be worth — the wait. Don't — go anywhere, Schmuck."

Perhaps, Buck thought, rummaging in his pockets for his phone, he could just take a quick snap of the coffee table when Niko Andrianakis's back was turned. He'd given up on the idea of writing anything about Mr Andrianakis himself; the man clearly had a problem with drink and drugs which had made him mentally deranged. But maybe he could compile something generic about the local drugs scene. A photo would be useful, he mused. Perhaps, when Mr Andrianakis had retrieved whatever it was he wanted to show him, Buck could ask if could take a few photos of the apartment as well.

Buck knew that the first thing readers like to know is someone's age, but a close second was where they lived. If you could give them a sneak preview inside a stranger's domain, then you were onto a winner. Especially if they were luxurious apartments like this one. Buck would challenge anyone to walk past an uncurtained window or an open door without taking a quick look inside. Obviously, a person's home and how they kept it was a direct reflection on the person themselves, and, Buck noted, Niko's coffee table spoke volumes. The story started forming in his mind.

Not all drug addicts will be seen in doorways or benches on our streets. Some hide away in ivory castles. This is a picture that I, Buck Witman, took whilst visiting such a castle. Showing no concern for my own safety, I infiltrated...

"Get out of my fucking apartment."

The request had been given in no more than a whisper, but a whisper that carried enough menace to make Buck's knees suddenly feel inadequate for the weight above them. He turned slowly. The sight of a gun pointing at his face was enough for Buck's knees to give up their fight and he found himself in a kneeling position with his hands held in front of his face. He could feel the contents of his stomach start to rise. Also, his hat had fallen off again.

"I said, get out of my fucking apartment," Niko repeated, pressing the muzzle of the gun against the top of Buck's head.

Buck had written many times about how people had adopted fight or flight as their means of dealing with a situation. In his experience, those who chose to fight either did so because they were under the influence of copious amounts of alcohol, were pretty sure the odds were stacked heavily in their favour, or were firmly convinced some higher authority was looking after their welfare. Sometimes all three. Buck was neither drunk, nor did he believe the odds looked good, nor did he believe in God. Therefore, he crawled as quickly as his quivering body would take him to the apartment's door, making strange guttural noises as he went.

It wasn't until he was back in his car, did he notice the damp, warm sensation running down his leg. He also fully realised that, this time, there'd be no going back for his hat.

Niko closed the door behind his unwanted guest, picked up Buck's trilby, and sat back on the sofa. He placed the hat on his own head and put the Glock amongst the items on the coffee table. He smiled. "Now, wasn't that just a hoot?"

Niko un-paused the television and started channel-hopping, but his focus was taken by the look on Buck Witman's face when confronted with a gun to his head. It was a look Niko was unfamiliar with. The six people Niko had despatched from the world had never been given the opportunity to wonder what might happen next. They'd never fully understood that a bullet was about to hurtle towards them at fifteen hundred feet-per-second from close range. Maybe, for the briefest of moments, their brains may have registered something; the slight sound of Niko's clothes rustling; the snap of a twig; a change in the air; something. And maybe that something got turned into a fleeting realisation not all was well. But it would have been miniscule; no more than the blink of an eye. No time for panic or alarm. No time to re-consider their life choices. No time to make amends. No time to wonder why. No time for goodbyes. No bother. No fuss. The T.S.A. way. And certainly, no time for them to piss themselves.

Niko picked up the Glock and tossed it from hand to hand. He sniggered as he recalled the wet patch appearing around Buck Witman's groin.

"So," he whispered. "Let's see what the prick was worried about." He quickly put the muzzle of the gun tight against his temple. "Get out of my fucking apartment," he said. He tried to employ the same menace he'd used with Buck. He closed his eyes and envisaged who it might be was holding the gun. He went through several options before settling on the Grim Reaper he'd stood next to at Bijan's funeral. He'd looked like the type who would put a gun to someone's head with no qualms about using it.

Niko's heart rate increased with the anticipation of what he knew a bullet could do from point-blank range. "Get out of my fucking apartment," he repeated, louder. He pushed the gun harder against his temple. Buck's hat fell off.

Niko's breathing quickened. He started to apply pressure to the trigger.

Niko felt a familiar stirring; one he'd felt every time he'd pointed the gun the other way. He slowly removed the gun and put it down on the coffee table. He looked down.

"Well, hello, old friend," he said. He quickly grabbed the remote and navigated to the soft-porn channels. He was sure he could manage this one without Cherie's help. Perhaps he'd use that prick's hat to collect the discharge.

After Niko had finished, he fell into a deep, satisfying sleep.

FRIDAY

Niko had tried his best with his clothes, but no amount of fancy apparel would take away the sight of his face. Ugly, purple-yellow bruises had started to appear in places where Niko had not even known he'd been hit, and the gash above his right eye was not healing well. It hurt to blink. But Niko was hungry. Hungry for food, but also hungry for the substances that would help him to *tatfu mae alsahub*.

He checked his pockets to make sure he had his keys and wallet. He looked at himself one last time in the mirror, winced, and left the apartment.

***

Greasy Joe's was full and noisy. There was a new roof being put on a wing of The Royal London Hospital, and one of the gangs had descended on Joe's for their mid-morning breakfast. In Niko's experience, builders liked to eat their own bodyweight in food, several times a day. Like hobbits, he mused, they were probably already on their third breakfast. Niko had momentarily thought about going elsewhere, but his hunger needed satisfying as soon as possible.

Niko tried to sneak to a single table tucked away in a corner, but it was impossible not to be spotted.

One of the builders took a double-take as Niko sat down. “Bloody hell, mate, what happened to you?” The question brought many more pairs of eyes in Niko’s direction, followed by all sorts of queries.

‘Wow, what does the other guy look like?’

‘Hope she was worth it, mate.’

‘Was it a car accident? Looks like a car accident to me. Gone through the windscreen, I bet. Weren’t wearing your seatbelt, were you?’

‘Did you lose any teeth? I’d bloody hate to lose my teeth. Women love my teeth.’

‘It’s not my teeth women love. They don’t even look at my face when I release the monster from his cage. I could even look like our friend here and they still wouldn’t notice.’

There followed what passed as banter to a group of builders, most of it directed at Niko’s expense. Niko sat quietly and fielded each question with a nod and as good a smile as he could muster. He distracted himself from the merriment by wondering which of the builders may be gay. There had to be at least one. His money was on the *monster in the cage* chappie. Although, the youngest-looking of the bunch, who’d not said anything, and only awkwardly joined in with a laugh or two, may also be a candidate. Perhaps *monster guy* was doing a lieutenant-commander on the youngster and using his superiority to get his kicks. Niko imagined holding his gun to *monster guy's* head and watching him piss himself just like that journalist prick had done. It brought a wider smile to Niko's face. The smile hurt. It was a pain Niko was happy to endure.

A very large black man with a different coloured hi-vis stood up, stretched, and said, "Right guys, let's leave Quasimodo here to have his breakfast. Break's over. Back to work. That roof isn't going to attach itself."

There followed the grating sound of many chairs being put back under tables, along with the general cacophony produced by a dozen well-fed men who all gave the impression they knew exactly where they stood in the world. Niko supposed if you spent most of your working life looking down on people from a great height, then you could easily adopt an air of superiority. After all, you were literally closer to God.

The café quietened as it emptied. After the builders had left, the only punters remaining were Niko and the regular two old dears sitting at their usual table. Both women found it difficult not to stare as they sipped their coffees.

The whispers of the old, Niko noted, are not exactly whispers anymore, and the topic of their conversation reached Niko's ears without hindrance. Somehow, the old dears managed to put the state of Niko's face down to Britain's lax immigration policies.

"I will just be moment," Greasy Joe said as he cleared away the builders' plates, cups and cutlery. Niko noticed that, almost to a man, the builders had not left behind any food. “I will just be moment,” Joe repeated.

Niko had always been convinced Joe’s Italian accent was exaggerated. Niko knew Joe, real name Giuseppe, had been born in this country, albeit his parents had come over from Sicily in the late 1940s.

Once Joe had cleaned the builders’ tables, occasionally shouting to some poor soul slaving away in the kitchen, he approached Niko. He took a small pad and pencil out of the front pocket of his grimy, black apron, along with a pair of half-moon spectacles. On donning the glasses, he gave out a long whistle.

“Mamma Mia, you face is one hell of a mess, my friend.”

Niko simply nodded. Joe was obviously one for stating the obvious. “I’d like a—”

“Who has done this to you?” Joe interrupted, waving his pencil in front of Niko’s face. “Who has made this mess to my friend?”

Niko wouldn’t exactly have classed Joe as a friend. Niko wouldn’t exactly class anyone as a friend. Cherie would be the closest to that description now that Mr M was gone, but he paid for her company. Niko calculated he’d been in Joe’s café no more than a dozen times, and only a few sentences had ever passed between them, most of which had simply centred around what Niko wanted to eat.

“Just some guy,” Niko said. “Nobody really. Now, I’d like a—”

"Was he Polish?" Joe said, pointing his pencil at Niko. "This, how you saying it? Just some guy. This nobody really. Was he Polish?" Niko noticed Joe's nose twitching wildly.

The question took Niko by surprise. Through the corner of his good eye, Niko could see the two old dears start to take extra notice in the conversation.

"I… I… I have no idea," Niko said. "He was big, I think. Definitely black. I never stopped to ask him his nationality."

"You see those builders?" Joe pointed to where the builders had been sitting. "Two of them Polish. I make sure I spit in food." Joe scribbled something on his pad and tore off the sheet. He placed the torn-off paper in front of Niko. "If you ever find this nobody really, this Polish scum, you call this number." He leaned into Niko and whispered, "You say you friend of Giuseppe Siciliano. You tell him you need Polish *feccia* to disappear." Niko could smell the grease on Joe's apron. "You tell him where to find this nobody really and he will make him go away." Joe made some gesture with his hands as if he was releasing a hidden bird. "Poof, just like that. You understand?"

The irony of being told he could make a stranger disappear was not lost on Niko, and he attempted to smile.

"Ah, I see you understand," Joe said. He turned to the two old dears. "Polish feccia did this." He pointed at Niko. The two old dears nodded in sage understanding, their views on the world obviously confirmed. Joe turned back to Niko. "Now, I get you Joe's special with extras. On the house." He disappeared into the kitchen and began shouting orders in Italian.

Niko now wished he had paid a visit to Camden Market before deciding on having his breakfast. He was sure a nice lungful of marijuana would have helped the surrealism of the situation.

***

Buck Witman had not slept well. Every time he'd closed his eyes, he could actually feel the weight of the gun against his head. He was sure if he put his fingers to the spot, there'd be an imprint. The feeling that he may lose control of his bladder again at any moment had also kept sleep at bay.

He poured himself an orange juice and sat at his breakfast bar in his mediocre flat. As he had lain awake, his mind had persuaded him he had two possible options. Option One — do nothing. Option Two — do something. He made two columns in his notebook with the relevant headings.

Under Option One, he wrote:

Carry on as if nothing has happened. Just like Lionel would do.

Under Option Two, he wrote:

Carry on as if something has happened. Just like Buck would do.

Something else now came to Buck. A third option. The option he really should be taking. The option to go to the police and tell them a complete lunatic had pointed a gun at his head. He knew his name, where he lived, what he looked like. Surely, he could give the police everything they needed to arrest the idiot. At the very least, they could lock Mr Andrianakis away in a psychiatric hospital, and they were even more difficult to get out of than prison.

Last night, as he'd been driving away from the scene, the thought had crossed Buck's mind to go straight to the nearest police station, but he had then become conscious of the wetness on his trousers and had decided to come home first. There was absolutely no need, he'd told himself, for anybody to know that when faced with a major crisis to his wellbeing, Buck Witman had pissed himself. Having got back to the sanctuary of his flat, changed his trousers, and taken several large slugs of whiskey, he'd then decided he needed time to think.

Maybe, Buck thought, sipping at his orange juice, he'd just write a piece up about the event and see what it looked like. The more he thought about it, the more he liked the idea. Was there an opportunity here? An opportunity to make him, Buck Witman — the greatest journalist The Hackney Gazette had ever seen — to be some sort of saviour, putting himself in harm's way in order to bring the true grit and grime of London's East End drug problem to the readership. Maybe the paper would win another award, all thanks to him. Images floated in his mind of Buck at some swanky ceremony, standing at the podium with a gleaming trophy in his hand, delivering a speech which would be talked about for years to come.

Perhaps he would type something up and leave it sitting on his computer. Maybe come back to it in a day or two, when the shock had worn off. See how he felt. Yes, he was liking the idea a lot. Under Option Two, he wrote:

'Write an award-winning piece, to include how I managed to better a drug-crazed lunatic with a gun.'

Buck scanned back a few pages in his notebook, looking to see if he'd actually written anything whilst at Mr Andrianakis's flat. The pages were bare. Given the circumstances, Buck was not surprised. Having a gun pressed against your head and writing things down at the same time did not go together. So, what could he remember?

What was it he'd called him? He'd asked Buck if he was a Jew. Then he'd called him something. Shuck? Stuck? Schmuck? Yes, that was it, Schmuck. Buck wrote the word down and then fired up his computer. He entered *Schmuck* into the search engine.

In common usage the term can mean a contemptible or detestable person, but in Yiddish the word Schmuck is a vulgar term for a penis.

"Bloody charming," Buck said.

Buck scribbled other things as he remembered them. The word *Promises* got written down — Buck couldn't remember exactly why. The first ten American states alphabetically also came to mind. He recalled how Mr Andrianakis had laughed himself almost to a stupor when he couldn't say the word alphabetically. He wrote *bloody mental*. He also wrote, *Get out of my fucking apartment*. He then also wrote, *pissed myself*, and, *lost my hat*, but then quickly scribbled them out.

Buck scanned what he had so far and came to the realisation that he still had no idea why Niko Andrianakis felt the need to put a gun to his head. As far as Buck could see, he'd neither said anything to upset him, nor done anything that would threaten him in any way.

Buck replayed every moment from entering the apartment to leaving it. What had he done that had peeved his interviewee so much? He offered up a silent prayer that Mr Andrianakis was looking after his hat. Maybe, given time — lots of time — he could go and ask for it back. He wrote down, *get hat back*.

Then he remembered the coffee table.

Buck switched on his phone and scrolled to where the photograph of the coffee table was sitting. It was a good photograph, Buck thought; very incriminating, and he would definitely use it in his award-winning article.

Had that been why Mr Andrianakis had been so upset? Perhaps he didn't appreciate people taking photographs of his flat. Okay, so it seemed a bit extreme to then point a gun at the photographer's head, but who knew how the mind of a drug-addled maniac worked. Buck stared at the photograph.

His eyes started blinking uncontrollably. He shook the phone just in case the image changed. When it didn't, he threw the phone onto the breakfast bar as if it were burning his skin. He jumped off his stool and stood up. His legs were telling his brain something wasn't right, and he toppled backwards into his cooker. His ears registered a noise, followed by his nose advising there was a smell. It took several seconds for Buck to realise the sound was the pilot-light of the cooker *click-clicking*, and the smell was that of unlit gas. He pushed himself off the cooker and very slowly, like a curious dog approaching something unknown, reached out to where he had thrown his phone. The phone had landed screen-down. Buck's shaking hand hovered over it. Buck knew as soon as he picked up the phone, and if the image was still the same, his life could change dramatically.

The image hadn't changed; amongst the items on the coffee table was a business card; a business card showing a single white circle on a black background.

***

Michelle had not had a good night. All of yesterday had been spent almost exclusively in bed, and, Stanley noted, her speech had become thicker. It was obvious, although Michelle would never admit to it, that she was also occasionally struggling to swallow properly.

Stanley had suggested taking Michelle to hospital, but she would hear nothing of the sort, insisting she would be fine with a little bed-rest. Stanley had taken her the occasional plate of food, but it had, in the main, remained uneaten. She'd also had to ask Stanley for assistance to go to the toilet, which Stanley knew she'd hated doing, but her thinning legs were finding it difficult to carry her weight on their own.

This morning had not started any better. On waking, Stanley used the experience twenty-five years of marriage brings to realise his wife was quietly crying. She had her back to him and was attempting to hide the fact, but Stanley's ears tuned in to the tell-tale sounds. He propped himself on one elbow and put his hand on her shoulder. Michelle tried to shrug it off.

"Don't," she said. "Don't touch me."

Stanley remained in physical contact. "It's not contagious, Michelle," he said, now putting his arm around her waist.

They remained perfectly still until Michelle's crying stopped.

"Why aren't you in work?" Michelle asked. "You should have gone to work by now. Haven't you got any criminals to catch?"

"Just thought I'd have the day to myself," Stanley replied.

"Bullshit!" Michelle said. "You're just feeling sorry for yourself because your wife's dying. Well, big deal, wives die all the time, so piss off and go to work."

"I'm sure if anything exciting crops up, the station will call," Stanley said. "Anyway, Patty's gone off on compassionate leave or something. You know what they say? When the cat's away, the mice will play."

"I really need a shower," Michelle said, moving Stanley's arm. She sniffed the air. "So do you. You smell like a dog who's been left out in the rain."

"Now there's gratitude," Stanley said. "I spend all this time cooking, cleaning, doing all the household chores, and keeping down a decent job, whilst my lazy, good-for-nothing, whore of a wife stays in bed."

"Oy!" Michelle tried to kick Stanley with the back of her heel, but there was little force in the effort. "Less of the whore if you don't mind. I'll have you know you're the only man I've ever allowed in me, Stanley Wood."

They both laughed at the known untruth.

Michelle had told Stanley — during that conversation all lovers have — that she had enjoyed three sexual relationships before he came along. Her virginity had been lost not long after her sixteenth birthday to a school acquaintance who'd got her drunk at a house-party. They had briefly continued to see each other until Michelle found it more interesting to start dating someone a few years older. *'Who could blame me?'* she'd said. *'He had a car.'*

Once the novelty of the car had worn off, Michelle had turned her attention to a drummer in a rock-band. It was, as Michelle had described, her *'experimental period.'* The drummer had never officially been dumped. He'd simply gone off to play some gigs in Germany and never returned. It was a standing joke between Stanley and Michelle that as the old boyfriend was leaving for Germany, the new one was coming in the exact opposite direction.

"Do you want me to run you a bath, instead?" Stanley asked. "I could light those candles you like?"

"You've always said they smell of despair."

Stanley was not a fan of candles. Apart from the obvious fire risk, in his eyes they symbolised death and destruction. People were always lighting candles in memory of some disaster or another.

"Yeah, well, I've changed my mind," he said. "So, what do you say — bath?"

Michelle swung her legs off the bed and planted her feet on the floor. She pushed herself up off the bed and took a few tentative steps. "It'll have to be the shower," she said. "I don't think I can get in and out of the bath."

Stanley watched as his wife slowly made her way out of the bedroom like someone negotiating a minefield. "You can run a bath for Poppy if you like," she said.

Stanley's mouth gaped. He replayed the words his wife had just said in order to satisfy himself she had actually said them. Not only said them, but meant them.

'You can run a bath for Poppy if you like.' As if it was something still happening on a regular basis.

Michelle and Stanley had been warned by the neurologist that one of the possible side effects of motor neurones degenerating was something known as *frontotemporal dementia.* He'd advised that Michelle may well display personality and behavioural traits that she'd never shown before, and this may well involve some memory loss.

Stanley heard the thrum of the electric shower. He glanced at the several pictures on the shelf underneath the bedroom television, his eyes settling on one, in particular. As far as he could recall, it was the only photograph they had of the three of them, courtesy of a kindly passer-by who'd agreed to take the snap. He believed it was on a day out to South Norwood Country Park; a memorable day, according to Michelle, because she'd actually persuaded Stanley to look at life south of the river.

In the photograph, the little fluffy terrier was trying to lick Stanley's face, much to Michelle's amusement.

The puppy had been Michelle's idea. Stanley had argued against it. He knew Michelle was only suggesting it as a way to fill the obvious gaps children would have filled, but he never said so.

Somehow, to Stanley's bemusement, despite him being the one who walked it, fed it, and cleaned up after it, it was to Michelle that it devoted most of its loving. When the little dog had to be put to sleep because of a growth in its stomach, Michelle had been inconsolable. That had been twelve years ago.

Stanley wondered if he should tell his wife what she'd just said. Was it necessary? Would it just upset her, or would it be a comfort for Michelle to know where the disease was in its progress? Perhaps he'd phone the doctors; see what they advised.

Stanley got out of bed and made his way to the bathroom.

He found his wife sitting in the shower with her head between her knees. She was still clothed in her pyjamas. She hadn't closed the shower door and the bathroom floor was puddling.

"Michelle?" Stanley whispered. He walked into the shower, closing the door behind him. He awkwardly manoeuvred himself until he was sitting behind his wife. He cradled her in his arms and gently rocked.

"Michelle, I'm going to phone the doctors, okay?" He felt his wife stiffen.

Stanley wasn't sure where his tears ended, and the shower-water started. He remembered how quiet and empty the house had felt after Poppy had left. How the hell would he ever climb out of the hole Michelle would leave?

"No, you're bloody not," Michelle said. "I want to do this on my terms, not theirs."

As Stanley and Michelle rocked back and forth in their watery embrace, the chirping of Stanley's phone went unanswered. If Stanley had paid more attention to the ring, he would have realised the tone: desperation.

***

"He's not picking up," the desk sergeant said. "I told you, he's taking the day off."

"But I don't think you fully understand the urgency here," Buck said. He'd already had to wait half-an-hour while the sergeant dealt with the language barrier of an Asian woman complaining about dog-shit in her garden, even though she didn't own a dog. "You really need to get him to answer. Haven't you got a special code or something? You know, so many rings then hang up, then ring again?"

"We're not lovers," the sergeant said, laughing. "He obviously doesn't want to be disturbed. You're unlucky though, I'll give you that. I can't remember the last time DCI Wood had a day off. Anyway, isn't it Delaney you normally see?"

"Yes, but… never mind. This time, it's got to be DCI Wood."

The sergeant pulled some paperwork in front of him. "In that case, I'd call back tomorrow, if I was you. I'll tell him to expect you. I'm sure he'll be delighted." The sergeant pointed his pen at Buck's head. "Where's your hat? I don't think I've ever seen you in here without your hat."

Buck reached up and stroked his hair. "It… it… it got blown off in the wind," he said. "Listen, never mind my bloody hat. Tomorrow's no good. By tomorrow… well, things may have changed."

Buck had stared hard at the photograph of the coffee table. He'd looked at it from every angle. He'd zoomed in, he'd zoomed out. He'd added all sorts of filters. He'd downloaded it from his phone to his computer and then deleted it off his phone. He hadn't been exactly sure why, it had just seemed the right thing to do. Somehow, it just felt safer.

A fleeting thought had crossed his mind to contact his editor and put her in the picture, but he'd quickly dismissed the idea. He may be the greatest journalist The Hackney Gazette had ever seen, but if the paper ran a story on the possible identity of a T.S.A. assassin, then Buck Witman did not want his name attached to it. He'd decided that everything he did from here on in would need to be done purely for his own self-preservation.

Since becoming Buck Witman, instead of plain-old Lionel, scared was not an emotion Buck had been used to. But when Buck had eventually digested what the photograph of that coffee table might suggest, he'd become petrified. How long would it take Niko Andrianakis to realise the business card was on the table and that Buck may have seen it? Even if he wasn't sure it had been spotted, surely Mr Andrianakis would not take any chances.

So, with thoughts of Niko Andrianakis tracking him down and blowing his brains out with that bloody gun, Buck had decided to unburden himself. Pass the buck, so to speak, onto someone else and then disappear for a few days, maybe even a few weeks, perhaps even a year. There was only one person who came to mind. Surely, DCI Wood wouldn't mind taking on T.S.A. After all, it was sort of his job. He could bloody well fight the fight while Buck took a long, well-deserved holiday somewhere far away, from where he could watch events unfold. Furthermore, he would insist DCI Wood promised never to reveal his source. Wasn't that a thing? A code the police had?

On the way to the station, Buck had found himself continuously looking over his shoulder like a skittish antelope that's caught the scent of a lion. He'd darted in and out of doorways, checking no one was following him. By habit, he had put on his Mackintosh. Why had he made himself so conspicuous? He'd considered maybe popping into a shop and changing it, but time was of the essence. The sooner he could off-load his information, the better.

"There's nothing I can do," the sergeant said, impatiently. "He's not here. I can't just magic him out of a bottle. I told you, you'll have to come back tomorrow."

Buck's mind was racing. If he stepped out of this station still being the only person who knew about the photograph, he firmly believed it would be knowledge he might be taking to his grave. He had to tell someone before he set foot in the outside world again. As his mind churned, another name came to him.

"What about his partner?" he blurted. "DI Chandler, right? What about her?"

"What about her?" the sergeant said, clicking the top of his ballpoint.

"Jesus Christ, man, is she here? Can you get hold of her?"

The sergeant stared at Buck. The stare held a hundred questions, none of which Buck felt like answering. However, it seemed obvious the desk sergeant wasn't going to do anything unless Buck could actually make him. Buck decided the situation was serious enough to gamble.

Buck leaned over the counter slightly and looked furtively from side to side. "Okay," he said. "I didn't really want to do this… but… you know I'm the greatest journalist this patch has ever seen, right? Of course you do. Now, you look like an intelligent man to me, sergeant, so I'm sure you'll understand when I tell you that I know things about certain people in this station. Things that those certain people wouldn't like me writing about, you know what I'm saying? And sergeant, those certain people may well include people like you." Buck smiled and allowed the words to hang.

The truth was Buck could not recall ever having had any dirt on the desk sergeant, but he would bet his bottom dollar there was something in the guy's past that he'd be worried about if it became common knowledge. As Buck now saw it, the sergeant would have to take a punt on whether Buck knew anything or not.

The sergeant's pen clicking got faster and more aggressive.

Buck continued to roll the dice. "So, why don't you just pick up that phone," he said, "and get me DI Chandler? If you do that, I may just be able to forget the whole messy business."

After some tense moments of silence, the sergeant picked up the phone.

"She'll be here in ten," the sergeant said, replacing the receiver. "Said for you to wait for her in interview three. Follow me."

Buck dutifully followed the man. He had the distinct impression he wouldn't be making the sergeant's Christmas list any time soon.

***

The Libyan had taken one look at Niko and decided he knew exactly what he needed. *'I have excellent opportunity,'* he'd said, circling Niko's face with his finger. *'Just come yesterday. Afghanistan.'* He'd said the name of the country in a whisper, as if any stock from that part of the world was biblical. *'No more pain. Purple Kush is answer. Purple Kush make you blind to pain.'*

And so it was that Niko had left Camden Market with several hundred pounds worth of Purple Kush from biblical Afghanistan secreted in one of the four pockets of his newly acquired jacket.

SATURDAY

Buck had suffered another sleepless night.

Every noise of the flat, every slam of a car door, the bark of a dog, even the chirp of a bird had sent his stomach into cartwheels.

DI Chandler had listened to his story, and, he believed, understood his worry. She had sympathised as to why he was so anxious to tell all and get the hell out of town, but she needed proof, she'd said. She'd need to see the photograph for herself. Buck had pleaded with her long and loud to accompany him back to his flat where he'd gladly show her the photograph on his computer. Why the hell had he deleted it off his phone? But she'd said she needed to put protocols in place, whatever the hell that meant. Said she couldn't just visit people's flats on a whim. A whim! Buck had suggested he could go home and e-mail it to her. That would be enough, wouldn't it? Why hadn't he thought of that before? Not a good idea, Verity had replied. T.S.A. were resourceful. They may be monitoring such things.

However, she had agreed to pay him a visit early today. Buck had persuaded her to make it as early as early could be. Even then, he'd told her, she may well find him face down in his carpet with a bullet-hole in his head. He'd asked if they could provide protection; put a police officer outside his door. She'd laughed at the idea. Bloody laughed! Said he'd been watching too many gangster movies.

The sound of his intercom buzzing made Buck scream. He pressed the view button which showed DI Chandler standing outside the main entrance to the block of flats. "Come on up," Buck said, pressing the release button. He stood inside his own door in readiness. Moments later, there was a light knock.

"Good to see you're not face down in the carpet," Verity said. She walked into the flat, closing the door behind her. She took off her coat and threw it on the sofa.

"I hope yesterday's visit to the station wasn't just a ruse to get me to your flat, Mr Witman. You know, a sort of *come up and see my puppy.* Although, in this instance, it's *come up and see my photograph.* Actually, that sounds worse."

"No ruse," Buck said, picking up her coat and placing it on a hook just inside the door. "Mind you, if it was, it's worked." He suddenly felt much calmer. He had survived the night, and, for the time being, at least, he felt safe. Right now, there was no way Niko Andrianakis could get at him. Not with a police officer in his flat. Within the next half-hour or so he'd be free of his burden and could concentrate on his exit strategy.

"Are you armed?" Buck asked.

Verity laughed. "Am I what?"

“Armed. You know — packing. Have you got a gun? Just in case Mr Andrianakis comes knocking.”

Verity sat in the one and only armchair. “Of course I’m not. This isn’t America, Mr Witman. Detectives do not carry firearms. Especially when they’re only going to look at a photograph. I have, however, brought my notebook.” To prove the point, Verity produced a notebook from the back pocket of her jeans and flourished it in the air.

Buck found himself wondering how Verity had squeezed herself into the jeans. How had she made herself look so good so early in the morning?

“I think it’s a little bit more than just looking at a photograph,” Buck said. He looked at the door to his flat. “I thought perhaps DCI Wood would have been with you. When I left you yesterday, you said you were going to fill him in.”

“Seven in the morning is too early, even for him,” Verity replied. “Don’t worry, I’ve left him a message.”

Buck had the feeling something wasn’t right. Verity didn’t seem to have the appropriate excitement about her. She looked far too comfortable. Here he was, giving her the opportunity to do something no detective had done — uncover a T.S.A. operative — and here she was, nonchalantly sitting in his flat as if she’d come round to talk about the weather. He reminded himself she hadn’t seen the photograph yet. When she had, her demeanour would surely change.

"Do you want to see the photograph now?" Buck asked, moving towards his computer.

"Of course I do," Verity replied. "But maybe a cup of coffee first. I came straight here this morning and haven't had my fill."

"Really?" Buck said. "Coffee? Now?"

"Yes please. White, two sugars. I'll make it myself if you tell me where everything is."

"No, no," Buck said, making his way into the kitchenette. "It's all right, I'll do it."

As Buck made the coffee, Verity stood up and meandered around the meagre open-plan flat. Off a shelf she picked up a photograph of a young Buck Witman, his arm around the shoulder of a slim blonde.

"Who's this?" she said, waving the photograph in Buck's direction. "You wouldn't be two-timing me, would you?"

Buck laughed. "No, that's my sister."

"Ah, that old chestnut," Verity said, replacing the photograph. "Is she local?"

"No, she fell in love with an Australian girl she met whilst working in a bar. They moved out there ten years ago now. We don't really keep in touch. The odd message at Christmas and birthdays." Buck realised he couldn't actually recall when his sister's birthday was.

"Any other family?" Verity said, sitting herself back in the armchair.

Buck hesitated. He was confused. This wasn't how he had planned the conversation. "Uh, no," he said. "There's an uncle somewhere in Burnley, I think."

"And what about girlfriends, Mr Witman?" Verity's voice had taken on the demure tone of a Victorian virgin. "Am I competing against anyone for your undivided attention? Do I need to be worried?"

It had been a while since Buck had found any uptick in his love-life. He found, when in front of women in an unofficial capacity, that Lionel Witman was the persona that surfaced. Unfortunately, Lionel Witman was about as exciting as putting the bins out.

"No, no need to worry," he said. "I'm all yours." He emerged from the kitchenette and passed Verity her coffee. She immediately placed it at her feet.

"Boyfriends then?" Verity said.

"Not my style, DI Chandler. Can we… you know?" Buck pointed to where his computer was set up.

"Of course," Verity said, without moving out of the chair. "But first, just give me the story again. From start to finish."

Buck sighed heavily. This was obvious police tactics. Verity would be looking for contradictions in what he'd told her yesterday at the station. He moved an ironing-basket off a small, white stool, and pulled it to the centre of the room. He made a mental note to be very careful not to add, or leave out, anything already said…

Buck paused mid-sentence. "Shouldn't you be writing this down?" he suggested.

Verity looked at the pad as if she had forgotten it was there. “Yeah, maybe,” she said. “Although, I’m sure I’ll remember it. Carry on.”

Buck carried on.

Buck noted, on the second telling of the story, whilst still being cautious, he could add emphasis where needed; he could inflect tone and pace, pitch and volume. He found he could also minutely manipulate the scenario to make him look more manly; more heroic even. In each telling, he’d obviously found no need to mention the loss of bladder control. He did, however, mention that Mr Andrianakis still had his hat.

“Right,” Verity said, jumping up off the chair as soon as Buck had finished. “Let’s have a look at this photograph, shall we? You fire it up, and I’ll just make a quick phone call. Get the wheels in motion.”

***

Despite being in excruciating pain, Esfir had managed to creep out of the store via the little-used back entrance. The two people Fahred had brought with him last night had been animals. Fat, rancid animals. Esfir could still smell them on her. In spite of the amount of vodka she’d been forced to drink, Esfir could still recall Fahred and his cousins shouting their encouragement as the two men went about their business. At one point, she’d noticed Fahred stroking himself with his mangled hand. When they’d finished, Fahred had leaned into Esfir’s ear and whispered *'Youse done well, innit.'* Fahred and the two men had then left. The two cousins were given instructions to make sure Esfir was *'looked after'* which they took to mean plying her with more vodka until she eventually passed out.

Having got outside, Esfir's mind now instructed her to run as fast as she could; however, her body would not allow it. Every step brought a sharp stab between her legs, and she had to use whatever support she could to make progress. She had little idea of the time, but from the dim light and the quieter streets — none of the shops were open yet — she knew it was early. She took solace in the notion the cousins had been so wasted by the end of the night they may well not surface for a few hours yet.

As she leant into a shop window, she caught sight of her face. The tears that followed did nothing to enhance the vision.

In her eagerness to escape the store, she had managed to find her blouse, which now only had three functioning buttons, her skirt, and one shoe. Her bra and knickers had never been fully removed. She had quickly scanned the room for her confiscated phone, but it had been nowhere to be seen.

Looking at her face in the shop window, Esfir tested her facial functions, slowly opening and closing her mouth. Her jaw felt painful; unhinged. An image came to her of one of the men forcing her mouth open.

Esfir tried to move but didn't feel like she could make it any further. She sat down in the shop doorway and bunched up her knees, which brought a new stab of pain, put her head down, and eventually fell into a sleep of sorts.

She was woken by a gentle nudge. It took a few moments for Esfir's brain to process where she was. It also reminded her she was hurting. She knew she hadn't got too far away from Ahmadi's store, and she inwardly pleaded that Fred or the cousins had not found her. She slowly lifted her head.

"Excuse me, miss, but I need to open the shop."

The voice belonged to a young, thin woman wearing a shop uniform. She waved a bunch of keys to prove the point.

Esfir mumbled an apology. "Can you help me up?" she said, holding out her hand.

The young woman looked up and down the street before helping Esfir to her feet.

"Thanks," Esfir said, and started to walk gingerly away.

She'd only managed a few steps when the young woman said, "Look, do you need a glass of water or something? You could sit quietly in the stockroom for a while if you like. But my manager will be here in about half-an-hour, and you'll need to be gone by then."

Esfir thought that a glass of water sounded like the best thing in the world at the moment.

The young woman helped Esfir to the stockroom and sat her down on a large cardboard box. She disappeared momentarily, reappearing with a glass of water and two digestive biscuits. "They're a few days out of date," she said. "But I'm sure they'll be fine."

"Thanks," Esfir said, accepting the water. She didn't think she could manage the biscuits.

"I have to go and get the shop ready," the young woman said. "I'll come and check on you in a moment, okay? Now, see that crate over there?" She nodded to a blue crate, the type bread is carried in. It was full of shoes. "That's full of returns. Due to be sent back when anybody can be bothered to do the paperwork. Why don't you have a rummage? See if there's any take your fancy. I'm sure the boss won't notice. He hates dealing with returns."

As soon as the young woman was gone, Esfir allowed the tears to flow. They turned the biscuits soggy.

The young woman returned shortly to find Esfir crying hard. She knelt in front of Esfir, putting her hands on Esfir's knees.

"Oh, you poor thing," she said. "Listen, we've only got about another fifteen minutes or so before my boss comes in. Do you want to call anybody? Have you got a phone?"

"No," Esfir sobbed. "It was — I gave it to someone."

"Well, do you want to use the shop phone? Or would you like me to call someone? Would you like me to call an ambulance? Maybe the police?"

Esfir snapped her head. "No, please," she pleaded. "No ambulance. No police. He'll kill me. I know he will. Promise me you won't call the police."

The young woman felt Esfir's body stiffen.

"Okay," she said. "I won't call them, I promise. But I think we should call someone, don't you? So, who can we trust, my lovely? Who's out there who can look after you?"

It only took Esfir a moment. "Sean," she said. "Sean Adams."

***

Miss Harford received the message from the school's attendance officer: Esfir Ardavan was not in school, again. Could she please ring Three Rivers to see if they knew where she was?

Kath at Three Rivers confirmed to Miss Harford that Esfir had not come home the night before, and they had no idea where she was. She was mid-sentence explaining the home's policy on overnight absentees when Miss Harford hung up on her.

Miss Harford pressed a few buttons on her computer screen and called up Sean Adams's timetable. His first lesson of the day was maths, with Mr Ford.

***

"He just took off," Derek Ford said. "One minute he's sitting there," he pointed to an empty desk, "the next he's picked up his stuff and flown off like an Olympic sprinter."

"Did he say anything at all?" Miss Harford asked.

Derek Ford shook his head.

"He had a phone call," one of the other pupils in the class shouted. Miss Harford was astounded at the boy's full beard. "I saw him answering his phone before he shot off."

"Is this right, Mr Ford?" Miss Harford asked.

"Yeah, come to think of it, I think I did hear a phone going off," Mr Ford said. "I was just about to lay down the law, and then Sean went off like he did. I guess it must have been important."

Miss Harford turned to the boy. "Any ideas who may have been calling him?"

The boy laughed. "Do I look like Sherlock Holmes, Miss?"

The whole class lurched into laughter. The girl sitting next to him high-fived him. "Sweet," she said.

Back at her desk, Miss Harford picked up her telephone.

***

Stanley sat at his desk, wishing he'd been more forceful with Michelle and stayed at home another day. He'd made her a light breakfast, but the only thing she'd attempted was the orange juice. He'd pleaded with her to let him phone the doctor. Michelle would have none of it. She also wouldn't countenance him spending any more time away from work.

"It's already driving you nuts, Stan," she'd said. "I can see it in your eyes. In fact, I can see it in your nose, ears, mouth and toes. I can see it everywhere. Get back to bloody work and catch some criminals. Anyway, I'm not sure how much more of your cooking I can stomach. If the disease doesn't kill me, your undercooked pork will. Get out from under my feet and give me a break for God's sake. I'll be fine."

Stanley looked around the office, it seemed eerily quiet. "Where is everyone?" he asked himself. More importantly, he thought, where was Verity? He needed a coffee.

Then his phone rang. After the second ring he got it: worrisome.

***

Buck couldn't entirely concentrate. He was sitting at his computer, indicating to Verity as best he could where the incrimination lay in the photograph. He was finding it almost impossible. Verity had one hand on the back of his computer chair and was leaning over his shoulder.

He could smell her perfume, feel the weight of a breast pressed against his arm, sense her breath in his ear.

"So, the only place this photograph can currently be found is right here on this computer," she said. "You've definitely deleted it off your phone?"

"Yes."

"And you haven't printed off any spare copies, or sent them to the paper in an e-mail attachment? Nothing like that?"

"No."

"And only you know the password to the computer, right? You've not given it to anybody else?"

"Why would I give my password to anybody else?"

Verity leaned away, much to Buck's relief. "Well, I know how close to the edge you journalists tread," she said. "I just thought maybe you'd given it to someone for safe keeping. You know, like they do in the movies. Popped it in an envelope and given it to somebody marked *Only to be opened in the event of my death.*" Verity air-quoted the sentiment.

"My death!" Buck never knew his voice could reach such lofty frequencies. He had to gulp several times to get air in his lungs.

Verity punched Buck in the shoulder. "Keep calm," she said. "I'm only joking. I'm sure if T.S.A. ever find out you've got this photograph, they'll be understanding. They'll probably just hold their hands up in meek surrender and say, '*Fair play. That Buck*

Witman, the finest journalist The Hackney Gazette has ever seen, has got us bang to rights.'"

"But that's why I've come to you," Buck said, his voice still in falsetto mode. He caught hold of Verity's arm. "Surely, I don't need to be involved anymore. Look, I'll just send the photograph to you, then delete it. You can take all the credit. Tell people they just fell into your lap from an unnamed source. That happens all the time, doesn't it? Police are always saying they never reveal their sources, right? It's a code, right?"

Verity gently removed Buck's hands from her arm. "You really do watch too many gangster movies, Mr Witman," she said. "But, let's try and put your mind at rest. The only people, so far, who know this photograph exist are you and me, correct?"

"And possibly Mr Andrianakis," Buck said. "And DCI Wood. You said you'd left him a message."

"Of course, of course. You're absolutely sure there's nobody else."

"Absolutely. Apart from you, I've not told a soul."

"Good, let's keep it that way," Verity said. "You know, sending the photograph to me and then deleting it off your computer probably isn't a bad idea. But if you think for one moment I'm letting you have my private e-mail address, you've got another think coming. You'd be sending me photos of certain parts of your anatomy every day. So, shift your arse."

Verity pulled Buck out of his seat and sat in it herself.

"And no peeking."

Buck turned his back and listened as Verity pressed buttons.

"Why your private e-mail?" he asked. "Wouldn't it be better going to your work e-mail?"

There was a slight pause before Verity explained, "I just want to be extra cautious, Mr Witman. Let's just say — and I'm sure you know where I'm coming from — that there are some police personnel who are not exactly above board. I just can't risk something as important as this photograph being seen by the wrong people. You know what I'm saying?"

Buck did know what she was saying, and he took comfort that Verity was finally starting to treat the matter with the gravitas it deserved.

"Okay — done," Verity said, vacating the chair. She made her way to the hook by the door and collected her coat.

"You're leaving?" Buck said.

"Of course I'm leaving." Verity laughed. "Did you think I was moving in?"

"Do you want to move in?" Buck had meant it as an attempt at a joke, but the question had come out with a hint of desperation. "What I mean is, you're actually leaving me alone? You haven't even touched your coffee."

Verity sighed. "Let's analyse exactly what we've got here, Mr Witman," she said. "Firstly, as you yourself have said, Mr Andrianakis is deranged. He's obviously got a problem with drink and drugs and held a gun to your head in order to steal your hat—"

"Actually, he didn't steal it—"

Verity held her hand up. "Secondly, he's got a business card which, on inspection, portrays a white circle on a black background."

"Exactly! A T.S.A. business card. A business card of an organisation that's been as elusive as a three-legged unicorn for ten years."

"Yes, but is it? We could go on your computer right now and print off the exact same card, Mr Witman. Anybody could. Including Mr Andrianakis."

"But why would he do that?" Buck pleaded. "Why would anybody print off the calling card of a known killing machine? I mean, I wouldn't, would you? It would make no sense. No sense at all. Might as well print off swastikas."

"And, as we know, some people do print off swastikas," Verity said. "But let's not compare T.S.A. to the Nazis, shall we? Anyway, who knows how the mind of an alcoholic, drug addict works, Mr Witman? Perhaps he thought it would be fun. Perhaps he uses them to impress the girls." Verity looked up at the ceiling in thought. "Would it impress me, I wonder?" She lowered her head and giggled. "Do you know, I think it might. Remind me if Mr Andrianakis was good-looking."

"No, he bloody wasn't," Buck said. "I've already told you, his face looked like a sodding war-zone."

“But didn’t you say he’d been in a nasty fight? One which he’d lost quite badly, if I remember your story correctly. So, what about when all the wounds heal, Mr Witman? Do you think he would impress me then? Actually, I’m quite partial to a man with scars on his face. Shows a certain danger, don’t you think? I do love a bit of danger, Mr Witman.”

Verity started putting her arms through the sleeves of her coat. The action raised the hem of her T-shirt, showing a glint of something bright and expensive dangling from her belly-button.

Buck stared at Verity’s taut stomach for longer than what could be considered polite before the coat was fully donned.

“So, what now?” he asked. “What are you going to do now? More importantly, what am I going to do now?”

“I’m going back to the station,” Verity said. “Catch up with DCI Wood and bring him up to speed. As for you, I’d suggest you stay right here and wait for further instructions. I expect DCI Wood will want to see you himself.”

“But I can’t just wait here,” Buck said. “If Niko Andrianakis doesn’t get me, a bloody heart-attack will. I spent most of last night peeking from behind the curtains. I’m telling you, the minute you walk out that door, I’m going to be back on that computer looking for long-haul, one-way flights.”

Verity reached the door to the flat and stopped, her hand on the catch. She turned slowly. "I once threatened to bury you," she said. "After you'd printed that photograph of me. I'm sure you know the one I'm talking about." Verity walked to Buck and put her hands on his face, squashing his cheeks together.

Verity could feel Buck's surprise travel from his face through her hands.

"I believe my exact words were, *I am going to bury that arsehole.* Do you know what DCI Wood said? Of course you don't. You weren't there. He said, *Best of luck, he's pretty much indestructible.* Are you indestructible, Mr Witman? You don't look indestructible. In fact, I'd say right now, you look very much destroyable."

Verity planted a kiss on Buck's puckered lips, laughed, then turned and left.

***

"Where are you taking me?" Esfir asked. "Sean, please slow down. I can't walk very fast."

Sean Adams did as he was asked. "I'm sorry," he said. "We just need to get you somewhere safe." He kissed Esfir lightly on the top of her head.

"I already feel safe," Esfir said. "Now I'm with you."

"Yeah, well — you're not," Sean said. "What the hell, Essie. I told you this is what he wanted. I told you all the booze and extra money was wrong. I mean, how stupid are you to think someone like him was just being your friend? Come on, let's keep moving."

"I tried, Sean," Esfir said, bursting into tears. "I tried to get away, honest. After my shift finished, I told him I was going home to change and that I'd be back for the party, but I would never have gone back, Sean, I wouldn't. He stopped me. Said he didn't believe me. The cousins were there and — well, I just couldn't get away. I'm so sorry, Sean. Please, I really love you. Please, please, forgive me."

***

Verity had only taken a few steps into the station when the desk sergeant stopped her.

"Two messages for you," he said, retrieving some scribbled notes. "DCI Wood says he's been called to a shoe shop on the Essex Road called Sole to Sole. Didn't say why; said he'd fill you in later. And a Miss Harford called. Says she needs to speak to you urgently about a young girl called Esfir Ardavan. I had her spell it for me."

"A shoe shop?"

"Yep, a shoe shop. I don't know, maybe he needs a new pair and wants your advice. He's not exactly fashion wise, is he?"

Verity shook her head. "Did Miss Harford leave a number?"

The desk sergeant handed over the scribbled notes. “Yep, it’s at the bottom there.”

“Thanks.”

***

“So, Poppy, you say her name was Esfir?” Stanley asked.

“That’s what I heard,” the young woman replied. “When she was on the phone. She said, *‘Sean, it’s Esfir. Please come and get me, I’m hurt.’* She then had to ask me where she was. By the way, my name’s Holly, not Poppy.”

Stanley quickly checked his notes. “Of course it is,” he said. “That’s actually what I’ve written. Sorry, I used to have a… never mind. Anyway, this Sean, he arrived?”

“Quick as a flash,” Holly said. “Probably no more than twenty minutes. He’d obviously run all the way. He was covered in sweat and completely out of breath.”

“Can you give me a description of him? Apart from being covered in sweat.”

“Ooh, let’s see — he was young. I’d say maybe seventeen, eighteen, that sort of range. He had wonderful hair with blonde streaks in it. Very trendy.”

“Height, build?”

“Tall. Probably hovering on six feet. Thin, but not stupidly so. Had the makings of filling out well, you know what I mean? It’s a good job my boss had been held up. I don't think he would have been happy to see a young girl in Esfir's state being escorted out of the shop by a sweaty, black man."

"Black?"

"Yes, black, Inspector. As in the colour of his skin."

Stanley couldn't believe it had never occurred to him to ascertain the boy's colour. How many times had his name cropped up in conversations over the last few days? And only now was he finding out Sean Adams was black. It changed nothing of course, but Stanley wondered if he'd missed something as fundamental as the colour of someone's skin, what else might he have missed?

"Why didn't you call as soon as you found the girl in the doorway?" Stanley asked. He kept the tone as light as possible. He didn't want to put the young shop-worker, Holly, on the defensive.

"My first thought was to get her off the street to safety," Holly said. "Well, actually, no, that's not quite true. My very first thought was she was just another homeless person and I needed to move her away from the doorway, but as soon as she lifted her head... well, I just knew."

"Knew what?"

"That she needed help. Apart from the obvious damage I could see, I just knew there was plenty of damage I couldn't."

Stanley forced himself not to roll his eyes. These days it seemed everybody, including shoe-shop workers, fancied themselves as life-gurus. “Okay, so you brought her in here,” Stanley rolled his head around the stockroom, “and gave her a glass of water.”

“And two digestive biscuits.”

“And two digestive biscuits. So why didn’t you just nip out and call us then?”

“She made me promise I wouldn’t,” Holly said. “No ambulance and no police. She was quite adamant. So, when I asked her who we *could* call, because there was no way I was letting her leave unless she was with someone she could trust, she gave the name Sean Adams. I let her use the shop phone because she said she’d given her phone to someone else.”

“Did she say who?”

“No, she didn’t. I phoned you the minute she’d left.”

“Did she say where she was going?”

“No. That lad, Sean, whipped her out of here as fast as he could.”

“Well, thank you, *Holly*,” Stanley emphasised the girl’s name by using his fingers. Why? It didn’t make any sense. It was her proper bloody name, for Christ’s sake. “You’ve been very helpful.” Stanley tapped his notebook. “The nearest tube station to here is Angel, right?”

“It is,” Holly said. “It’s the stop I use to get here.”

Two thoughts came to Stanley at the same moment.

During his conversation with Esfir at the station, she’d said she thought Miss Harford hated Sean and everybody like him. Why had he not picked up on that? Why had Esfir added, *and everybody like him*? If only he had simply asked what Esfir meant by that, he believed Sean Adams being black would have been something he would have known about by now.

The second thought was he remembered Esfir telling him Sean Adams had a — what was the word? Boss — yes, that was it. Sean Adams had a boss body since he'd been attending a boxing club not far from Angel tube station. The only boxing club Stanley knew of in this part of the world belonged to Jack 'Puncher' Norris.

***

Back at her desk, Verity rang Miss Harford.

"Thanks for calling back, DI Chandler," Miss Harford said. "I thought it best to speak to you. For some reason, I don't think your colleague likes me very much."

"Ah, don't worry about him," Verity said. "I don't think DCI Wood likes a lot of people at the moment. He's having a few personal problems. Now, what can I do for you?"

"It's about Esfir Ardavan."

"What about her?"

"Well, she's not turned up for school again, which isn't uncommon as you know. But I'm a bit concerned that the home has confirmed they haven't seen her since yesterday, either. What's equally concerning is Sean Adams seems to have disappeared, as well."

"Disappeared?"

"Yes, he was here, in maths with Mr Ford, but then, according to one of the other pupils, he had a phone call and took off."

"Took off?"

"Like an Olympic sprinter, apparently. I think the only reason he would do that was if there was some promise on the end of it. I told you he was no good. In fact, I've told you several times, but you don't seem to want to take it seriously. I know you said these things take time, but the boy is having… you-know-what… with a fifteen-year-old girl. Why can't you just arrest him?"

Verity gritted her teeth and silently vowed to make Stanley pay for making her deal with Miss Harford.

"I'm sure you're right, Miss Harford," Verity said. "It does sound like Sean fancied whatever promise you're talking about better than an hour or so of maths." Verity almost added, *'Can you blame him?'* but stopped just short. "But I'm sure he and Esfir will turn up shortly. In the meantime, I'll ask our officers to keep an eye out for them, okay?"

"Oh, I suppose so. I just thought you may know where people like Sean Adams go?"

Verity paused as she digested Miss Harford's words. "People like him?" she repeated, slowly.

"Yes, I just thought you, of all people, may know where people like him hang out. Where their little hidey-holes may be. You know, corners and tunnels. Maybe a group of derelict garages or something."

There was a silence in which Verity's mind raced.

"DI Chandler, are you still there?" Miss Harford said.

"Yes, I am," Verity replied. "Miss Harford, from what you're saying, I'm assuming Sean Adams is black."

"Well of course he's black. What did you think he was?"

"Ah, right. In that case, I know exactly where he is."

"You do? That's wonderful."

"Yes, there's an area where all black youths congregate. Right in the middle of Bethnal Green, it is. We normally find them there at all times of the day and night, taking drugs, drinking, singing songs, summoning up the Devil, raping white virgins, and oh, the worst of it, Miss Harford, is what they eat. Do you know what they eat, Miss Harford?" Verity didn't wait for an answer. "They eat white babies — that's what they eat, Miss Harford. The whiter the better. I expect Sean is there right now, Miss Harford, chomping on a nice, juicy limb, freshly torn from a screaming, lily-white baby."

Verity's phone went dead.

Verity took a while to calm down. She vowed to make it her mission to ensure Miss Harford would not be employed for very much longer.

When she was back to somewhere near thinking straight, Verity got the distinct feeling Stanley's visit to a shoe shop and Esfir's whereabouts were intrinsically linked. She looked at the piece of paper the desk sergeant had given her. "Essex Road," she mumbled. "The same road as Ahmadi's."

She grabbed her coat, but before she left, she tapped into her private e-mails and sent Buck's photograph to her boss.

***

Stanley could see Esfir through the glass. She was sitting opposite Norris with her head bowed and her shoulders heaving. Even from a distance he could feel her pain. No, pain wasn't correct. He searched for the appropriate word. Misery: he could feel her misery. There were a few die-hards at the gym, all going about their business, but, Stanley noticed, even they seemed to know something was very wrong. There was a silence to the place that spoke volumes. They all looked at Stanley with an understanding as he walked towards the office. An understanding that said: *if you don't sort this out, DCI Wood, we will.*

Norris spotted Stanley, and to Stanley's surprise, a look of relief fell across his face. He waved for Stanley to enter, then put his fingers to his lips.

Stanley opened the office door quietly. Esfir was crying hard.

Norris and Stanley exchanged a quick nod. "Hello, Esfir," Stanley said.

Esfir's face snapped up. She jumped out of her chair and flung herself at Stanley, burying her head in his chest. The force almost pushed Stanley back out through the door. She mumbled something that Stanley didn't quite catch. It sounded like an apology.

"Whoa, tiger," he said.

He glanced at Norris who just shrugged. Stanley had a strange feeling; a feeling he could not compartmentalise. It had nothing to do with police-work; it was coming from somewhere more personal. Gradually, he wrapped his arms around Esfir and allowed her to sob.

When Esfir's crying eventually subsided, Stanley slowly manoeuvred her back to her chair and sat down beside her. He remained holding her hand.

"Esfir," he said, quietly. "I need you to tell me exactly what's happened."

Esfir shook her head. "I can't."

Stanley turned his head to Norris. "Norris?"

Norris looked out into the gym. "Not sure it's my place to say."

Stanley felt Esfir's grip tighten. "Norris, if you don't put away your God-forsaken bullshit and tell me what's happened here," he said, "I swear I'll find some way to shut this place down."

Norris turned his eyes back to Stanley and drummed his arthritic fingers on his desk. "Don't make idle threats to me, son," he said. "I'm not some fresh-around-the-gills bum who can be intimidated by the likes of you. I don't care who you are. I've learnt if you hit someone hard enough, it'll fucking hurt. So, like I said, I'm not sure it's my place to say. Easy, see?"

There followed several moments when the only sound was that of Esfir's sobs.

Norris continued drumming his fingers on the desk. He looked back out through the glass at the gym. "God, give me strength," he said. "Right, on one condition."

"What's that?" Stanley asked.

"Easy, see? You keep that goddamned partner of yours away from my fighters."

Stanley nodded his head. "Okay," he said. "I can do that. But whether I can keep your fighters away from her is another matter."

"Are you sure you want him to know, Sweetheart?" Norris asked Esfir.

Esfir nodded her head slowly and mumbled, "Please, don't let Sean get into any trouble."

"I'll try my best," Stanley said.

"Okay," Norris said. "Sweetheart, you let me know if I get any of this wrong, okay? And DCI Wood, you didn't hear any of this from me."

Norris got out of his chair and made his way to the door to the office. He opened the door and shouted, "What are you lot gawping at! Either get on with what you need to be doing, or get out!" He made sure the door was firmly closed before settling himself back down.

"Right," he said. "I'll make this quick because the sooner I get you out of here the better it's gonna be for everybody concerned. Easy, see? So, this young-un gets brought in here by Sean Adams. He's a good boy, is Sean. Can see him going places with the right coaching. Sean sits right where you are now, Inspector, and he asks young-un exactly the same as what you just did. He asks her to tell him exactly what's happened."

Norris paused.

"And?" Stanley said.

Norris shook his head. "Are you sure about this, Sweetheart?" he said.

Esfir didn't reply.

"Okay," Norris said, obviously taking Esfir's silence as approval. "Well, young-un here tells Sean that last night, Fred Ahmadi, his two imbeciles, and a couple of randoms fed her on vodka and cocaine—"

"I didn't take the cocaine," Esfir said, without looking up. "I didn't take the cocaine. Honest, I didn't. Fred said I wasn't worth wasting good cocaine on, anyway."

Stanley turned to Norris.

Norris rubbed his face with his gnarled hands. “Jesus Christ, you’re the bloody detective! Ain’t you worked it out yet?” he said. “Just look at the girl!”

“Okay, okay,” Stanley said. “You’re right. I can imagine the rest.” He turned to Esfir. “So how did you get out, Esfir?” he asked, softly. “How did you end up here?”

“I got out through a back door,” Esfir said.

“Was Fahred still there?” Stanley asked.

“No, he left with the two old men sometime last night, after they’d… finished. The cousins were still there, though. But they were asleep.”

Norris obviously decided the story was taking too long and took up the narrative.

“She didn’t get too far before collapsing in a shop doorway,” he said. “A woman took her into the shop and allowed her to phone Sean. Sean brings her here. I tell him I wished he’d taken her somewhere else and we argue for a while. Sean then phones his eldest brother and we argue some more. Sean disappears, leaving young-un here behind for me to bloody well deal with. Then you turn up. Now, if you don’t mind, I think you both need to get the hell out of my gym. Easy, see?”

“Hang on,” Stanley said. “Did you say Sean phoned his eldest brother?”

“Did I say that?” Norris said. “I don’t remember saying that. Now, off you go.” He stood up, made his way to the door, and put his hand on the handle.

"Not just yet, Norris," Stanley said. "Esfir, who is Sean's brother?"

Esfir raised her head and looked at Stanley. "Promise Sean won't be in any trouble," she said.

"I can't promise, Esfir," Stanley said. "I can't promise anything. The only thing I can do is try my best. But I can't do that if I don't know who or what I'm dealing with. If you want me to make sure Fred doesn't give you to his friends again, you're going to have to help me. Do you understand?"

Esfir slowly nodded her head.

"So, Esfir, who is Sean's brother?"

"He's got three," Esfir said. "Three half-brothers. The eldest is Terrell. Terrell Williams."

Norris groaned loudly. "Oh, Jesus," he said. "There go my body parts."

***

Stanley rang the station and requested two officers be sent to Norris's gym to collect Esfir. "Make sure at least one of them is female," he said. "Tell them to be quick about it. Norris is really not happy about keeping her here. Get her back to the station and give her anything she wants, okay? Don't let anybody see her without my permission. I'll be back as soon as I can."

He then rang Verity.

"I'm standing outside a shoe shop on Essex Road," she told him. "But you're not here. I've had a lovely chat with Holly, though. She tells me you've met."

"Meet me outside Ahmadi's as soon as you can."

***

"Hey," Fahred said, shaking one of the cousins awake. "Where the girl? Where she gone, man? When I leave here last night, she about to pass out in that chair right there, innit? Now, unless my eyes deceive me, she nowhere to be seen."

The cousin rolled over, broke wind loudly and merely grunted.

Fahred wafted the smell from his nostrils and then shook him harder.

"Hey!" he shouted louder. "Youse stinking hump, wake up and go and find her, innit? Get your sorry, fat, fetid arse out of my shop and go find her. Make sure she ain't done nuttin' stupid, you know what I'm saying?" Fahred was proud of the use of the word *fetid.* He'd learned it off a fellow inmate who'd been university educated, no less.

'You are one small, fetid apology of a human,' the inmate had told him, then went on to explain exactly what he'd meant when he realised Fahred thought he'd been complimenting him.

The cousin seemed to have gone back to sleep. "Hey!" Fahred gave up shaking him and kicked him instead. "I is paying you top dollar to looks after me, not to clog up my store with you stinky smells, you git me? You… you… you fetid apology of a human."

The cousin grunted and rolled off the sofa he'd slept on, leaving his bulk indented into its cushions. Fahred turned his attention to the second cousin who was sleeping in Bijan's old armchair, snoring. Fahred pinched the man's nose until, unable to breathe properly, he woke with a start.

The man mumbled a few unintelligible words. Fahred slapped him across the face.

"You needs to wake up quick smart," Fahred said. "I needs you two imbeciles to go find the girl, innit? Remember the girl? The one who was here and now she ain't."

He pointed to the only other armchair in the room. The second cousin looked at the chair and rubbed his eyes. He then scratched his crotch.

The two cousins rummaged around for shoes and odd bits of clothing before heading for the connecting door to the store.

"Not that way!" Fahred said. "Use the back entrance, innit? Can't have you two upsetting my customers."

The two cousins bumped into each other as they turned for the back entrance.

"And when you find her, you tells her she already late for her shift, you hear me?" Fahred watched and tutted as the two men fumbled their way out of the living quarters. "And when you gets back, youse cleaning this place up all fancy until it gleams like the top of the Chrysler Building, you hear what I'm saying?"

The saying brought a smile to Fahred's face as he recalled watching the film Annie over and over again as a child. The smile faded as he remembered the eventual fate of the criminals.

Fahred slumped into Bijan's armchair and sighed. He closed his eyes and pinched the bridge of his nose with the two remaining fingers on his right hand. Should he be worried, he thought. Would the girl go to the police? Surely not. Not after everything he'd done for her. He'd given her a job. Given her extra shifts and bonuses. He'd supplied her with free food and alcohol from the store. He'd shown her a good time. Anyway, even if she did go to the police, would they believe her? Who was she? Just a nobody really. If she'd had any sense, she'd have arranged for one of the others to turn up like he'd asked: it would have shared the burden.

Slowly, Fahred drifted into sleep.

Fahred was aware someone was in the room. He could sense a change in the atmosphere. Even with his eyes closed he could tell the room had darkened. A small grunt was followed by a loud, long breaking of wind and a very quiet, mumbled apology. The air turned *fetid.* Fahred slowly opened his eyes to see the two cousins standing side by side, looking at him, their eyes wide with panic.

"You have got to do something about that arse, you git me?" Fahred said, again wafting the air around him. "So, have you found her? Where is she, innit?"

The cousins said nothing. It was only then that Fahred digested the whole picture in front of him. The cousins were not alone, but it wasn't Esfir they'd found.

Each cousin had a gun pressed against the back of his head. The two people holding the guns were big. Most people looked big to Fahred, but these two looked like they'd been spat out by giants. They stood a good head and shoulders taller than the cousins and were infinitely better shaped. If there'd been a mould for the perfect menace, these two were it. Perhaps he could get rid of the cousins and hire these two. He'd feel a lot safer. They smelled better, too.

The scene stayed frozen for a few seconds before a voice boomed, "Excuse me, gentlemen."

The two gun-wielders pulled the cousins apart and through the gap came one more man: he was holding a cricket bat.

"Allow me to introduce myself," said the voice. He was the biggest of them all. "My name is Terrell." He glanced either side of him. "And these fine specimens with the guns are my brothers, Zane and Kemuel. Say hello, boys."

The two brothers mumbled a greeting.

"And this cute little tyke," Terrell said, turning in the direction of the back entrance, "is my half-brother, Sean. Come on in, Sean. Don't be shy."

Sean Adams entered the room. To Fahred, he didn't look shy at all. In fact, he looked the angriest of them all.

"Now, if you look close enough, I'm sure you'll notice he's not quite as dark as the rest of us," Terrell said. "That's because after our beloved father died, my mother, in a moment of weakness, took up with a North-African dipshit who wasn't quite as coal as he should have been, you know what I'm saying?"

Fahred said nothing. He knew he was in serious danger. If he'd learnt anything during his dealings with criminals, it was they didn't give named introductions or potted life-histories. He looked at the cousins and tried to use facial expressions to indicate they were in grave peril, but the cousins obviously took the friendly introduction as a sign things were improving; their bodies had visibly relaxed.

Terrell spotted the exchange, but simply laughed. "Anyway," he continued. "As soon as our North-African dipshit caught wind Mama was expecting, he high-tailed it back to Algeria, or Morocco, or wherever the hell he was from, and we never heard from him again. Now, I cannot tell you the pleasure it gives me and my brothers when people we don't like disappear. It makes us all fuzzy inside, doesn't it, boys?"

The brothers mumbled their agreement. The one called Zane added, "We best get on with it, Terrell. We don't want to be here longer than we need."

"My brother has a point," Terrell said. He pointed at Fahred. "The last time I was in here, you weren't in. Which is a crying shame because it meant I had to have a conversation with your grandfather. By the way, my condolences. He was a good guy. I hope my visit didn't upset him too much. If it did, I hope you can forgive me."

Fahred nodded his head quickly. "All forgiven," he said. "No hard feelings, innit?"

"You see, little Sean here told me and my brothers what he thought you was planning on doing, and we thought we'd pop in and tell you, politely like, that we didn't like the sound of it, but, like I said, you weren't here to accept our message."

"Uh, Terrell, we really need to get moving, man," Zane said.

"Of course," Terrell said. "Now, where was I? Oh, that's right, I was telling you about Sean here. Well, you see, despite young Sean being the product of a North-African dipshit, I'm sure you'd agree he's the cutest one amongst us. Mama certainly thought so." Terrell ruffled Sean's hair. "And here's the thing. We brothers sort of feel, what's the word I'm looking for? Responsible, yes, that's it, responsible for his welfare." Terrell passed the cricket bat to Sean and leaned in to Fahred, putting his hands on Fahred's shoulders. Fahred didn't think he'd ever seen hands so big. "Now, you'll never guess what's happened to young Sean," Terrell said. "Can you guess?"

Fahred shook his head, sending a spray of spittle across both his cheeks.

“He’s gone and fallen in love,” Terrell said, quietly. He elongated the word love, so it came out as *lurve*. “Got it so bad you wouldn’t believe.” Terrell moved his hands, caught hold of Fahred by the front of his shirt, and picked him up as if he weighed no more than a toy. Terrell pulled Fahred to him until their faces were practically fused. Fahred’s feet windmilled as he tried to find some purchase with the floor. “And now he tells me that, last night, someone messed with his girl — real bad. Really, really bad.”

“Please,” Fahred said, his voice barely escaping. “I can explain, it wasn’t—”

With one push, Terrell flung Fahred back into the chair. “When I want you to speak, I’ll tell you,” he said. “And right now, I’m thinking I never want to hear another word come out of your ugly face.”

“But it wasn’t me,” Fahred said. He pointed at the cousins. “It was them. They got—”

Terrell took one quick step forward and slapped Fahred across the face. It brought a strangled squeak from Fahred and a wince from each cousin. “I said, when I want you to speak, I’ll tell you,” Terrell repeated. He turned and pointed at the cousins in turn. “Now, you two half-wits we’ll get to in a minute, but…” he turned back to Fahred, “right now, I’m looking at you.”

Fahred rubbed the side of his face. The force of the slap had brought stars to his eyes, and a loud ringing in his ear.

"Please," he said. "Take anything you like, innit? Money, alcohol. Drugs! I have drugs. You want drugs? Cocaine. Pure." Fahred started fishing in the pockets of his sweatpants. "My cousins they have drugs also, you git me? Show him — show him you have drugs."

Fahred was stopped with another slap across the face which almost made him black out.

"Right, I think we've heard enough," Terrell said. He looked at Sean and smiled. "I think it's only fair you have the first blow."

Sean shook his head and passed the bat back to Terrell.

"No, please," Fahred said. He curled into a ball on the chair and started crying. "It wasn't me."

Terrell took a few steps back to give himself enough room to swing the bat.

One of the cousins fainted and the air turned *fetid.*

"Dirty bastard has shit himself," Zane said. He then shot him in the knee.

***

Stanley arrived at Ahmadi's and had to fight his way through a small scrum of people standing outside the store. He spotted two youngsters wearing yellow tunics. He didn't bother clocking their names. "Police!" he said, holding out his badge. The scrum of people started to disperse until only the two youngsters remained. Stanley reckoned neither of them looked much older than Esfir.

"Okay," Stanley said. "Why the hell are you out here?"

The two looked at each other. "We heard gunshots," the slightly older-looking of the two eventually offered.

"And screams," the other added. "Really bad screams."

"We rung the police," the older girl said. She looked up and down the street. "Are you all they've sent?"

"There'll be more on their way," Stanley said. "Where did the gunshots come from?"

"In there," the older one said. She nodded to the door of the store. "From the back."

"Any ideas who's in there?" Stanley said.

"I know Fred is in there," the younger girl said. "I saw him come in. I think I heard voices, but…" she shrugged her shoulders.

"How long ago did you hear the gunshots?" Out of the corner of his eye, Stanley could see Verity approaching on foot.

The two once again looked at each other and exchanged knowing nods. "About ten minutes. Maybe a bit longer."

"How many?" Stanley said.

"Pardon?"

"How many gunshots did you hear?"

"Oh, at least four," the older worker said. Stanley thought there was a hint of pride in the statement.

"It was four," the other said. "I heard four."

"Yeah, like I said, *at least* four." The older girl poked her tongue out at the younger.

"And you've seen nobody leave since?" Stanley asked.

"No." The older one waved a set of keys in the air. "I've locked the door," she said.

"What's up, Boss?" Verity asked, reaching the scene. She was slightly out of breath. "The school said Esfir is missing. Is she okay?"

"Not really," Stanley said.

"Esfir!" the older worker said, before Stanley could say anything further. "What about Esfir? She hasn't turned in this morning." An image must have formed in her mind. "Oh my God!" she put her hands to her mouth.

The younger girl, sensing danger, caught hold of her colleague and her eyes watered. "What's wrong, Anna?" she said. "What's wrong with Esfir?"

Stanley put a hand on the shoulder of each girl. "No, no, it's okay," he said, quickly. "Esfir is safe. She's a bit… well, she's a bit… look, she's safe, we're looking after her." The girls visibly relaxed. Stanley exchanged a nod with Verity.

"Right," Stanley said, releasing his grip on the girls' shoulders. "Why don't you two tell my partner here exactly what you've told me so far. Leave nothing out, okay? Don't worry, she's very friendly. She doesn't bite — well, as far as I know." Stanley turned to Verity.

Verity understood and said, "Come on, girls. Let's leave DCI Wood take care of things here. I know a nice, little coffee shop down the road. They sell the most amazing cakes."

"Uh, Anna, is it?" Stanley asked the older girl. The girl nodded. "I wonder if I can borrow those keys of yours?"

Anna looked at the keys. "I… I'm not sure," she said. "Fred will go mental if he finds out I've lended the keys away."

"Lended?" Stanley said.

Verity shook her head at Stanley and mouthed, *don't*.

"I promise I'll get them back to you before you know it," Stanley said. "Fred will never know." The girl looked to Verity, who nodded. "Thanks," Stanley said, taking the keys off the girl.

The sounds of sirens could be heard nearby. "Okay, girls, let's go get that cake," Verity said. She gently started ushering the girls away, then turned to Stanley. "Be careful."

***

Stanley quickly briefed the eight armed-response officers who'd arrived in two squad cars. He instructed the six uniforms, who'd also appeared, to cordon off the area. "Fifty metres in every direction from this door," he said. "No traffic, no pedestrians. Tell those ambulance crews to be ready." Stanley indicated to where two ambulances had arrived.

The armed officers formed a plan based on Stanley's information. Four of them would find the rear entrance to the store and the remaining four would enter through the front door that Stanley would open for them. If it could be confirmed the main store was clear, they would then make their way to the connecting door. When everyone was in place, all eight would co-ordinate their entrance into the living quarters.

Stanley noted the area outside the front entrance of Ahmadi's store had become eerily quiet. Birds that, under normal circumstances, would never be noticed, no matter how hard they shouted, could be perceived enjoying the new-found freedom to communicate with each other. Stanley could also clearly hear the deep breathing of the response officers, who were double-checking their equipment.

Stanley could feel sweat running down his back. The words of Verity, *be careful*, played over in his mind. They'd seemed genuine, he thought. There'd been a real concern in the way she had delivered them. His thoughts were interrupted by a message.

The officers sent to the back entrance came over the radios loud and clear in the silence. "We're in location. Rear door is open. Repeat, rear door is open."

"Entering front door now," replied one of the officers close to Stanley. "Remain in position and wait for my instructions." He nodded to Stanley who opened the front door.

There followed a cacophony of noise as the officers went about their business. No shots were fired: there was no need.

The two cousins had taken two gunshots each. One in each knee. Both were unconscious and were being furiously attended to by the ambulance crews.

Fahred Ahmadi was dead, lying face up on the floor, his arms and legs splayed out like a starfish. If it hadn't been for the missing digits on his hands, Stanley would never have recognised him.

"Doesn't look like this one's been shot," one of the armed officers said, waving a hand in Fahred's direction. "Looks like they've just used his head as a Pinata."

"He's been held in that position as they've done it," Stanley said. "Otherwise, he'd be curled up. My guess is they've shot these two in the knees to stop them running, then, if they were still awake, made them watch as they've gone about Ahmadi's head."

***

"Why am I still here?" Esfir asked. "Why can't I go home? Where's Sean? Have you found him? Is he in trouble?"

"I'm not going to lie to you, Esfir," Stanley said. "If we find Sean, or his brothers, he could be in serious trouble. They all could. The best thing for Sean right now would be for him to walk into this police station and give himself up."

"Did they beat Fred up?"

Stanley and Verity exchanged glances.

"Like I said," Stanley replied. "If Sean gives himself up it would be far better for him than if we have to carry on looking for him."

Esfir looked at the floor.

Stanley passed a phone over the desk. "We found this," he said. "Stuffed behind a cushion. I believe it's yours."

Esfir lifted her head and took the phone.

"I bet you've got Sean's number on speed-dial on that phone," Verity said.

"There's no way I'm ringing him," Esfir blurted. "You can't make me. There's no way I'm telling him to come here. You'll lock him up. I know you will."

"If we have to go and find him, Esfir, and we will find him," Verity said. "Things will be a lot worse. He'll listen to you. If you love him, Esfir, and I know you do, he'll listen to you."

Esfir rolled the phone around in her hands before eventually pressing some buttons. "The battery's dead," she said, throwing the phone on the desk. "Can I go back to The Rivers now?"

"Not just yet," Verity said. "We're waiting for a doctor to come and examine you. Just to make sure—"

"Examine me!" Esfir screamed. "Examine me for what?"

"Just to make sure you're all right," Verity said. "Esfir, you've had a harrowing ordeal. We can't just send you back to the home as if nothing has happened."

"But I'm fine," Esfir said. "I'm…" Esfir looked from Stanley to Verity, then put her head on the desk and cried.

Verity leaned over and stroked Esfir's hair. "There's another reason why we don't want you to go back to the home, Esfir," she said. "You see, I had a lovely chat with two of your friends earlier. Anna and Tuhina."

Esfir's head lifted sharply. "Oh, God," she said. "Are they all right? I wouldn't… I couldn't… Fred wanted me to…"

"They're fine, Esfir," Verity said. "Absolutely fine. They were very worried about you, though."

Esfir put her head back on the desk and continued to cry.

"Anna and Tuhina told me all three of you arrived at the home within a short time of one another. Is that correct?" Verity asked.

"Yes," Esfir mumbled.

"And that the home found all of you jobs at Fred's store. Is that also correct?"

Stanley felt his skin crawl. There was a constriction at the base of his throat, and he started taking gasps as he tried to get more air to his lungs. He recognised the feeling. It was the same feeling he'd had when Michelle's diagnosis had been given.

"I need some air," Stanley said, standing up. "I won't be long. I'll see if I can find a charger for this." He picked up Esfir's phone. "Is there anything you want, Esfir? Anything at all? How about a Big Mac meal with a strawberry milkshake?"

"Large," Esfir said.

"Large," Stanley repeated.

Stanley opened the door to the interview room and literally bumped into Delaney. Stanley ushered him out to the corridor and shut the door behind him.

"Sorry, Stan," Delaney said. He was holding a piece of paper. "But none of these brothers you're looking for are at their home addresses." He checked the piece of paper. "And none of them has appeared at the boxing gym, either."

"Thanks," Stanley said. "Has anybody spoken to their mum?"

"Said she saw Sean this morning before he went to school. Apparently, hasn't seen any of the others for a few days."

"Okay, let's bring her in anyway. And get a search warrant for the house." Stanley paused. "Tell you what, bring Norris in as well. If they see all their friends being pestered, it might flush one of them out."

Delaney nodded. "Will do," he said.

"Oh, one more thing," Stanley said as Delaney went to leave. "There's a woman who runs the Three Rivers children's home out in Hornsey. Name of Kath somebody or another. Tomorrow morning, I'm going to bring her arse home in a bucket, and I want as many people as possible watch me do it. Set it up for me, will you?"

SUNDAY

Lukas had travelled from Vilnius first class. As was normal, he'd insisted T.S.A. arrange for him to spend his one night in the UK at a top-class hotel. As this was London, he'd suggested The Ritz, or The Savoy; he didn't mind which. Whoever picked him up at Heathrow could let him know. He also reminded T.S.A. that his favourite musical was *Les Misérables*, and a top-price ticket would be expected at the box office for that night's performance.

During the conversation, he'd pointed out that he would be missing his son's tenth birthday. Not the celebration — that would be held on the weekend coming — but the actual birthday itself. Maybe something a little extra for the inconvenience would not go amiss? Then, of course, there was the issue of there being two targets to deal with. That had never been the case before: negotiation was needed.

Eventually, a compromise was met. Lukas would agree to eliminate the second target at a reduced rate, as long as T.S.A. would secure him a pre-theatre dinner reservation at The Ivy, and maybe a little female company waiting for him at the hotel after he'd returned from his evening at the theatre.

***

Niko was surrounded by Polish soldiers. They were dressed as chess pieces and didn't look happy. Niko's mother was by his side, stroking his hand.

"It won't hurt, Niko," she said. "It'll be nothing but a scratch. Double promise."

Niko turned to his mother, but her place had been substituted by Greasy Joe. He winked at Niko. "Call on my friend," he said. "Tell him, Giuseppe Siciliano sent you and you need to get rid of Polish *feccia*. I'll see you soon, my friend." Greasy Joe skipped away with the two dears, one on each arm. The three of them were singing something in Italian.

"But there's so many of them," Niko said. He started counting the soldiers, but they kept moving. "Keep still!" Every time he counted them, he came to the same number: eleven.

"Oy, who's the Schmuck?" one of the soldiers shouted. Niko squinted his eyes to get a clearer look. The soldier, obviously a knight, was completely naked and sitting on a rocking-horse. Niko recognised the soldier's circumcised, erect penis.

"Put this on!" a voice boomed from behind Niko. Niko turned slowly. "I said, put this on, arsehole!" The lieutenant-commander, dressed as a black bishop, was holding out a blindfold. He was smiling broadly.

The request had not held any notion of choice, and Niko dutifully donned the blindfold. The darkness was absolute. Not a glimmer of light penetrated his brain. Had he gone blind? What was it the Libyan had said about Purple Kush making him blind to pain? Niko was struggling to breathe.

Niko thought he heard the tell-tale click of a gun being readied, followed by a slight pressure against his forehead, right between his eyes. He smiled, knowing how his body would react. He'd need to get Cherie on the case as soon as possible. He'd make her wear that prick's hat, as soon as he could find some air.

His mother's voice floated to him once again. "It'll just be a scratch, Niko. Double promise. Triple promise. Super promise." There was an air of finality to the tone of her voice. This time, the promises sounded genuine.

Niko made one last attempt to find oxygen. If he'd had more time to clear his head and figure out what was happening, it may have answered the chronic question of what had happened to Operatives One, Two & Three.

The Lithuanian removed the pillow from Niko's face and checked the bullet had found its mark. It had.

One more, then he could relax; take in some sights before his dinner. Perhaps he'd visit The National and seek out his favourite, *The Fighting Temeraire*.

Lukas pressed the star button on the phone he'd collected from a security box at Heathrow. "Reverend Lukas here," he said, straightening his dog collar. "The first is done. I'll leave the door unlocked."

On his way out, he collected what was left of Niko's Purple Kush off the coffee table. It seemed a shame to leave it for the clean-up team. He might as well treat himself to the trilby as well. He always thought he looked good in a hat. And maybe that watch was too good to leave behind.

***

Buck had not slept well, again. But tomorrow — tomorrow he'd be on his way to Guatemala. Buck had been amazed at how cheaply he'd managed to find a flight. He'd also found a reasonably priced apartment. Once he was there, safe and sound, he could spend time deciding what to do next.

Overnight, he'd repeatedly checked and double-checked his computer to make sure there was no trace of the photograph, but it seemed DI Chandler had been thorough. There was no sign of it anywhere.

Buck had also checked his sent e-mails, but there was nothing there, either. The latest entry being the one he'd sent to the paper to say he was taking some time off. He had been deliberately vague as to why.

Buck tried to persuade himself he now had nothing to worry about. It was all in the hands of the police now. Nothing to do with him. He was a little surprised that Stanley had not contacted him yet, but was that a good sign? Was it further proof he was out of the loop?

Buck started to envisage the headline he might write — maybe from his new home in Guatemala —

when T.S.A. were finally uncovered. There would, of course, be no mention of his own involvement.

Or would there?

Buck quickly tried shaking the thought from his head. "Jesus, Buck," he said. "Get a grip. You're a reporter on The Hackney Gazette, not The Washington Post. Who do you think you are — Bob Woodward?" He made his way to the kitchen and put the kettle on.

He put his hands on the work-surface and bowed his head as the kettle boiled. He'd just have a nice cup of tea, he thought, and then look up where Bob Woodward had started his career. For all he knew, perhaps he'd started on a small provincial rag like The Hackney Gazette. After all, everybody has to start somewhere. Maybe the Watergate thing had fallen into Woodward's and Bernstein's laps just like T.S.A. had landed in his.

And he'd given it away! The story of the century, maybe even bigger than Watergate, had shown itself to Buck Witman, and Buck Witman had got scared and turned his head the other way. Pure bloody Lionel.

The click of the kettle switching off was followed by another. Buck spun around.

There was no time to release his bladder this time. The last thought he had was someone had returned his hat.

The Reverend Lukas pressed the star button. “Reverend Lucas here. The second is done. I’ll leave the door unlocked.”

Lukas checked his newly acquired watch. Plenty of time to get his son a special present from Hamleys.

3 DAYS LATER

The room was lit only by a large desk lamp. Buck's photograph, printed off onto an A4 sheet was laid out on the desk.

"You did not need to send me this. When you say we have a problem, then we have a problem. Please do not send me anything of this nature again." The photograph was put away in a desk drawer. "Tell me, how is Patty?"

"She's fine. It was best we just got her out of the way for a while. The pressure was starting to show."

"Good. We need her back as soon as possible. Where did we send her?"

"One of our safe-houses. Sunny Bournemouth. It was her choice. I gave her several. If it had been me, I'd have gone for Jersey, but there's no accounting for taste. I've made sure there's a dishy hunk doing the garden with instructions to say hello. Perhaps he'll help her get over what that stupid, idiotic husband of hers has gone and done."

"And you think introducing sex into the equation will help?"

"Who said anything about sex? I've just told him to say hello, that's all."

"Then why have you got that knowing smile?"

"Can I not smile?"

"Of course you can. It is one of your many God-given attributes. I am sure your smile has loosened many a tongue and sent many a man to his doom."

"A bit melodramatic, don't you think?"

"Am I wrong?"

"Probably not. You're very rarely wrong."

"One of *my* God-given attributes."

"Indeed. So, what is it you wanted to talk to me about? It sounded important."

"Yes. I have proposed that we do not yet move our operations out of London. There is still a lot of work to do here. All our friends — you know, of course, of whom I speak — agree with this proposal. In fact, they have already given me a few options for our next venture. I have told them we need to find a new operative first."

"Will sticking around be wise?"

"Why do you ask?"

"Well, there may be some heat around the sudden disappearance of Buck Witman."

"I thought you said nobody would worry about him."

"And they probably won't. He's got a sister in Australia and an uncle in Burnley, but he hasn't seen either of them in years. There's no love lost there."

"So, what is your concern?"

"I'm just wondering if his paper may ask a few questions. Even try and get a few headlines out of it. Star reporter suddenly ups and disappears, that kind of thing. We are aware that they do actually have some decent reporters on their books. We wouldn't want them sniffing about."

"I see. In that case, in a month or so, we will start circulating sightings. Somewhere exotic. Costa Rica comes to mind. We will give The Hackney Gazette some photographs of Buck Witman checking into a hotel with a beautiful woman on his arm. You will not see his face, but he will be unmistakable in his coat and hat. Just to add mystery, we will give The Hackney Gazette a tip-off about a secret bank account with relatively large sums of money appearing from an unknown source. We will make it look like he was leading some sort of double life. I am sure he would appreciate the sentiment."

"I'm sure he would. Although, we never actually found his bloody, stupid hat."

"You cleaned out both properties thoroughly?"

"Of course. Don't worry, there's not a scrap of either Buck Witman or Niko Andrianakis anywhere to be found."

"And the bodies?"

"Like I said, there's not a scrap of either Buck Witman or Niko Andrianakis anywhere to be found."

"Then we will find another hat. I am sure it was not unique. I must say, I think it is a shame about Niko Andrianakis."

"It was the drug use that failed him. He'd started to get sloppy."

"I must also tell you having to dispose of two people in such quick succession does not sit well with me. We have never had to do it before, and it makes me nervous. The more people involved, the more likely things are to go wrong. The only person who benefited was our friend from Lithuania, the Most Reverend Lukas Vitkus. We had to pay him five thousand pounds more than usual because he was missing his son's birthday."

"Mm, about Lukas. I wonder if you could have a word with him about something?"

"And what is that?"

"Well, the clean-up team reported the Andrianakis hit was fine. Mess nicely confined to a bed, they said. There was even a rolled-up rug that came in handy. Bloody images of cats all over it, apparently. But they've complained bitterly about the hit on Witman. They've asked why Lukas had to blow Witman's head off. Wondered why he couldn't have just strangled him. Even stabbing would have been less labour intensive, they suggested."

"You have to understand Lukas is set in his ways. He does not like imponderables. He prefers the absolute certainty of a bullet from close range. It was he who first proposed it be our method. However, if it makes you feel better, I will mention these concerns to him."

"Thank you."

"Apart from a missing hat, is everything else under control?"

"Yes. As you instructed, I've made arrangements to transfer Niko's apartment to one of our companies in the Caymans. It could come in handy, especially if we're staying in the area. Hell, might even move in myself. I've also got the bank to close his account and transfer the balance to one of our working funds. All the normal safeguards are in place. It'll never be found."

"Good. Anything else?"

"No — well, yes. If we're staying in the area, there's a woman by the name of Joanne. Works at the station. I'd like your permission to start the conversation. She'd be a real asset."

"How confident are you?"

"She loves this place with a passion. I'm sure I'd be able to convince her to share our vision."

"Be very careful."

"I will. Maybe I'll use Niko's new Mercedes as a carrot. It's quite nice. I've got it in one of our storage units at the moment, undergoing the usual transformation. As soon as it's all done, and the new paperwork is in order, I'll make the offer."

"Very well. Like I said, be careful."

"I will. Um — can I ask one last favour?"

"I doubt if it will be the last, but go ahead."

"There's another woman. Name of Harford. Works in a local school. Can we arrange it so she sees the error of her ways and never sets foot inside a school again?"

"I hope this is not personal. Why do you want this woman to lose her livelihood?"

"Oh, trust me, I'd like her to lose a lot more than her livelihood. But it will do for starters. And it's not personal. She's a boiled in the bag racist."

"Racist, or not, we remain silent on such issues. The more influence we exert, the more attention we draw to ourselves. Great pains are endured to ensure those we remove will not be mourned too heavily. If we start interfering in people's livelihoods just because we do not like their politics, or their religion, or their viewpoint, our situation becomes tainted. It is not what we are here to do."

"She has the ear of children, for Christ's sake."

"Please do not blaspheme."

"I'm sorry. Will you do something about her, or not?"

"I have a feeling if I do not, you will."

"Probably."

"Then we shall leave it at that. This woman, Harford, will be your concern, not mine. But I will not stand in your way."

"Thank you."

"I feel I must ask, are we to be concerned about DCI Wood?"

"Concerned?"

"Is he likely to cause any problems? What is the saying? Ruffle any feathers?"

"I don't think so. His mind is currently occupied with a children's home possibly offering up teenage girls for sale."

"I heard about this."

"I'm not surprised. Stanley made sure there was a big fuss when he brought the manager in."

"I also heard you are trying to find some brothers."

"Of course you've heard. We haven't exactly kept it quiet."

"And how is that going?"

"The brothers are all still missing. Well, I say missing…"

"What is it?"

"Well — I think I know where one of them is."

"Sorry, you say you are aware of the whereabouts of one of these brothers?"

"Possibly."

"And you have not told anyone?"

"No."

"Why? Why would you do this?"

"Because, if I'm right about him…"

"Go on."

"If I'm right about him, I think he would make an excellent operative."

"No! I do not like this. This does not sound like a good idea. We cannot have operatives who are wanted for murder. You are obviously not thinking straight."

"Don't worry, everything is fine. No one will find out. And at least he doesn't have Libyan friends on Camden Market. Hopefully, he won't call me Delores, either. Or have terrible Sean Connery imitations."

"Perhaps I should order you to give up his location."

"You could try."

"Would it be futile?"

"Totally. Don't worry, I told you, no one will find out."

"Until they do. Would DCI Wood, for example, not fully turn his attentions to finding these brothers once he has finished with the children's home?"

"DCI Wood is only a hop, skip and a jump away from retiring. His wife is also dying. Don't you worry about DCI Wood. I have him totally under control."

"Maybe we should arrange an early retirement for DCI Wood."

"What?"

"I mean it literally, not figuratively."

"Oh, I see."

"I am getting the impression you care about this man."

"What? Don't be daft. He's old enough to be my father."

"And do you not care about your father?"

"Of course I do. You know I do. What I meant was… well, never mind what I meant."

"Do you think DCI Wood would ever join the cause? I would imagine he has had his share of liberal justice in his time. Maybe he is frustrated."

"I should imagine having me around makes him very frustrated indeed."

"That is not what I meant, and well you know it. Please do not be flippant. And do not get complacent. Do not allow any feelings you may have to cloud your thoughts. This is a very dangerous game we play. The most dangerous of all. You may not be worrying about DCI Wood, but do not give him any cause to worry about you."

"I won't. I'll be careful. I've always been careful. Have I ever let you down?"

"Apart from not accepting God's wisdom, no, never."

"And on that note, I shall take my leave."

Verity stood up and looked tenderly around her father's office. All the smells were still there, along with the Bible and the cigar box. Verity opened the box and counted the fat, brown sausages. There were still ten. Engraved on the box, along with the brand of cigars, there was also her father's full name.

Tayo **S**apele **A**debayo.